SIX YEARS

SIX YEARS

MK BROOKS

Copyright ©2024 by MK Brooks

All rights reserved.

No portion of this book may be reproduced in any form without written permission from the publisher or author, except as permitted by U.S. copyright law.

CONTENT WARNING:

Dear Readers,

As much as I would love for everyone to read this novel, your safety will always be the top priority. Six Years does include difficult topics such as sexual assault, abortion, and suicide.
If these topics are too hard for you to read, please do not read any further.

To my own personal Brad, *fuck you.*

ONE

Auden

Spring 2017

    I knew I should've never agreed to come to this party. I have one month left until high school graduation, and the last place I want to be is standing in line for the bathroom with a bunch of drunk classmates.

    My knees bounce together in a restless rhythm, my bladder dangerously close to bursting. I try to distract myself by counting the three people in line ahead of me over and over again. Normally, I could recite each person's middle name, their parents' occupations, and the street they live on without hesitation. But with my urgent need for the bathroom growing by the second, I doubt I could even tell you what color shirt they're wearing.

    As the door swings open, a petite girl with dark hair steps out. Her eyes are wide and her nose looking like a powdered donut.

    "Two more people," I whisper to myself, swaying my hips in the opposite direction to let her by.

Before the girl can make her way out of the bathroom, the next girl in line grabs her by the arm and pulls her back inside with her. The moment the door closes, Sarah releases a loud sigh and raises both of her hands in frustration.

"I won't judge what you put up your nose, but I sure will judge you on your clear lack of human decency!" she yells, bringing a fist down on the wooden door.

Sarah pivots towards me, her porcelain cheeks flushing crimson as she cracks her knuckles. With a satisfying rip, she peels one foot off the sticky floor, tilting her head to the side and meeting my gaze.

"Do you think occupying a restroom without the intent of actually using it could be considered abuse? It has to be a health risk at least!" she exclaims, removing her round, vintage-framed glasses from her face and proceeding to clean them with her shirt.

I bite my lip, suppressing a smile. Sarah always poses questions that never cross my mind. Her quirkiness captivates me.

"There's just something medieval about pushing someone to urinate on themselves in front of their peers," she continues.

Shaking my head, I look up toward the ceiling, taking in all of the colorful streamers hanging from the wooden beams, a happy birthday sign already half fallen from the pole barns middle beam. My gaze lingers toward the familiar faces of the kids I've known since childhood. I can't help but feel a pang of sadness at the thought of no longer hearing Sarah's insightful theories on life and passionate rants about society once we graduate. I already know that she will be heading to Duke in the fall to pursue political science.

"I guess that's just *one* more law I'll be enforcing when I get into office," she says, running her fingers along the newly painted wall as she turns back towards the closed door.

"Feel free to hold me accountable for that one," she says over her shoulder.

As soon as the doorknob starts to turn, I feel a tap on my left arm. My nostrils fill with the overwhelming smell of Creed cologne, and without looking I know Bradley Mallehan Montgomery is standing right behind me.

Since eighth grade, Bradley has been dousing himself in Creed, a fragrance he had stolen from our local department store. He's the only person I know who wears it, and I'm certain he might be the only person on the planet who does, given its overpowering aroma that could knock the breath out of an elephant. Bradley proudly refers to it as his signature scent, drawn to anything that sets him apart. And he certainly nailed it with that choice!

"Well, look who decided to show up." The words slowly roll off Bradley's tongue.

Covering my scrunched nose with a hand, I fish my phone out of my pocket, anticipating a text from Taylor with her ETA.

"Have you heard from Taylor?" I ask Bradley, looking back toward the bathroom line.

Bradley rolls his eyes while bringing his hands up into quote marks.

"She said that she wasn't *feeling well* and can't make it," he says.

I narrow my eyes in frustration. Why wouldn't she tell me? I'm only here because she practically begged me to come. Bradley's birthday hardly seems like a valid reason for me to waste time that I should be using to study for finals.

I quickly text Taylor to confirm that Bradley is telling the truth, drowning him out as he goes on about all the other people who thought his birthday *was* a good enough reason to come out tonight.

"Well, Happy Birthday, Bradley," I say as I turn back in the direction of the bathroom.

He quickly steps in front of me, blocking me from the line that is now two people longer.

"Hold on," he says, raising his hands up between us. "Just because Taylor can't make it, doesn't mean we can't still have a good time."

My leg trembles with increasing intensity as my fear of not reaching the bathroom in time escalates.

"I really need to pee, Bradley."

He chuckles before grabbing my hand and leading me through the crowd of drunk, dancing teenagers. The mingling scents of various cheap, fruity liquors make my stomach churn, and my sneakers struggle to lift off the sticky floor with every step, making a sucking sound. I can't shake the image of how furious Bradley's dad will be when he sees the state of the new floors.

He lets go of my hand as soon as we make it outside, the cool night air sweeps across my face.

"Every tree on this property is at your service," Brad declares, extending his arms as he spins around, gesturing to the lush green ash and towering red maple trees that line the landscape under the bright moonlight.

This property is my ideal vision for a future home. With no neighbors nearby, the grass soft and velvety, like silk beneath your feet. Giant red maples create the entrance, leading to a cluster of trees in the back so vast you could easily lose yourself in them, their leaves transforming into a deep, apple red hue come autumn.

I notice a cluster of trees planted in the distance and begin to walk towards them. As I get closer, I pick up the pace, eventually breaking into a jog and unbuttoning my jeans as I approach.

As soon as I make it to the trees, I squat down, ripping my jeans and underwear down to my ankles in the process to pee. *Thank you, sweet baby Jesus.*

Scanning my surroundings for something to clean myself with, I hear Bradley clumsily making his way over, twigs snapping under his feet. He stops just a few feet away from me, leaning against a tree and taking a swig of his beer.

"How come you and I never hooked up?" He asks, releasing a hiccup before wiping his lips across his cuffed sleeve.

I fasten my jeans and brush the dirt off my hands as I process Bradley's absurd question.

"Did you forget you have a girlfriend, Bradley?" I ask sarcastically.

Before I can slip around him, he steps back in front of me.

"That's true," he says, his eyes slowly scanning up and down my body. "But that doesn't mean you've never thought about it."

Feeling a vibration in my pocket, I reach for my phone, but he snatches it from my hand, holding it above his head just out of my reach.

I jump up to grab it back, but he raises his arm even higher, chuckling like the playground bully he's always been.

"Bradley, give me my damn phone back," I demand. "I just want to go home."

Bradley lowers my phone within my reach, teasingly holding it out in front of me. As I go to grab it, he swiftly raises it back up, using his other hand to deftly slip my dad's truck keys from my pocket.

"Let's play a game," he teases, stepping back and waving my belongings in his hands. "One question for each item."

I throw my head back with a groan.

"Come on, Bradley, hurry the hell up. I'm tired," I reply, trailing after him as he heads towards a patch of grass nestled between two ancient maples.

He settles onto the grass, patting the space beside him. He reclines on his elbows, tucking my phone and keys into the front pocket of his khaki chinos. With a smirk, he gazes up at me, his frosty blue eyes locking onto mine, gesturing once more to the grassy spot next to him.

I let out a grunt as I reluctantly lower myself to the ground and sit beside him, creating as much distance as I can. However, Bradley promptly shuffles closer, rolling onto one elbow to align his body with mine.

"So, tell me, Auden," Bradley asks, making a trail through the grass with his finger. "How far have you gone with a guy?"

My lips part in surprise as I glance towards him, noting his complete lack of filter or boundaries. I guess you can get away with saying whatever comes to your mind when your dad owns half the town.

"Excuse me?" I ask, my tone louder than I intended.

"I know you were with that loser Danny last year," Bradley says. "But I doubt the kid had the balls to fuck you, and even if he did, I'm sure he didn't know how to do it right!"

I feel my fingernails digging into the skin of my palms.

Bradley taps his fingers against his pocket before raising an eyebrow at me. I interlace my fingers and rest them in my lap, closing my eyes briefly as I try to steady my breathing for the upcoming conversation.

"Not that it's any of your business," I answer, my jaw clenching as I pull at a loose string on my sock, "but I'm not a virgin."

I extend my hand toward him, fixing my gaze and releasing the tension in my jaw as the distant call of an owl reaches my ears. He laughs lightly as he retrieves my phone and places it in my hand. I quickly pocket it and then turn my head back to face him, observing him as he continues drawing lines in the grass with his fingers.

"So, if I was single . . ." Bradley begins to ask, taking his time with each word.

His finger starts to trail up my knee in the direction of my thigh, "Would you want to hook up with me?"

I swat his hand away and rise onto my knees, the anger dissipating and morphing into a growing sense of discomfort in my shoulders.

"Not a chance," I answer, my heartbeat gaining momentum. "Give me my damn keys Bradley!"

He reclines back on the grass and lets out another chuckle, shaking his head as he looks up at the moon, its light obscured by wispy clouds.

"Why do you refuse to call me Brad?" he asks, his tone turning stern.

The question takes me back to a memory from two summers ago. It was a day when Bradley's father, Mr. Montgomery, unexpectedly returned home early from work while we were all swimming in their pool. He brought out a bag of hotdogs and buns, firing up the grill for everyone. As soon as Mr. Montgomery appeared, Bradley exited the pool and stayed out, sitting alone on a chair, looking down at his feet as if he felt sick. Taylor encouraged him to join back in, but when she addressed him as "Bradley," Mr. Montgomery burst into laughter, leaving Bradley frozen at the pool's edge. Mr. Montgomery then turned to Bradley and commented on how rare it was to come across someone who still preferred Bradley over Brad. Bradley didn't find it amusing; he didn't even meet Mr. Montgomery's eyes or ours for the remainder of the day. The following day, Bradley requested that we all refer to him as Brad instead. Without a word, we all complied, understanding his unspoken reasoning behind the change.

"I don't know," I lie with a shrug of my shoulders. "I guess I'm just used to it."

I had always refrained from calling him Brad because I didn't think he truly wanted that nickname. I believed he might appreciate having someone who addressed him by his full name. If he hadn't started behaving like a complete jerk around that time, he would have likely had numerous chances to question me about it long before tonight. I wasn't going to try to console him, especially not while he was in the process of eliminating any remaining comfort I felt in his company.

I pull my phone out to check the time. It's almost midnight and my eyelids are becoming heavier by the second.

"I need to go home," I say. "Give me my keys, Brad." I'll call him whatever he wants if it gets me home in the next twenty minutes.

Brad taps his pocket, causing the keys to jingle inside.

"Come and get them," he says, flashing a grin that sends shivers down my spine.

Before he even completes his sentence, my hand instinctively moves towards his pocket. As soon as my finger hooks through the keyring, Brad's right arm envelops me, drawing me close against his chest.

I struggle to free myself, my arms flailing as I attempt to steady my fall into Brad's chest. His left arm shifts, allowing me some room to maneuver. I try to free myself, but he swiftly flips us over before I can fully move.

"Get off me!" I shout, pushing against him to dislodge him.

He presses against my shoulder until my back is pressed flat against the grass, leaning in so close that I can smell the beer on his warm breath.

"You don't really want to go home, Auden," he whispers, brushing a stray hair away from the corner of my mouth.

I struggle to shove his chest with all my might, but he remains unmoved. Sweat trickles down my neckline to push him off. Each knee jerk, elbow jab, and head butt is met with laughter. My body grows weary quickly, and my hands drop to my stomach in defeat as the realization sets in that he's just stronger than me.

My heart races as I scan the surroundings for the barn, spotting its faint glimmers in the distance, the music from inside muffled. There's no way anyone can hear me if I attempt to scream for help. A surge of cold air brushes against my skin as Brad lifts the hem of my shirt, sliding his hand beneath my back until he reaches my bra strap.

"Brad, stop!" I yell.

Brad leans in, pressing his lips to my hair before whispering in my ear, "It's okay," as he releases my bra strap.

I beg him to stop, but he ignores my pleas, kissing my neck and letting his hands and lips roam freely. He tries to reassure me with soft "it's okay" and "just relax" for a few minutes before abruptly slamming his fist on the ground beside my head.

    My entire body tenses as I see his smirk fade into a flat expression, the anger in his eyes burning fiercely. In one swift motion, he flips me onto my stomach, forcing my wrists together behind my back.

    The maple trees blur as I fight back the tears welling up in my eyes, trying to maintain control over my emotions. I go limp as Brad yanks my leg out of my jeans. I give in and surrender, closing my eyes and retreating into my mind as I brace myself for what's about to happen next.

    The rustling of the wind in the trees draws my focus, and I try to guess the direction of each gust. I'm used to tuning into the sounds around me. My mama used to get on my case all the time for not fitting the stereotype of how girls are supposed to behave, so I learned at a young age how to tune out her lectures and focus on the things I really loved like nature.

    As I concentrate on the sounds around me, a sudden noise of his zipper being undone snaps me back to reality. Panic sets in, and I start to kick frantically in a desperate attempt to break free, my heart pounding fiercely in my chest. But despite my efforts, I remain completely trapped.

    As he begins to position himself between my legs, his weight against me suddenly disappears, along with the grip on my wrists. I swiftly bring my arms forward, propelling myself off the ground, and sprint toward the barn.

    A shadowy movement catches my eye, and I glance back to see a second figure in my peripheral vision. Slowing my pace, I come to a halt, frozen in place as I recognize Asher towering over Brad's body, clutching him by his shirt collar.

"No wait!" I yell, trying to take a step forward but my feet feel glued to the ground.

I glance around and begin to feel dizzy, running my hands up and down my arms.

"This isn't right," I whisper under my breath.

Asher pivots to face me, his expression blank, his eyes drained of emotion.

"But you weren't here," I say with confusion, rubbing the side of my head. "You weren't even at the party."

I stumble to the ground, closing my eyes and feeling my surroundings slowly fading. Blackness.

When I open my eyes again, I see a popcorn ceiling above me. I sit up and rub the fog out of my eyes before noticing a small yellow alarm clock on the side table with a tiny sticker pasted above the time: *wake up bitch.*

Wake. Up. Bitch.

TWO

Auden

2023

  The barista slams my coffee down on the table so hard that hot droplets splash out and burn her wrist.
  "I called your name four times," she says frostily, rolling her eyes as she stomps back to the counter.
  I lift the paper cup up and turn it in my hand, looking for my name written on it. *Autumn.* I knew it. I've been coming to this same coffee shop for three years now, and for some reason, they can't get my damn name right.
  The only reason I keep coming back is for the amazing aromas and the ratio of people on Saturdays. There are never too many people to prevent me from grabbing a table for my laptop, but there's always just enough customers to keep anyone from spotting me and wanting to chat. I value this workspace so much that the thought of going by another name to avoid coffee conflict has honestly crossed my mind.

The coffee warms my lips as I take a sip, looking over at the counter as the barista takes the next customer's order, her eyes glaring directly back at me.

There's fifteen different tabs currently open on my laptop as I try to draft multiple emails in hopes of getting a new software program approved. The hospital I'm contracted with is running anything but smoothly. My fingers hover over the keyboard but my mind is still stuck on my dream last night.

I've worked my ass off to build a new life for myself here in Minneapolis, and I've done a pretty great job at avoiding thinking about anything relating to my past. In fact, the only person who knows anything other than the fact that I'm from a small town in Louisiana, is my roommate, Dec, and even he hasn't heard my real accent. So why the hell am I dreaming now about the worst night of my life?

A pigeon flies into the window, causing everyone to stop for a brief moment and stare. I watch longer than the others, waiting to see if he'll get up and fly away when my eye catches a flyer on the door. I squint until I can make out the words: "Like us on social media for a free bagel." It instantly makes me second guess my rule of never getting a social media account.

I had an Instagram when I was younger, but I deactivated it the day I left my small hometown of Monroe. Being untraceable has been incredibly easy so far, and I'd hate to jinx it all for free carbs. Although if I did have a social media account, I feel like I'd find it hard not to look up Taylor. As badly as she hurt me, I will always have a soft spot in my heart for her, full of the memories from the best years of my life. I even kept the last few voicemails she sent me before it all happened. I haven't listened to them since she left them, but for some odd reason, knowing I still have the chance to hear her voice is comforting.

    I take another sip of my coffee and realize it's already cold. Leaning back in my chair and letting out a sigh of defeat, I realize this day is going nowhere positive. I shut my laptop and start cleaning up my space when the chair on the other side of the table is pulled out. It's Dec.

    "Tell me the truth," he says, his face looking completely distraught as he sits down. "This shirt or my grey button up? I don't want to stand out."

    He's wearing a gold, short sleeved button-up top with a glittery gold bowtie around the collar. I soak in every inch of the shirt, enjoying the distraction, but Dec's patience is too short.

    "You hate it. I'll go change," he says before grabbing my coffee cup and taking a big swig. "Gross! How long have you been here?"

    He starts to stand from his seat, checking the time on his phone.

    "Not long enough to get anything done," I answer.

    He looks over at the door and then back at me before sitting back down.

    "You wanna talk about it?" he asks.

    I know Dec has a big event tonight. He's receiving an award for best dance choreography in the third grade division. Dec teaches dance at the local community center a few days a week, and tonight he gets to be honored for all their hard work. He's been looking forward to this for over a month, and the last thing he needs is to be distracted by my issues.

    Dec and his two younger brothers, Liam and Patrick, were raised Catholic in a small town in Minnesota. His parents say that he was dancing in the womb, so when Dec was ten years old and finally decided to come out to his parents wearing a sequined leotard that he found at a garage sale, they couldn't help but laugh. They knew longer than he did, and they decided to support who he is, even if their church didn't.

By eighth grade, his parents had packed the whole family up and moved to the Twin Cities so that Dec could attend dance classes and be in a neighborhood where he was accepted. Once a month, we have dinner with Dec's family. The way his dad accepts him for all that he is reminds me of my own dad, so I look forward to those dinners more than they probably realize.

"I'm okay," I answer, faking a smile to try and reassure him.

He rolls his eyes, leaning across the small square table and grabbing both of my hands in his.

"Auden, I am your best friend, tell me what's going on or I'll break a million hearts tonight by not showing up because I'm dealing with my top priority."

How the hell did I get so lucky? I'm not sure if I believe in God anymore, but if I did, I'd like to think he made Dec just for me.

"I had a nightmare last night," I start to say. "It was about . . . that night."

I don't have to say more. Dec is one of the only people in the world who knows about that night and right now, without me having to say it, he knows how badly I'm hurting.

He lets go of my hands and walks around the table to me, crouching down on his knees and wrapping his arms around my shoulders.

"Do you want me to cancel tonight? We can eat spaghetti and watch Gossip Girls. I could use a little Chuck Bass in my life right now."

I let out a hardy laugh. There is no issue in Dec's world that can't be solved by Chuck Bass.

"No, don't be silly. You need to go tonight, and I'll be completely fine."

Dec pulls his chest away from our hug, just far enough so he can look into my eyes.

"Are you sure?" he asks, raising his eyebrows.

I give him another smile. It's genuine because he already reminded me how loved and safe I am by spending these extra five minutes with me.

"Yes, go get that award, Dec, and wear the gold shirt," I reply.

Dec would never let me pretend to be anything I'm not and pushing him towards an option that takes attention away from him would be me allowing him to pretend to be something he's not. And Finnegan Declan Lindell is anything but a dull, grey shirt human.

*

I'm determined to turn the rest of my day around and not allow my past to take anymore away from me. I exit the coffee shop and feel a rush of warmth on my shoulders as the sun decides to peek out and show itself. I pause on the sidewalk, closing my eyes and breathing in the fresh air, the melodious chirping of birds drowning out the people passing by.

My gran used to have me sit on her porch after every rain. We would close our eyes together, trying to guess what birds were singing as the sun dried away all the rain that the clouds had just left us. A smile takes over my cheeks as that peaceful memory floods in. I miss those simple days with my gran.

Just as I am about to open my eyes, I feel something wet landing on my forehead before trickling down my temple. With a sense of dread, I open my eyes and instinctively wipe at it with my hand, only to find white pigeon droppings smeared across my fingers. Letting out a frustrated grunt, I realize that I have officially lost the battle for today.

I walk back into the cafe with my eyes glued to the floor, hoping the barista doesn't notice the bird shit on my face as I head to the bathroom. If I can't salvage my day, I refuse to be the one to brighten hers.

I finish rinsing my face off when my phone start to ring. I don't rush to answer because I already know it's my mom calling. As bad as it may sound, letting her go to voicemail during our weekly Saturday phone call makes me feel a little better. I'll call her back in a second, I just need a moment before I go from literal shit to feeling like shit.

Don't get me wrong. I love my mom, and I appreciate the fact that she wants to check in on me, but she asks the same questions every single week and it never makes me feel excited to talk to her. She always asks if I've found the man I'm going to marry yet, and when I say no, she finds a way to blame that on me. She never stops reminding me that my career choice should be my top priority. She'll then ask when I'm coming home and will get upset when I don't have an answer. I used to be honest and say never, but then she'd be heartbroken for the rest of the conversation and sometimes even through to the next week.

This is exactly why I love working on Saturdays at the coffee shop. I feel accomplished, like I have a head start on the upcoming week. That feeling is hard to beat. So when my

Mom calls, no matter how our conversation ended, I wouldn't allow it to ruin my day.

But today I woke up from my real-life nightmare, got yelled at by a barista, didn't accomplish a single thing for work, and then literally got shit on. This phone call is probably the last thing I should be adding to the list, but here I am dialing her back.

"Was I interrupting a lunch date?" she asks, her voice rising in pitch as she spoke, the excitement of her assumption evident.

"No, I was just cleaning bird poop off my face," I respond, hoping for a chuckle instead of disappointment.

"Oh," she says, letting out a sigh. "Well, I have some good news for you, Auden. There's a new guy at church. His name is Tucker. He just moved to Louisiana from Vermont and has the sweetest accent to match his big blue eyes."

I lean against the bathroom wall and slide my back down it until my butt lands on the floor. I don't care how disgusting the cold tile floor is, I have a feeling this conversation isn't ending anytime soon.

"He's twenty-eight and runs his daddy's cement business. They just added a new location here in Louisiana, and he was sent down to run it a few weeks ago. I was telling him all about you and showed him a picture. I could tell right away that that boy was excited to meet you!"

"Mama, you know I love living in Minneapolis," I say, silently wishing she would stop showcasing my college photos to every eligible guy she encounters at church.

"Well, you loved it *here* a lot longer. Can't you play on your computer here at home? You work at home already, why not do it here?" she asks.

Her lack of interest in my own interests is something that used to bother me. I still believe that has a lot to do with why we don't have a strong relationship. Growing up, she always wanted me in a dress like all the other little girls, but after ruining most of them with mud and rips, some self-inflicted, she finally gave up forcing me to wear them. She still pushed for me to join the church choir and take etiquette classes, but she gave up pretty quickly on those as well. I think she's always resented me for not becoming the girly girl she always dreamed of. Taylor was exactly what my mom dreamed of in a daughter. She loved sundresses and baby dolls growing up, so when my mom got the chance to braid Taylor's hair or paint her nails, I would run off and fish with my dad or help him work on his latest project. I was grateful my mom had a distraction.

"I do work wherever I want most days, but I also do a lot of meetings and tours and I need to do those things in person, and you know I'm not just 'playing on my computer,'" I answer shortly.

I understand that she wishes I was back home, looking for a husband and popping out grandbabies for her, but it would make life a lot easier for the both of us if she would just accept that I'm different and have built something that I'm just as proud of as she is for starting a family.

She's silent for a moment, I can hear her fiddling in the kitchen as the sound of cabinet doors opening and closing are in the background.

"If you say so. Tucker sure will be heartbroken."

Tucker will be just fine.

The conversation ends sooner than I anticipated, filling me with a glimmer of hope that I can make it back to my apartment without any further mishaps. Tossing my phone into my bag, I begin to push myself off the germ-ridden tiles when the door swings open. To my dismay, it's the barista, her expression even more irritated by my presence than before. She firmly shuts the door, arms crossed, and gazes down at me with disdain.

"You can't hang out in here," she states, reopening the door as a clear sign for me to depart.

I push myself off the floor, "I hope you have the day you deserve." I say sweetly with a grin, ignoring her mumbled response as I exit the restroom.

THREE

Auden

Dec's event went amazing. His students had a surprise performance lined up to say thank you after he accepted his award, causing him to ugly cry on stage. His ugly cry always tugs at my heartstrings because it's so genuine. If you ever see Dec cry and look good while doing it, he's faking.

We head toward home, both of us struggling to walk with our arms full of bouquets from students' parents.

"Where do we put all of these?" I ask Dec, trying to peek my head through a face full of dahlias.

"The room that has the best lighting," he replies, knowing already that the room with the best lighting is mine.

I bury my nose in the bouquets of flowers cradled in my arms, savoring the intoxicating fragrance that fills the air. Typically, I would resist the idea of cluttering my windowsill with plants, but in this moment, the aroma and sight of these vibrant symbols of life seem to be just what my soul craves.

My phone starts to ring, and I stumble to find a safe place on the sidewalk to set down the paper wrapped bouquets.

Once I finally get my arms free, the phone stops ringing. I pull it out of my bag and notice an unknown number with a Monroe area code. Weird. My parents are the only people I speak to from back home.

Dec must sense my uneasiness because he starts to set his armful of flowers down next to mine.

"Who was it?" he asks, walking closer to me and trying to peek over my shoulder at the phone screen.

"I'm not sure, but it's someone from back home," I reply, looking up from my phone and watching Dec's expression and waiting for his reaction.

It takes him a minute to realize what I'm implying, and then his eyes widen as he shifts his body so he's facing me.

"Well, are you going to call back? Did they leave a voicemail?" he asks, the speed of his voice quickening.

Before I can answer him my phone beeps and I receive a text from the same number.

Asher: Hey Auden, this is Asher Landry. Can you give me a call back?

I freeze, running through all the reasons Asher would be reaching out. I never changed my phone number. I just blocked a few people from my old life and never thought about it again.

Why would he be getting in touch? Is Taylor wanting to make amends and didn't have a way to reach me?

Dec leans over my shoulder and reads the message for himself.

"Who's Asher Landry?" he asks.

My stomach starts to feel queasy as I contemplate replying, calling, or ignoring that this ever happened.

"Asher is Taylor's older brother," I answer, breaking out of my silence and turning to face Dec. "I haven't seen or spoken to him in six years."

Dec grabs one of my hands and squeezes it before pulling me out of the way of a couple trying to pass by.

"Dec, Asher was in my dream last night. He saved me from Brad, but in real life, he wasn't even at the party. This all feels too weird."

Dec's eyebrows furrow as he takes in the new information.

"Is he a bad person?" he asks.

Asher was never someone you could describe as bad. He always seemed to keep to himself when others were around. When he did speak, it was always short and to the point, leaving you no room to continue the conversation. Taylor always knew how to get him to laugh though. It was nice when he had a laugh that made everyone else automatically join in. He was always much taller than Taylor and had strong, broad shoulders even though he wasn't on any sports teams. Taylor always managed to have him wrapped around her finger, even though he had almost a foot of height on her. He was usually off fishing in the summers and spent a lot of time in his room during the school year.

The last summer I spent in Monroe, before our senior year, I remember running down to their old lake house dock. Right as I was going to jump off the end, I noticed Asher emerging from the water, running his fingers through his messy, brown hair. The sight of him caused me to trip and fall right off the edge, cutting my foot open on a rusty nail on my way down.

Asher came rushing out and helped me. He brought me inside their house to clean the cut and put on a bandage. He was always kind to me, but we never had a lot of conversations over the many years I occupied his parents' home.

"No, he was always great," I answer, looking back at the message on my screen.

"Then you should call him back. It'll eat you up if you don't. Let's rip this Band-Aid off," Dec says with another squeeze of my hand.

He's right. I need to find out why Asher is calling, and I need to do it now before I lose my courage. I clear my throat and click his number, straightening my posture as I bring the phone up to my ear.

"Hey, Auden."

I freeze. His voice is much deeper than I remember, and I've suddenly forgotten every reason I decided to call back.

"Auden, can you hear me?" he asks.

Dec nudges me to snap out of it and respond.

"Hey Asher, it's Auden Sterling, what's going on?" I finally respond, my hand hitting my forehead as I regret how awkward I'm already being. Of course, he knows who this is. He called me first.

"Hey, I'm sorry to reach out like this, but I wanted to talk to you before the rest of the town heard the news."

My eyes dart to Dec when I hear Asher's reply. This can't be good.

"What news?" I ask as I start to count the cracks in the sidewalk beneath me, trying to ignore my quickening heartbeat.

"I go over to Taylor's house every Saturday morning to pick her up for brunch," Asher begins. I can hear him taking a deep breath before proceeding. I can feel the bile making its way up my throat the moment he says Taylor's name.

"And this morning she didn't answer, so I assumed she overslept."

He pauses again, this time I hear a muffled sniffle before his deep breath.

"I walked into the house and headed straight for her bedroom, and she . . ." his voice becomes quieter.

"She was . . ."

His voice cracks and he's holding back tears. I grab Dec's hand, bracing myself for bad news.

"She committed suicide, Auden."

The phone falls out of my hand, crashing to the cement, my body shortly behind it.

FOUR

Asher

    I set my phone down on the kitchen table and take a seat, my eyes scanning the many pieces of paper sprawled out in front of me. I started filling out my monthly incident reports for the fire department late last night, but now I can't bring myself to touch any of it.

    I pick up Taylor's letter to Auden and hold it up to the ceiling light above me, unable to make out any words other than the name written outside. My thumb rubs across the front of the envelope, the image of Taylor's cold, stiff fingers holding it this afternoon is flashing through my mind.

    I shake my head and toss the letter back on the table, there's no address on the front of it. I knew Taylor and Auden had a falling out before they graduated, but them not knowing where the other ended up just doesn't make sense.

    When I called Auden, I didn't know what to expect, and even now, I'm still uncertain how to proceed. I never had the opportunity to tell her that Taylor had left a letter for her before she abruptly ended the call. I had rehearsed the conversation in my mind multiple times before dialing her number, but her reaction caught me completely off guard.

The sound of vibration pulls me out of my thoughts as I reach for my phone, our mother's face smiling on the screen. My stomach starts to turn as I stare at the picture—is she even "our" mother anymore? I pause before answering the call.

"Asher?" I hear my mother ask, her voice shaky on the other end.

My father's voice echoes in the background among the beeping machines and the continuous ringing of telephones.

"Asher we're at the hospital right now with Brad," my mother continues, "and he's hoping you could run to his house and look for Taylor's wedding ring. She wasn't wearing it when . . ."

Her voice goes silent, and I can feel her struggling to find the words no mother should have to speak.

"I can do that," I interrupt.

"We're about to head over to the funeral home," she says. "Your uncles are flying in this week, so we're planning to have the ceremony on Friday. I'm assuming the Chief doesn't expect you to return to work by then."

I walk over to my living room and spot a photo from Taylor and Brad's wedding, gazing at the big smiles on all our faces, my mouth turning upwards as I remember how beautiful Taylor looked that day, just like every other day of her life.

Retreating to my weathered leather chair, I reminisce about the times Taylor sat in it, tracing my fingers over the worn seams. I recall a particular memory of her laughing so hard that water came out of her nose. Rushing to the kitchen to get her a paper towel, I found her staring blankly at her phone upon my return, her once joyful expression replaced by a solemn demeanor and slumped shoulders. Before I could ask about her sudden change in mood, she excused herself, mentioning that Brad was coming home early, and she needed to be there before he was.

"Asher?" my mother asks, waking me out of my memories.

My jaw clenches as I hear Brad laughing in the background, forcing me to bite my lip to keep silent.

"The Chief said I can take all the time I need," I answer.

After I hang up the phone, I stare back at the photo of Taylor's wedding, noticing my mother's arm linked through Brad's, an even bigger smile on her face than Taylor's.

During the wedding toasts, my mother took the microphone and went on and on about how she knew Brad and Taylor were meant to be together since they were little. She told the story of the time when Brad pushed Taylor off our old swing set, and she ended up having to get stitches. The next day, Brad and his mom showed up at the house with flowers to apologize. Both sets of parents loved telling that story as if Brad had made a mistake in love and made up for it with such sweetness the next day. I don't think they ever knew that I was in the tree fort when Brad and his mom were getting out of the car. I heard him tell his mom that he didn't want to give flowers to some stupid girl. I never told Taylor about that part because she seemed to love the idea of it being the beginning of their story as well.

Finding a way to deliver this letter to Auden seems like an impossible task. The fact that she still has the same phone number from when she lived here was a stroke of luck, but locating her current address will be a whole other challenge. I settle down at my kitchen table, opening my laptop, and stare at the familiar Google homepage. Where do I even begin? I type in her name and sift through numerous LinkedIn profiles and unrelated individuals. Just as I begin losing hope, a link to a bar named Jerry's catches my eye with Auden Sterling's name highlighted. Intrigued, I click on it and discover a Facebook post praising a woman who had organized a fundraiser to repair the bar's leaky roof. In the photo attached to the post, I instantly recognize Auden. She looks older, more mature, yet just as beautiful as I remember. Without hesitation, I scribble down the bar's address and contact number on the back of an envelope lying in front of me before closing my laptop.

Time seems to stretch on endlessly as I stare at the piece of paper in front of me. My knee starts to bounce up and down involuntarily, a nervous habit I can't seem to shake. To clear my mind, I instinctively reach for my laptop again and start scrolling through the local flight lists. It's something I've always done, finding solace in the idea that there are places I can escape to at a moment's notice, making Monroe feel less suffocating. My eyes come to a halt when I spot a flight departing for Minneapolis in just a few hours.

I pull myself out of my chair and walk over to my closet, throwing a few random items into my backpack, smelling socks and shirts along the way.

The morning Taylor chose to end her life was the same morning that she knew I was supposed to visit. Taylor had a penchant for planners that dated all the way back to third grade. She wouldn't go anywhere without one, and every Christmas, without fail, a new planner would find its way into her stocking. I used to tease her about how she seemed to know my schedule better than I did myself, and in truth, she probably did.

I grab the letter from the table and hold it up against my chest. Taylor planned on me finding it, and she wanted me to make sure Auden received her final words.

My pocket vibrates and I huff as I yank the phone out of my pocket.

A text from my mother.

Mom: Did you find her ring?

I shove my phone into my backpack before carefully zipping the letter into its own section.

"I don't want to give that stupid man the ring," I mutter under my breath as I reach for my car keys.

FIVE

Auden

Dec slept in bed with me last night, and he finally passed out around 3:00 am. My mind was stuck on memories of Taylor and the many assumptions I've formed as to why she ended her life. It doesn't feel real, and I can't find a way to accept this new reality.

I knew sleep was out of the question and headed to Thunderstruck, my local boxing gym. When I had finally opened up to Dec about the reason I left Monroe, he suggested we take a self-defense class and Thunderstruck was the best fit being only a block from our apartment.

My gloves smack against the worn-out bag, sending the stiff smell of sweat back towards my face. Being the only girl in any establishment usually sends me into flight mode, but Thunderstruck is more of a sanctuary for me. Most of the men at this gym know me by name and seem to respect that I keep to myself. We're all here for a reason and making new friends isn't usually one of them. Besides, I doubt many of the other members are too interested in a girl who only wants to grow muscle, not tone a perfect ass.

"Hot water heater is out again," I hear a man say across the room.

When I turn around, I see a guy talking to Kevin, the owner's son, who must've shown up to help his parents again. Kevin looks back in my direction and gives me a smile while helping the man who's complaining in only a towel and shower shoes.

I haven't seen Kevin in about three months, and he looks better than ever. His thick blonde locks are pulled back in a black headband, highlighting his strong chiseled jawline. The morning light is finally starting to shine in through the window lined walls, hitting every angle of his defined shoulders, peeking out of his cut off Thunderstruck t-shirt.

I walk over to the wall where I left my water bottle, leaning over and picking it up for a well-earned drink. I can feel the sweat soaking my t-shirt and realize I forgot to coat my inner thighs with baby powder because they feel as raw as a fresh cut steak.

Dec and I met Kevin through our self-defense class that he was teaching a few years ago. He doesn't actually work at Thunderstruck. He just helps when his parents need him. Kevin's the total package. He does very well for himself in finance and owns a beautiful home right outside of the city. On weekends, he mows the lawns of a few of his elderly neighbors, walks the dogs at the local animal shelter on Thursdays, and volunteers at the homeless shelter on Sundays. You would think his flaw must be in his romantic relationships since he's a little too perfect in every other area of his life, but even that he manages to ace as well.

I would know. We dated for a few months this last year, and I can say from my experience that it doesn't get any more perfect than Kevin.

Kevin finishes his conversation, sending the towel man back to the locker room. Looking back in my direction, his eyes meet my gaze. I give him a smile but try not to look too happy since our last interaction wasn't the greatest.

Three months ago, I decided to finally call it quits with Kevin, and boy was that hard.

We dated casually for a few months, the first and only guy I've given a chance since moving to Minneapolis. Everything was great, he was always respectful and never pushed anything on me. We spent so many nights walking around and talking about life, our families, and everything in between. But as our relationship progressed well beyond the usual stage of becoming physically intimate, I realized I wasn't ever going to be able to give myself to him fully. Kevin taught me for eight weeks how to protect myself physically, and even after all of that, his touch sent me into flight mode.

We never talked about my past and why I've built such a tall wall around myself, but we didn't have to. He's been teaching his classes for long enough to recognize who's there for fun and who's there for protection. That's another reason I felt so comfortable in his presence.

But three months ago, I had to make the decision to let him go and be loved by someone who could give him everything he deserves. Unfortunately, as badly as we both wanted it to be me, it never can be. He took it well, but I knew asking him to stay in my life as less than he wanted wasn't fair, so I let go of him completely.

"Well, look who's back," he says, walking over with a towel.

I grab the towel from him, wiping away the sweat around my neck as it continues to cover me.

"How are you, Kevin?" I ask, giving him a bigger smile to match his.

"Better now that I see you back to working on your technique."

I stomp on any hope the man has for a relationship with me, and he still manages to care about my own health and safety. *The total package.*

"Do you have time for a little coaching?" he asks.

All I have is time if it includes a distraction. I nod my head yes and grab my gloves back off the gym floor, following him over to one of the boxing rings.

My thigh burns as I lift myself up onto the canvas covered mat, squeezing under the ropes. Kevin leans down and grabs my arm, helping pull me to my feet.

He puts both of his gloves up, covering his face and I mimic him, starting to gently jog in place as I ready myself.

"Let's see what you've got, Auden. Think you can get me with a face shot?" he teases, trying to get me riled up.

Little does he know that I'm already as high strung as I can get.

I swing and hit the side of his glove, his head moving swiftly to miss a face shot before taking a step back and realizing I'm ready to go full force.

But I keep swinging, pushing him further and further back on the mat. My mind warps Kevin's face into a resemblance of Brad's, and I feel the rage building inside of me. Each blow is coming out stronger and faster, my ears ringing so loud that I drown out my own grunts. My arm pulls back, and I take one more full swing, landing my punch directly into his jaw and sending him flying backward into the ropes.

"Woah, woah, you got me, Auden!" I hear him shout, snapping me back to reality.

My arms drop to my sides as the situation comes into focus, looking over at Kevin and seeing the shiny red mark I just added to the side of his face.

"Oh shit, Kevin," I say, ripping my gloves off and walking closer to him. "Are you okay?"

My eyes start to fill with tears when I recognize how out of control I'm becoming, my shoulders shaking up and down as I try to desperately hold my composure.

I hate crying and always have. I've always felt out of place when others would cry around me. The vulnerability that crying makes me feel, even when I'm alone, makes me uncomfortable in my own skin, so doing it in front of others is something I avoid at all costs.

Kevin lowers his hand from his cheek as I start to lower myself to escape the ring.

"Where are you going?" he asks, his hand reaching out and touching my shoulder.

Without a response, I feel his arms tucking underneath my armpits and lifting me back to my feet. He turns my body towards him and wraps his arms around me snuggly.

"Auden, it's okay. You're okay," he whispers in my ear as I flood his t-shirt with tears and snot.

My blubbering eventually calms down, and Kevin leans back, pulling my face from his chest and wiping away the snot trailing between his shirt and my nose.

Once the tears finally subside, I scan the room, noticing the many men silently watching me as I try to get myself together. Kevin pulls my chin back, so that my attention is only on him, and he tells me to follow him.

We walk into his dad's private office, and Kevin opens a cabinet, pulling out a clean towel, sports bra, and shorts.

"These were left behind a while ago. They're clean. I promise," he says, handing them to me.

"Why don't you cool off for a minute, Auden, and I'll be waiting when you're done." He unlocks a second door leading into his dads' private shower and holds the door open for me.

This bathroom is much nicer than the ones attached to the locker room—there aren't any loose hairs or rusted pipes exposed, and the smell is surprisingly lemony instead of the usual musty aroma.

The cold shower trickles down my face, and I start to feel my heart rate slowing down. I close my eyes and embrace the wetness, calming my dry and swollen eyelids.

Back home in Monroe, when I would feel out of place or overwhelmed, Taylor would take me to our secret spot. She'd sit with me quietly while we took in the sounds around us and splashed our faces with the chilled water from the stream. I keep my eyes closed a moment longer, and I imagine that I'm back there without a care in the world and no dead friend.

Once I get dried off and dressed, I open the door back to his dad's office, noticing Kevin sitting behind the small, black metal desk, waiting for me just like he said he would.

"Feeling any better?" he asks, a smile creeping across the concerned look on his face.

I hand him the wet towel and nod my head yes, taking a seat across from him.

"Thank you, Kevin. I'm so sorry I got out of control."

Kevin stands up and walks around the desk, pulling a chair from against the wall and taking a seat next to me.

"Don't apologize. I'm not hurt, but I am a little worried that you are."

He lifts his hand and rests it on top of mine, ducking his head so our eyes meet.

Instead of looking back at him, I lean my whole body in his direction until my shoulder is resting against his chest.

"Do you hate me for not being able to give you what you wanted?" I ask.

I feel his body shake a little and realize he's starting to giggle. I pull myself off him, leaning back until I can see his face, confirming he is indeed laughing at my question.

"This can't be what's bothering you, can it?" he asks "Do you really believe I'd be wiping your boogers from my shirt with my favorite gloves if I hated you, Auden?"

A small grin forms across my face with the realization of how ridiculous I sound before I join in on his laughter.

"I guess you're right. I think I just wish I could've given you more," I say.

The office door opens and Kevin's dad walks in, stopping the moment he notices his office is occupied.

"Oh sorry, I didn't realize anyone was in here," he says before recognizes me. "Oh hey, Auden, so glad you're back."

Kevin's dad could be his twin, except for the gray hair and the foot of height he's missing. He used to be a pro wrestler and went by the name Thunderstruck, hence the name of his gym. On Friday nights, he still turns the boxing rings into wrestling rings and allows the locals to come in for a $5.00 show, and any gym members can participate as wrestlers. He donates all the proceeds to the winner's charity of choice too. There's no mystery where Kevin gets his giving nature from.

"Thanks, Mr. Thunderstruck. I was just leaving," I reply, standing up.

Kevin walks me out of the office, holding a bag of my damp clothes.

"I'll wash these for you and throw them in the cabinet for when you return," he says before pulling me toward him for another hug.

My arms tighten around him, letting him silently know how much I appreciate him. He leans down before letting go and plants a soft kiss on the top of my head.

"Do me a favor, Auden, come back and let me help you master that uppercut before you use it on the person who clearly deserves it."

SIX

Asher

I land at the Minneapolis-Saint Paul International Airport at 7:00 am. The only flight I could find was a "red eye," but I doubt I would've slept back at home anyways. I rub my eyes and check my backpack again to make sure I have Taylor's letter, wondering if I'll really get the chance to deliver it to Auden.

I wave down a cab and give the driver the address to Jerry's Bar. I already GPS'd the time it'll take to get there and start to feel the sweat building on my forehead knowing I'm only fifteen minutes away. The bar probably isn't even open this early, especially on a Sunday, but the small chance of running into her is enough to raise my blood pressure.

The cab turns down Tellsman Rd., pulling up to the curb in front of a strip of old brick buildings. I step out of the cab and notice a small unlit sign that says Jerry's. I hand the driver cash before he points at the door of the bar.

"Think you might be a little early," he says.

I nod my head, staring at the bar and regretting showing up without putting any real thought into what I'm doing. The door has its hours posted so I walk closer to read it. To my surprise, they're open on Sundays but not until noon, four hours from now.

I spot a bench facing the bar and decide to take a seat while I figure out my next move. I set my backpack down next to me and reach inside, making sure the letter hasn't somehow unzipped the pocket and walked away on its own. The smell of coffee fills the air around me causing me to look around, but I don't see a coffee shop anywhere. But there are people smiling as they round the corner with their to-go cups still steaming in their hands.

The sun warms the front of my black t-shirt and I lean back into the bench, allowing its rays to reach my face, running new scenarios of how I'm going to get in contact with Auden once the bar does open.

People keep passing by for what feels like hours, their heels smacking against the concrete and the occasional siren behind me. I can't find a way to force myself off the bench to walk around before the bar opens. The thought of missing Auden if I leave this bench feels too risky. I was in such a rush to get here that I guess I never took the time to consider what I was really doing.

I'm not an idiot. I know I'm avoiding my own pain. I feel as if I've been floating through the last two days. My feet are on the ground but even when I'm staring directly at them, my brain is still trying to convince me that I'm in the air. I don't know how I've been doing anything—drove myself to the airport, got on a plane, waved down a cab, and walked to this bench and took a seat. It's like I've been watching myself doing everything from above.

Am I the one that died?

Am I just a soul now, trapped and floating around this world searching for my body? Because I know I've been moving but my body is so numb that I can't feel it.

The smell of smoke grabs my attention, and I notice a short guy around my age with curly red hair with, if I had to guess, very expensive sunglasses resting on the tip of his nose. He's leaning against the brick building, taking another drag off of his cigarette, and looking back at me with a smile.

"Why are you so curious about my building?" the guy asks, pushing his sunglasses back up his nose.

He has a shirt on that says "ask me to dance" and neon green short-shorts with socks that match his clean, white sneakers.

I look around for the person he must be talking to, finding only myself in his eyeline. He walks over and takes a seat next to me on the bench.

"The bar," he says, pointing at Jerry's. "I manage Jerry's, you look like you're very interested in what's inside, but I don't remember ever seeing you here before."

My mouth feels dry as I try to swallow and find the right response that won't make me seem like the stalker Auden has spent years hiding from.

"You're right. I've never been here, but I'm looking for someone that has" I answer, unable to make eye contact. I hope that didn't sound as creepy as I think it did.

He takes another drag off on his cigarette before flicking it into the street and blowing the smoke above both our heads. I can feel his stare.

"I know everyone that walks into that bar, and depending on who you're looking for, I may be able to help," he says.

I think I'm making him nervous and, based on how sweaty my palms are, I'm making myself nervous as well. I pull out my phone and show him the article about Auden raising money, hoping he'll recognize her.

"How do you know Auden?" he asks, his eyebrows rising as suspicion covers his face.

"We grew up together, and now I don't know how to find her," I answer, putting my phone back into my pocket. "I tried to look her up and this is all I could find online." "You're from Monroe?" he asks.

He must know Auden well if he knows where she's from. Not many people have even noticed Monroe on a map.

"Yeah, I am. Do you know where she lives?" I ask, instantly regretting my directness and trying to back track. "Or how to get a hold of her?"

He stands up, pulling another cigarette out of his crossbody bag and lighting it up before crossing his arms in front of his chest.

"Depends. What do you want with Auden?"

I look over at my backpack and then down at the cement, thinking about the reality of why I traveled all this way.

"We kind of grew up together," I start to answer. "She was good friends with my sister." I pause for a minute, feeling like their relationship deserved more than what I was giving it.

"They were best friends," I state, tilting my head up to feel out his reaction.

I watch as his eyebrows furrow before his eyes widen, the cigarette between his lips falling to the ground.

"Taylor's your sister?" he asks.

My posture immediately straightens with his response, feeling a rush of hope.

"You knew my sister?" I ask, feeling much more curious about how this colorful man is connected to Auden and Taylor.

He shakes his head before pushing the toe of his shoe into the cigarette laying on the sidewalk. He takes a seat back on the bench next to me, this time much closer and reaches one arm around my shoulder, pulling me in for a side hug.

"No, I didn't, but I'm so sorry for your loss."

I lean into his hug, and I notice he smells of cigarettes and pears. I'm not an affectionate person, but for some reason this little man's arm reaching up over my shoulder calms my nerves.

"I'm Dec by the way," he says. "Are you Asher?" I sit back up, turning my body so I can face him.

"Yeah, I am. How do you know Auden?" I ask.

"We've been roommates for a few years now," he answers, before checking the time on his watch. "We actually live right in this building. Do you want to come inside and wait for her?"

I look up at the tall brick building next to the bar, the hair on the back of my neck starting to stand as I realize how close I've been to her this whole time. Dec must sense my hesitation because he pats me on the back and stands up, pointing his head toward the building.

"Come on, it'll be fine. I promise. I have another hour until I need to open the bar anyways."

I follow Dec into the building, taking in the modern artwork and grey cement flooring. We walk into the elevator and ride up to the third floor, my nerves building as each floor dings on the way up.

We step out into the hallway, and I follow behind him until we reach a door with the numbers 308. Dec unlocks the door, and we step inside their apartment, the shiny cement floor continuing inside. I notice immediately the floor-to-ceiling windows lining the walls, wondering if there was any chance Auden had already looked down and seen me sitting on the bench below.

"Can I get you anything to drink? Water? Coffee? Vodka?" Dec asks.

I turn around and set my backpack on the small island in the kitchen, nodding my head yes. "Just water, please."

Dec scoops some ice into a glass and fills it with water before setting it down in front of me.

"So, when's the last time you spoke to Auden?" he asks. "Besides last night."

I pull the cold glass away from my lips and take in a deep breath, scanning the room until my eyes stop on a painting of a magnolia tree.

"Around the same time she left Monroe. I'm sure I'm the last person she'd expect to see standing in her apartment," I answer, looking over at the front door.

Dec walks around the island, blocking my view of the door and waving in the direction of the living room, my eyes following him.

"I know why Auden left Monroe, and I think you're right that she'll be a little shocked to see you here. But I also think this little reunion might be exactly what Auden needs to help her heal and move on with her life," he says before plopping down on their fluffy, cloudlike couch.

"Heal and move on with her life" catches me off guard.

I push off the island and walk over to join him, taking a seat in a green velvet chair with wooden armrests.

"I think you may know more about why Auden left Monroe than I do." I reply, looking back over my shoulder. This time my eyes noticing the doorknob starting to turn.

Dec stands before the door opens all the way, heading straight in its direction. My heart starts to beat rapidly, and I'm suddenly no longer feeling like I'm floating because I can feel every inch of my body starting to tense and shake at the same time as I wait to see how my impulsive actions play out.

"Hey, Aud. Don't freak out," he starts to say.

I recognize her piercing green eyes immediately, but her slim figure and defined waist are new to me. I was expecting the eighteen year-old girl I remember from six years ago, not this grown woman who stands in front of me now. She's wearing baggy athletic shorts that seem to be tied as tightly as possible, a red sports bra stained with fresh sweat and a pair of boxing gloves hanging over her shoulder. Her chestnut brown hair is pulled back in a ponytail, and I can't help but smile about the fact that this big city has failed to alter her core essence.

The Auden I remember was always fierce and ready for a challenge, which is why Dec's comment about healing threw me off. The Auden I knew growing up was always the one helping others heal from their own issues, never the one who needed support. I never felt the need to worry about Taylor when Auden was around. She made sure she always had Taylor's back. I'll never forget when they were in sixth grade and Taylor had sat in some chocolate milk at lunchtime. She didn't realize it until a few kids cornered her on the playground and were teasing her about having an accident. Auden ran right up to the kids and shoved one down so hard that he had to go to the nurse's office for stitches in his elbow. Taylor was always safe with Auden around and I loved their friendship because of it.

I stand up from the chair and make eye contact with Auden, her eyes staring blankly back at me as if she's seen a ghost. Her jaw drops open as I take a step toward her.

"Hi, Auden."

SEVEN

Auden

    I suddenly feel small as I look up at the boy that I used to know standing in my living room. He was always taller than me, but it feels like he's grown another foot in the last six years. His untamed, mahogany hair falling in unruly waves match his aged-oak colored eyes. I notice his scruffy jawline start to move and snap out of the trance he had me in.

    "Asher," I whisper, feeling the sweat from my chest trickle down to my stomach.

    "I'm sorry to just show up like this," Asher says, rubbing the back of his neck as his eyes trail back and forth between the sight of me and the backpack sitting on my kitchen counter. "I'm not quite sure what I'm doing but when you hung up last night, I wanted to make sure you were okay."

    Asher rubs his hand down the side of his backpack, stopping at a zipper along the side.

    "She left you something."

    I pause, not understanding. Then I excuse myself quickly and retreat to the bathroom, frantically searching for a pair of jeans and a t-shirt to throw on, my mind racing.

What could she have left me?

Am I the only person she left something for?

I spot the leg of dark skinny jeans and pull them out of the laundry hamper, sliding them on as my hands shake. I continue to dig through the hamper for a few moments, listening to the muffled sounds of conversation in the kitchen.

I'm not sure how Asher ended up here, or how they're now in the kitchen talking as if they've known one another forever. I'm so glad Dec is here, and I wasn't in the apartment alone when he showed up. I spot my plain white t-shirt and grab it, pulling it over my head and checking for wrinkles in the mirror.

Why do I even care what I look like?

Why would Asher even care what my clothes look like? His sister died. He probably won't even remember what I looked like in a few days with how much his mind must be racing.

I sit down on the toilet seat and think back to my gram's funeral. I don't remember who attended or what was said. I just remember the color of her coffin and how the funeral director didn't notice that half the lilies were dead.

Before leaving the bathroom, I lean my head down into the sink, splashing cold water on my cheeks in hopes of waking from the second dream I've had with Asher in it.

What the hell could Taylor have left me?

We haven't been a part of each other's lives in so long that we could be considered strangers. I shake my head and take a deep breath, trying to find any form of composure I can. I don't think I'm ready to see what she left me. Her brother standing in my Minneapolis apartment is enough of a shock for this moment.

As I make my way back to the kitchen, I hear Dec's voice, the tone full of excitement.

"So, Aud said you were always a kind kid. Is that why you decided to become a firefighter?" Dec asks, followed by a crunching sound which means he's broken back into my secret stash of rice cakes again.

"She said that?" Asher asks. "She was always easy to be nice to."

I lean against the hallway wall and keep listening. I like that Asher thought I was easy to be nice to.

"I'm not one who likes to sit around doing the same things over and over, so when the opportunity to check out the fire academy came up, I decided to take it."

"So you aren't scared when you have to run inside a burning building?" Dec asks.

"There are a lot of things in this world that scare me more than fire," Asher replies, standing up straight when he notices my presence.

I sit down at the counter and Asher takes a seat next to me, the air stirring an enchanting blend of sandalwood and natural musk in my direction.

"How long are you in town?" I ask.

Asher fiddles with the strap of his backpack.

"I haven't really booked a flight back," he says quietly. "I sort of just ended up here without a plan."

His voice is filled with such deep sorrow that it tugs at my heartstrings.

I reach out to grab a rice cake and my elbow brushes Asher's arm, sending a wave of goosebumps all the way down the back of my neck. I pull my arm back, my cheeks flushing like a school girl. I'm not sure why my body just reacted that way. Am I embarrassed that he's here and I wasn't expecting it? Or is that extra foot of height he's grown taking over my mind. The last thing that should be catching my attention right now is how attractive he's become.

"Well, the couch is available for as long as you would like," I say without thinking it over or asking Dec.

Asher looks over at the couch and then back at me. I spot a small smile creeping along his lip line as his fingers trace the zipper on his backpack.

Just as Asher opens his mouth to respond, Dec jumps in to remind me that it's my day to do the grocery shopping. He wipes the crumbs from the corners of his mouth before swiftly picking up his keys from the countertop and turning toward Asher, placing a reassuring hand on his shoulder.

"Thanks for coming," he says before heading to the door. "I'll be around later after my shift."

Asher smiles back at Dec and I love the way he seems so comfortable around him. Dec isn't always taken seriously with his loud expressions and flashy clothing choices. But anyone who gives him the time of day quickly learns to love him as much as I do. Dec closes the door behind him, and Asher turns in my direction.

"I don't mean to intrude on ya'll," Asher says. "I just wanted to make sure you were okay, and that Taylor's letter ended up with you."

He starts to unzip his backpack, my throat closing as the zipper opens.

She left me a letter?

Me of all people?

My heart sinks into my stomach and the fear of what she could have written overcomes me. I'm not ready to read a letter from Taylor. I'm not ready for her brother to be sitting at my kitchen island. Shit, I'm sure as hell not ready for Taylor to be dead.

I lean forward and put my hand on top of his before he can reach into the bag. His hands are rough and dry, reminding me of my father's.

"Nonsense," I say, pulling his hand away from the backpack. "You just got here and I'm sure you haven't eaten. Why don't you join me at the grocery store and help me carry back some groceries?"

EIGHT

Asher

I grab three bags of groceries from the cashier, one filled with Auden's pasta ingredients and two full of organic, meatless imitations of food for Dec. I giggle at the idea of a gay man who doesn't enjoy meat.

Auden's silky hair falls in front of her face as she puts her wallet back in her purse before tucking her hair behind her ear, exposing a small scar along the left side of her neck.

Everything about her seems to catch my attention. I don't usually find myself captivated by much, I can't even keep my attention on my favorite hobbies for long. But so far, I've taken every opportunity this morning to absorb how much she's changed, even though she also seems like the same girl I've always known.

"If I knew I wouldn't have to carry all of this by myself, I would have invited you to Minneapolis years ago," she says as we exit through the automatic doors.

The sun beats down on my black t-shirt as we walk back in the direction of her apartment, making me realize that black wasn't the best color choice for such a sunny day. I can't believe how many people are out and about during the day here, going on with their lives, not pretending that there isn't a letter a few blocks away whose contents are burning in the back of their minds.

A familiar sound plays in the distance, causing Auden and I both to stop. Right as the theme song pops in my mind, Auden turns to face me and sings, "Who ya gonna call?"

Both of our faces light up as we notice a small thrift shop across the street with a Ghostbusters movie poster in the window.

"Do you remember how obsessed Taylor was with those movies?" I ask.

"Do you remember how scared *you* were of those movies?" She replies as she trails back toward the cross walk.

I follow her lead as we head toward the shop. I like how comfortable she seems around me. We haven't seen one another in so many years, and we were never very close, but there's just something about her that makes me feel at ease. I like that she seems to feel the same way.

"I wasn't scared," I protest, trying to keep up with her fast pace.

She rolls her eyes, and I can't help but smile back at her. The feeling of being with someone who's known you your whole life is so comfortable, and I haven't realized how rare it is for me to feel that way until now.

We walk into the dimly lit shop, a small bell dinging as we step in, the smell of musty antiques filling my nose. I watch Auden's eyes widen as she takes in the many dust-lined shelves that are filled to the brim with an array of Ghostbusters memorabilia—posters, action figures, and even a life-sized replica of the iconic Ecto-1 tucked in the back corner. She looks like a kid in a candy store.

Auden wanders off into the shop while I explore the random picture frames still holding memories in the form of photos inside of them. My finger trails across the glass of an old wooden frame, wiping away the dust from an old wedding photo. I wonder if twenty years from now, Taylors wedding photo will be left in a thrift shop in Louisiana, convincing strangers that it was the start of a happy and long life.

The sound of Brad laughing on the other end of the phone last night pops in my mind. What the hell could have possibly been so funny when you're in the same building as your dead wife! I wonder if the person who finds their wedding frame will wonder if he truly loved her as much as I wonder now.

I hear a crashing sound and turn the corner down the next aisle, spotting Auden trying to pick up an old, black phone, its curled wires tangled around her arms as she tries to stop it from repeatedly asking, "Who you gonna call?"

She finally gets the phone back on the shelf and looks up at me, a flush creeping across her cheeks.

I can't help but start to laugh, and the moment I do, Auden bursts into a fit of laughter with me. We stand there laughing together for what feels like a full three minutes until I notice a tear start to fall down Auden's face, her eyes starting to fill with sorrow.

She tries to hide the quiver of her bottom lip with her hand, but a sudden urge forces me to take a step forward and pull her hand gently away, wiping her tear in the process. She doesn't need to hide her sadness, not with me.

"Do you remember the Halloween when I ate too much candy at school and puked all over my costume?" Auden asks me as she rubs her thumb across a ghost figurine.

"Yes, that was the year Taylor convinced you to go as Ghostbusters and made Sandy the ghost."

"I ruined my costume at school and didn't have time to clean it before trick or treating," Auden continues "Taylor gave me her costume to wear and she went as a ghost instead. She swore up and down that she secretly wanted to be a ghost anyways."

My eyes become blurry as the memory comes back to me. I wonder if there will ever be a time when the memories of Taylor don't sting to my core.

"That's the Halloween Taylor got grounded for cutting up mom and dad's white bedsheet."

"She begged me for months to go as the ghostbusters, and by the night of Halloween, she was a silly sheet of a ghost so that I could have a costume," Auden says, a smile creeping back across her face.

She reaches her hand out and touches the top of the shelf, running her fingers along the dust. I wonder if she feels the same stabbing in her stomach each time that she realizes our memories of Taylor are all we have left.

NINE

Auden

     The oven's heat comes blasting out on my face as I lean down and place the uncooked lasagna inside, setting the mitts on the counter after I close the oven door. I decided to make lasagna because I don't really know how to make anything else, and for some reason I feel the need to not admit to Asher that Dec does most of the cooking.
     Asher decided to go for a run after we got back from shopping. He got pretty quiet before he left and said he needed to clear his head. I tried to get some work done while he was gone but kept getting distracted by the thought of him not being okay. It must be hard losing your sister and then traveling so far away from home less than twenty-four hours later. I wish I knew how to help him, but in my short time on earth, I've learned that my only coping mechanism is to run away. So far, he seems to already have that part down. When he got back to the apartment, he seemed to be feeling a bit better so maybe I should stop overthinking it.
     I hear the water turn off from the shower and my heart starts to race because I know there aren't too many more

excuses that Asher and I can make up before we have to finally read Taylor's letter. Today has been an emotional rollercoaster. But after almost 24 hours since my past caught up with me, spending the rest of my day with Asher has surprisingly brought me a lot of happy moments.

I look over at his backpack, still sitting on the kitchen counter like a piece of gold being dangled in front of a homeless man.

How can I want to know something so bad and be terrified of its contents at the same time?

Asher walks into the kitchen, his hands rubbing a towel around his head, squeezing the water from his wet hair. My eyes drift down to the waistline of his grey sweatpants, his glistening V-shaped belly exposed sends a wave of heat down my neck. I think he noticed me looking because when I looked up to his face, his eyes squinted, and he smiled before pulling his white Monroe Fire Department t-shirt on. His work shirt makes him so much more attractive. I'd hate to find out how seeing him in his full uniform would make me feel.

"So, what do you do for work in this big city?" he asks, taking a seat at the counter across from me.

I set the timer on the oven and turn back toward Asher, resting my elbows on the counter before answering him.

"It's not as exciting as saving people from burning buildings." I give him a smirk. "But I have a degree in information technology."

"Information technology?" he asks, his face displaying honest curiosity.

"I work for a local hospital right now, making sure everything is running smoothly within all the departments and adding new systems while replacing old ones where they're needed," I answer, trying to keep my explanation as short as possible. "I work from home most days, which is nice, and the money is good, which is even nicer."

I turn around and grab two plates from the upper cabinet, remembering that I have an interview with a different organization in two days.

"Well, it may not be a burning building, but you're keeping the building that saves even more lives running smoothly," he replies. "So I think that means we make a pretty good team."

His comment makes me smile. I was right, Asher is good even when his life is turned upside down. He's trying to make someone else feel important.

He leans down and smells one of the vases of flowers Dec set on the kitchen island.

"Didn't you want to do something in nature before?" he asks. "I feel like I would've noticed Taylor being more upset your last year of school if you were planning to move all the way up here."

How does he remember that?

I was planning to attend the University of Louisiana in Monroe for a degree in wildlife conservation. Taylor was going to attend with me and get her degree in education. We planned on buying an apartment together once we had saved up enough money. Nature had always been a passion of mine, but when my life got flipped upside down, I guess I left that passion behind in Monroe as well.

"I was planning on attending college locally for wildlife conservation but changed my mind last minute, and luckily U of M was still allowing new admissions," I answer, not wanting to go any further into the details of how his sister broke my heart.

My phone beeps and I reach for it, seeing a text from Dec displayed on the front screen.

Dec: **Terrance asked me to stay and do inventory tonight. Might sleep over at his if it goes well. I can come straight home if you'd prefer but I wouldn't want me interrupting my time with a man who looks like Asher does ;)**

I let out a snort. He's so ridiculous but I love when he reads my mind. As much as I'd like for Dec to be here as a buffer for awkward moments, it really hasn't been that awkward between Asher and I. Without knowing how long I'll have with him, I want to take advantage of every second. "Dec has to work late, so it's just us two," I say to Asher, taking note of the smile he isn't trying to hide with the news.

"I kinda like Dec," he replies.

"It's hard not to like Dec once you get to know him."

"His accent is entertaining too. It's like a Canadian movie."

I can't help but laugh at Asher's comment. It's one of the first things I thought when I arrived in Minnesota, or MiniSO-da as the locals say it.

The lasagna still has an hour left to cook, and Asher and I have already gone through all the small talk I could come up with. My finger fiddles with the ribbon wrapped around a flower vase.

"Would you like to have Taylor's letter?" he asks, pulling his backpack closer.

I watch as he slowly unzips the bag, his eyes flooding with sorrow again as he pulls out a long white envelope, running it between his fingers as he stares down at it for a moment. The sound of his knees bouncing against the counter catch my attention, and I notice him reaching back into his bag and pulling out a small pill before tilting his head back and away from me to swallow it. I look away and back down at the envelope as soon as he turns back to me, not wanting him to know I was watching.

My chest begins to pound as he reaches over the counter to hand me the last words his dead sister ever wrote, the unspoken grief passing through us as he lets go and I grasp on.

My name is written on the front, and I recognize Taylor's handwriting immediately, my disbelief of her death evaporating as my hands tremble.

Asher stands up and walks around the counter, positioning himself directly next to me before reaching one arm around me and squeezing me into his side. The feeling his arm brings me as he wraps it around me is something foreign. I can't say that it's lust, but it makes me feel a little stronger than I felt before he walked over.

"I can leave you alone, or you can wait to read it when you're ready," he says.

I doubt I'll ever be ready. I hear Asher's stomach growl and check the timer, still 50 minutes left. I shake my head. I can't delay this anymore than I already have.

"You said you found her on the day you two always go for brunch, right?" I ask Asher as I walk around the counter and take a seat on one of the stools.

"Yeah, I assumed she was sleeping still so I went inside, and . . ." his eyes stay glued to the ground as he sits in the stool next to me. ". . . I found her there with the letter in her hand."

The image overwhelms my mind as I'm sure it did Asher's. He turns his head away, concealing his face from my view, cracking his knuckles as he brings himself to a stance again before he circles the counter and then the coffee table in the living room.

"Taylor planned every aspect of her life, she must have meant for you to be the one to find her," I say, looking back down at the letter still sealed in my hand. "She wanted you to find it, and she must have intended for you to read it at some point."

Without glancing back at me, Asher's posture drops as his shoulders slump. I start to carefully rip the top of the envelope open.

"Maybe," I hear him whisper under his breath.

TEN

Auden

My fingers start to tremble as I pull the letter out of its envelope, still folded perfectly between my hands. The piece of paper feels heavier than any I've held before, maybe it's the weight of all the secrets it holds.

I glance at Asher, noticing he's now cradling his head in his hands as he attempts to sit still on the couch. His anticipation seems to mirror mine, but I wonder if he's just as scared as well. I doubt he is, or at least not for the same reasons. He seemed so close to Taylor, and I doubt he has any fear that his influence or lack thereof had caused her as much pain as I fear I may have.

This is the last communication I will ever have with Taylor, once I read it, our story officially ends. I want to know the truth. I need to know why Taylor, the happiest girl I ever knew, could ever feel as if death was her only escape. But how do I read my old friend's pain and desperation knowing that I'm already too late to help her overcome it, knowing the last conversation we had brought nothing but pain.

The image of Brad's cunning grin invades my thoughts, igniting a surge of fiery rage in my heart. I need to make sense of all of this. I must find out what happened after I walked away from Monroe forever.

I brace myself, taking a deep breath as I unfold the letter, the creases cracking softly in the quiet room. The ink seems to jump off the page as Taylor's handwriting comes into focus.

Auden,

It feels unimaginable, ending my life without knowing who you have become for the last six years of it. Which is why I couldn't leave this earth without you knowing that I have written to you every year since the day that you left. You can find your answers within those letters that lay in our old tin box, along with our other memories.

Please forgive me, for now and for then.

I have always loved you.

And please give Asher a hug for me. Tell him I love him dearly, and I am so sorry I had to leave him. He was the only one I could trust to get you this.

He is the best brother a girl could have.

Until we meet again,

Taylor

I read it over three times, and then three more. Each time, slower and slower, trying to absorb every bit of its information.

Asher stands up and stretches his arms above his head, resuming his pacing around the opposite side of the counter. He hasn't stopped moving or readjusting since the moment the letter left his fingers. I stand and make my way over to him, gently placing my hand on his shoulder to bring him to a halt. He looks down at me then at my hand, still holding the now opened letter. I wrap my arms around his waist, pulling him closer until my head is nestled against his chest. His arms encircle me, one secure around my back and the other tenderly resting on my shoulder. With a gentle touch, he guides my head to rest beneath his chin, holding me in a comforting embrace.

I melt into him, listening to every beat of his heart, hoping he can't feel mine and its quickening pace. Taylor even managed to plan out a hug that I had no idea I so desperately needed. But here I am, thanking her silently for comforting me even in death.

After a few moments, I let go of my grasp, taking a small step back and bringing the letter in between us. Asher's eyes slowly leave mine and look toward the letter as I bring it closer to his hand, his lips curling in as he reaches forward.

"Are you sure?" he asks, his fingers suspended just above the letter.

I force a smile on my face, nodding and gently place the letter into his hand.

As he carefully opens the letter, he brings it closer to him, momentarily blocking my view of his face. I lean in to get a better look at a small spot of writing I notice on the back, trying to make out what it says.

And, Auden, I believe you.

ELEVEN

Asher

    The timer dings and I watch Auden grab a pair of oven mitts. She quickly slides on the sparkly pink mitts over her fingers, prompting me to think of Dec and the excitement he must have felt when he bought them. I feel like I'm really getting to know Auden, and I feel confident in assuming that she didn't purchase those for herself. She isn't a flashy, happy girl that people are drawn to like Taylor. She's someone you could easily overlook, maybe even feel intimidated by, but if you give her the time of day, she may become one of your favorite people.
    She pulls the oven door open, the heat escaping and blowing her hair back a little, the scar on her neck becoming visible again.
    When she stands up, she looks over at me and notices the small grin across my face, tilting her head to the side and giving me a soft smile back. She has no idea how much relief just being around her for less than 12 hours has brought me. Having Auden with me today and reading her letter from

Taylor has brought me the tiniest bit of hope that I may make it through this nightmare.

I have friends back home, ones I've made over the years in school and then at the fire station. But I wouldn't say they were the type of friends I could show my emotions to or be open with about my fears and desires. I'm not even sure if that's something men do in general. Taylor was that person for me. Taylor could always tell when I wasn't feeling my greatest or needed a break from reality, and I never once felt judged by her. I always thought she felt the same way about me, but how could she if she felt so alone that she gave up on life? She gave up on me being able to help her, and she gave up on being that person for me.

I have my parents, and I love them for who they are in their own ways. But any emotion is a sign of weakness in the Landry household. Growing up, Taylor and I were always taught to be mindful of our environment. We understood that anyone could be observing us, and that those who were watching could easily spread rumors or gossip about us. If I could see my mother now, I'd bet she's been cleaning nonstop, preparing for company while my dad cries in his den. I'd bet she's holding back tears and making food for all the guests that will stop by to bring my parents grief food. She's probably telling jokes and quietly reminding my dad to smile so no one else feels uncomfortable. My mother does love us, she is a wonderful parent. She just believes that making us seem like the perfect family is just as important as spending quality time together. I wish she would've spent more time with us while we were under the same roof, rather than solely focusing on readying us for the future.

I was always full of emotions as a kid. I was constantly bouncing off the walls and being way too loud and impulsive. I could never forget the night when my parents took us to a dinner at the Mayor's house. Taylor and I were dressed in our best clothes and told to behave a hundred times before we had even arrived. I tried my hardest to stay still, even though my shirt felt like stiff needles against my skin. But when I saw a glass vase that allowed the light to shine through it in a way that made rainbow patterns sparkle across the marble floors, I made the quick decision to reach out and touch it, accidentally sending it to the floor and shattering everywhere. I didn't sleep that night because of my parents' disappointment mixed with my own. The next day I was in my pediatrician's office being prescribed medication for ADHD, and I focused much harder on staying still, quiet, and out of the way.

Auden doesn't seem to be put off by my sadness. The way she held me after I finished reading the letter made me feel accepted in a way that only Taylor had made me feel before. I would've stayed in her embrace all night if she hadn't left to change out of her t-shirt covered in red sauce.

We serve up the lasagna and sit down side-by-side at the counter, my knees bumping against the edge as I struggle to squeeze onto the little wooden stool.

"Alcohol," she says, pushing herself up from her stool and making her way to the cabinet.

"Vodka or gin?" She asks.

I glance at the lasagna and then back at Auden, debating which option would have the least impact on the flavor.

To this day when I think of vodka, I think back to when I was a junior in high school and had received a text from Taylor asking me to come outside. I found her and Auden two sheets to the wind and both crying hysterically. When I asked them what was wrong, they said they were never going to drink vodka again. I learned that evening that I could hold two sets of ponytails at once while they puked. I guess it wasn't bad enough for Auden to swear off vodka all together.

"Vodka," I answer, wishing the answer could be wine.

She pours us each a drink, pouring more vodka than soda into the glasses. She takes a sip, her face twisting in distaste before nonchalantly placing my glass in front of me. I follow suit, taking a sip and mirroring her expression as the potent liquor stings my throat. Vodka isn't my favorite choice, but with how intense this room currently feels, I would drink battery acid to take the edge off.

*

I watch the clock on the oven, it's been 19 minutes of us silently eating our lasagna. The only sound in the room is the scraping of our forks and the clanking of our glasses hitting the counter after each drink.

A sudden boom shakes the floor, followed by the sound of heavy rain hitting the windows, causing Auden to whip her head up startled.

She looks over at me, and I give her a closed-lip smile that she doesn't return. She lifts her glass and finishes her drink before standing up to refill it.

Her eyes never leave the glass as she pours even more vodka into her second serving.

"You mentioned Brad wasn't around when you went to pick up Taylor." She pauses, taking another drink and swallowing half of it before continuing, "So, they stayed together?"

I swallow my last bite of lasagna and walk my plate to the sink, turning the faucet on and rinsing the sauce off, watching as the red liquid swirls down the drain.

"Yeah, they did." I turn around and lean my back against the sink. Auden turns her body to face me, but her eyes meet the floor instead of mine.

"Brad proposed to her right after you left, and everything moved quickly once they were engaged. Some of us thought she might be pregnant, considering how rushed the wedding felt," I respond.

Auden's fingers turn white as she grips the glass in her hand, bringing the other hand across her stomach and holding it there for a moment.

The way her hand is gripping her glass feels like a perfect representation of how I feel about Brad. His chuckle at the hospital keeps replaying in the back of my mind, and I can't help but wonder if he'd be laughing with my hands around his throat.

"Was she pregnant?" she asks, lifting the glass back up and finishing her second drink.

Without a chance to respond, she forcefully brings the glass down onto the counter, causing it to shatter. Blood begins to trickle from her palm, and instinctively, I grab a paper towel. Taking hold of her wrist, I lead her over to the sink, holding her hand up to prevent further bleeding.

"Fuck," she repeats over and over as I rinse away the blood, carefully checking for any small shards of glass.

I look at her as the cold water runs down her palm, her eyes glazed and starting to fill with tears. I want to know everything that's going through her mind right now. I want to know why the thought of Taylor and Brad having a baby would bring her such anger.

After turning off the faucet, I gently dab away the remaining traces of blood. Pressing the towel firmly against the cuts, attempting to stop the bleeding.

"Hold this here," I instruct her. "I don't think you need stitches, but we need to stop the bleeding."

She uses her other hand to hold the towel in place, still refusing to look in my direction.

"Was she pregnant?" she asks again.

"No, they never had kids," I reply, observing the relief that washes over her face.

She turns around and grabs a new glass out of the cupboard and sets it down, heading toward the bottle of vodka still out on the counter. She grabs the neck of the bottle, lifting it up to her mouth and using her teeth to twist off the cap.

I lean forward and cover the rim of the glass with my hand, slowly sliding it away from her.

"I don't think that's the best idea right now," I say, watching her eyes dart in my direction.

I can see the anger starting to burn inside of her when she makes eye contact, a part of her I have never seen before. She looks at my seat across the counter and leans over it, grabbing my drink that I had barely touched all dinner. Before she gets the chance to bring it up to her lips, I grab it with my free hand and take a step back, ensuring it's out of her reach before returning the unused glass to its place in the cupboard.

"What the hell are you doing?" she asks, her voice harsh with irritation.

"Auden you've had enough," I insist. "You're bleeding, and the alcohol won't help it stop."

Her eyes roll, and she lets out a huff. I know I shouldn't be trying to control her actions, but something inside me has shifted since she walked through the front door this morning. I've always cared for Auden. It's inevitable when you've known someone for so long and shared so much of your childhood. But now, a deep curiosity about her has ignited within me. The light from the kitchen illuminates the outline of her collarbone, drawing my attention. An impulse urges me to reach out and touch it, but my focus is diverted as I see her raise the bottle of vodka to her lips again.

She turns away from me, preventing any attempt to grab the bottle from her. Placing it back on the counter, she picks up the cap and twists it back on. When she faces me again, she wipes her mouth with the back of her hand, her eyes challenging me to respond.

"Now, I've had enough," she says firmly, keeping her eyes focused on mine.

I can tell she's waiting for a reaction, probably a negative one from the defensive tone in her voice, but she won't get that from me. I don't want to scold her or tell her how dumb that was. I want to wrap her in my arms and tell her it's okay. And, honestly, this feisty side of her is more adorable than maddening.

The temperature in the room seems to rise, causing sweat beads to form on my neck. I make a conscious effort to maintain eye contact with her, resisting the temptation to let my gaze drift back to her collarbone that I so badly want to touch. I look down at my glass still in my hand and lift it in the air.

"Well, evidently I haven't," I say before taking a big drink and praying this will help me resist the urges I'm having a hard time controlling.

She smiles but it fades quickly as she heads to the living room, grabbing a big green blanket from under the coffee table and covering herself as she takes a seat on the couch. She's becoming more difficult to read as the minutes go by, and usually I would be halfway home by now if she were any other girl. But I feel a brightness around her even during this dark time, and no other girl has given me that feeling. I'd be crazy to run away from that, especially at a time when I need it most.

"Was she happy?" she asked, pulling her knees up to her chest and wrapping her arms around her legs.

I finish the last sip of my drink and make my way to the couch, settling down next to her. She turns her head towards me, but her gaze remains fixed on the floor, silently anticipating my reply.

"She was still Taylor." I pause, the weight of speaking about my sister in past tense sinking in. "She always tried to appear happy, no matter the circumstances. But deep down, I sensed something was wrong."

I shift my gaze away, struggling to contain my emotions as I fixate on the window as raindrops race down the glass. I did know something was off. I knew something was going on with her, and I failed to ask the questions that could've saved her life.

"I should have asked her if she was happy. Maybe I could have stopped her from feeling like this was the only escape."

I sense Auden's weight on the cushion as she inches closer to me then lifts her hand and places it gently on my knee. Her touch sends a vibration all the way through me.

"Don't do that, Asher," she says, her face now close enough to mine that I can feel her breath on my neck.

I turn my gaze downwards to her hand, reaching out with mine to intertwine our fingers.

"She would never want us to play the 'what if' game."

She's right. Deep down, I know she's right. But still, I can't shake the feeling of guilt, wondering how I could have possibly saved her life. Maybe if I would've gotten there sooner, I could have.

Auden picks up on the lingering pain despite her words, and she rests her head on my shoulder for comfort. We stay there for a few moments until she finally breaks the silence.

"I wish you weren't the one who had to find her."

Her comment stabs straight to my heart, and my body automatically stiffens.

"I keep replaying that moment in my mind over and over. I haven't even slept because every time I close my eyes, I see . . ." My voice breaks and the pain crashes back over me.

Auden kisses my shoulder. It doesn't send the normal electric tingles through my body like our other touches have. In this moment, it felt warm, comforting, like her only intention was to tell me she's right here.

"The more I think about it, I think she really did have everything planned out," I continue to tell her about when I found Taylor. I'm not sure why I feel the urge to tell her. It was by far the worst moment in my life, and I continue to try to erase it from my mind. But right now, right here with Auden, I want to finally say it out loud. I want someone to understand what my last memory with my sister will always be, and the thoughts that keep popping up in my head alongside that memory.

"When I walked in, the place was cleaner than normal. The house was always spotless, but it was as if it was cleaner because it was emptier. I think she may have packed up some of her things to make it easier on everyone afterwards. When I turned into her room, I assumed she was asleep. I even remember letting out a sigh because I was annoyed that she overslept. When I noticed the letter in her hand and how she wasn't waking up from me barging in, I froze. I remember standing still in her doorway, just staring at her hands and unable to move. I couldn't even blink. I'm not sure I was even breathing. Eventually, I walked closer. I remember reaching down and . . ."

My breathing becomes shaky and a lump starts to form in my throat. Auden runs her hand up and down my arm, letting me know it's okay. I keep going, knowing if I don't get it out now, I probably never will. And if I wait another second, the tears will return, and I won't be able to stop them.

"And her hand wasn't cold. I don't think she had been gone long enough for that yet. But they weren't warm either. The reality hit me like a semi-truck, and I went flying back so hard that my back hit the wall across the room. I became frantic, and that's when it all starts to become blurry. I was scanning the room with my eyes, my body paralyzed against the wall as I searched for anything to make sense of or undo the reality before me. Then I noticed the empty pill container on her nightstand. I didn't know it was empty, it was sitting on the other side of her bed, the cap secured as it was neatly set right next to a glass of water. I picked it up and knew it was empty. I'm a certified EMT, and I know better than to waste time like I did. But I sat down next to her, my back facing her body so I couldn't see how lifeless she was, and I cried. I cried for 45 minutes while I begged her to wake up. And then it was like my heart shut off. The feelings all left as I stood up, took the phone out of my pocket, and called 9-1-1 just like I would do with any other call when I'm on duty. I took the letter out of her hand while I waited for an ambulance to come. I shoved it in my back pocket without even reading who it was addressed to. And after they left with her body, I drove straight to my parents' house, and I broke their hearts as well."

Auden pulls my arm up and wraps it around her shoulder, leaning into me and letting out a big breath. The weight of her body on mine calms my shakiness, giving me a moment to finally catch my breath. She doesn't say anything and that's okay. She doesn't have to, and honestly there's nothing anyone can say. The few people who did see me yesterday, mostly people at the hospital that I work hand in hand with, all said different versions of, "That's something no loved one should ever have to go through," as if Taylor did something horrible to me.

Was it horrible to find my dead sister's body? Yes! Hell, yes. It was absolutely horrible. But it wasn't as terrible as whatever my sister had been going through that made her think this was her only option. Staying silent is much better than any other mindless thought anyone can try to magically heal me with. I'm broken, period. Let's accept that first.

A sudden flash of lightning illuminates the room, redirecting my focus to her collarbone. The temptation to use her as a distraction, as I've done with many other girls before, briefly crosses my mind. However, Auden is unlike any other girl. She's someone I've always seen as my sister's friend, almost like a second sister to me.

But now that six years have passed between us, I see her as the woman she's grown into. The woman that grieves the loss of my sister, her old friend, and understands the pain I feel in Taylor's absence. I don't want to ignore my pain by escaping inside of her, I want my heart to beat with hers, cradling it until the pain subsides.

She sits up and faces me, still close enough that her breath can be felt, this time against my lips. She silently stares at me, her eyes following the stubble across my chin and then locking onto my lips.

I feel like she wants me to kiss her, just as badly as I want to feel her lips against mine. I look away, knowing that the liquor and our emotions are a bad combination. The thoughts she may have now might not be the same tomorrow, although I doubt my one glass, no matter how strong, has altered the way I feel in this moment.

I reach my hand toward her neck and graze the scar on the left side, noticing as goosebumps form on her skin in reaction.

"How did you get this?" I ask.

She immediately brushes my hand away and turns away from me, filling me with regret that I just crossed a line. She keeps one hand covering her neck, staying silent for what feels like eternity. Before I get the chance to break the silence, my phone begins to ring in my pocket.

Reaching for my phone, Brad's face lights up the screen. The atmosphere in the room suddenly feels stifling as I meet Auden's distressed gaze as she leans away from the phone. Standing up, I answer and make my way into the kitchen, hoping to alleviate Auden's uneasiness.

"Hey, man, where the hell are you?" Brad asks.

I remain quiet, my eyes fixed on the floor as I walk back and forth in the kitchen, searching for the right words in reply. The tension between Auden and Brad was evident by her reaction to seeing his face on my screen, and, honestly, I feel a burning hatred for him at this moment as well. I hesitate to mention where I am, as it may not benefit any of us.

"I'm just taking care of a few things out of town. Do you need something?" I ask, hoping that was good enough to keep Brad from pressing for more information.

"Well, I'm packing up Taylor's things and your mom suggested that I ask if you wanted anything before I donate it. I told her I doubt you'd fit into any of her bras, but she insisted I ask anyway."

I wince at his comment about my dead sister's bras, but as the words sink in, more anger bubbles up inside me. I halt my pacing and glance over at Auden. She remains cocooned in her blanket, tapping her fingers against her teeth as she gazes back at me with a blank expression.

The urge to confront Brad and give him a piece of my mind surges through me. It hasn't even been 48 hours since my sister's passing, and here he is making light of her belongings as he prepares to give away her entire life to strangers. However, as I look at Auden, I'm reminded of the bigger picture and the unanswered questions that still loom over us. Despite my anger, I realize that Brad may have valuable information that could be helpful in the future. I keep my eyes locked on Auden, the sight of her bringing me calmness.

"I can take care of all of that, just leave it alone for now and I'll grab it when I get home," I say.

I hear Brad whispering to someone but can't make out if it's a man or woman.

"When will you be home?" he asks. "I didn't want to say anything, but it's pretty fucked that you just left in the middle of all this. Don't you think you should be, I don't know, supporting your parents? Hell, or even supporting me?"

I lean forward, resting my elbows on the counter, my forehead cradled in the palm of one hand.

It does all feel fucked. Every single bit of it. The fact that her husband is currently with someone that is helping pack up my sister's things. The reality that Taylor killed herself and purposely planned on me to find her. The letter she made me pry from her fingers and deliver to her friend. Or exfriend? I don't even know what happened between them, but I guess I didn't really know what was ever happening with Taylor.

"I'll be home tomorrow," I respond, looking over at Auden and watching as disappointment comes over her face.

TWELVE

Auden

My stomach feels like it's being ripped from my body when I hear Asher tell Brad he'll be home tomorrow. I feel so foolish for allowing Asher in and beginning to let my guard down when time has taught me to know better.

Brad is once again proving that his hold on people will always be stronger than mine.

I stand up from the couch, throwing the blanket on the cushions behind me. My stomach feels as if it's eaten the sun, boiling me from the inside out.

Asher watches me as I head in his direction, passing by him and reaching back into the liquor cabinet, this time bringing the vodka with me to my bedroom without speaking a word to him. I can hear him calling my name as I close the door behind me.

I don't owe him an explanation. Taylor had many chances to explain to the people in her life, the ones I left behind for a reason, why I left and why we had no future left together. Clearly, she wanted to keep her inaction a secret and who am I to reveal the secrets of the dead?

I twist off the cap from the bottle and throw it in the waste bin by my desk. I don't plan on leaving a drop in this bottle tonight. My back starts to cool off as I lean against my window, listening as the rain continues tapping against the foggy glass.

A knock at my door comes shortly after my first swig, but I ignore it. What could Asher possibly say now that can fix anything about this situation. He can't bring Taylor back and save her from her marriage with Brad. He can't turn back time and force Taylor to do the right thing, or erase the moments in time that led to the painful reality of the last six years.

"Auden, please talk to me," Asher mumbles through the door.

My eyes roll as I tilt my head back again, taking note of how much vodka I can swallow in one gulp. I was talking to him. We were talking all day and night up until he decided to talk to Brad. At one point, I think I even wanted to kiss him. I usually have to talk myself into kissing someone, but I know there was a moment right before the devil called that I felt like wanting to be kissed by him.

Thank God that I didn't.

I set the bottle on the windowsill and look down at the blood crusted to the inside of my palm, shaking my head in disgust that Brad found a way to give me another scar from over a thousand miles away. He truly is capable of anything.

I reach over to grab the bottle and smack my fingers against the glass, accidentally sending it to the ground and covering the floor with shards and vodka.

"Fuck!" I yell, the desperation in me more upset that I wasted the last of the vodka than the mess I now have to clean.

The door flies open, and Asher comes in, heading directly toward me, his face covered in concern.

"Auden, are you okay?" he asks, grabbing me by my elbow and trying to help me navigate around the glass-covered floor.

My elbow pushes against him, forcing him to let go of me. He's not going to be the superhero in my story. I've already proven I'm more than capable of rescuing myself.

"I'm not a damn child, Asher," I yell, taking a step around him. "I don't need you to rescue me."

Trying to take another step, I suddenly become dizzy and struggle to keep my balance. Asher grabs my arm again and helps me over to my bed, setting me down on the edge.

"I doubt you've ever needed rescuing, Auden," he whispers, kneeling down and starting to remove the socks from my feet.

The hatred inside of me starts to subside as I watch him gently pull each sock off, inspecting them for glass.

How can he allow someone so evil to be in his life when he seems so good? How could he allow his sister to marry such a dangerous man when he clearly wants to keep people safe?

My eyes start to fill with tears as he pulls the last sock off, pulling each foot up one more time to ensure they're glass free before lifting both of my legs and laying them onto my bed.

"How can you be so nice to him?" I ask, laying my head down onto my pillow.

Asher takes a seat on the bed next to me, covering me with my comforter and slowly tucking it around me.

"I don't know what to do, Auden," he starts to say as he brushes his hand gently through my hair. "I never really liked Brad. He seemed to have a weird hold on Taylor, but I don't have any real reason to dislike the guy other than his arrogance."

I close my eyes, trying to keep the tears from Asher, but I can feel them pushing their way through my eyelids and running down my cheeks. Asher's fingers trace my jaw, trying to catch the tears as they make their way toward my neck.

"Auden, you can trust me, please tell me what's wrong."

His voice is so soft and comforting. If sounds could heal wounds, his words would be all I needed, just like Taylor's words used to convey.

The memory of the last time I saw Taylor flashes into my mind. I can see her standing on her front step, the look of disappointment and disbelief consuming her face as she ripped every ounce of trust that I had from me.

"I thought the same thing about your sister," I whisper, causing Asher's hand to freeze along my shoulders. "But you can't save me, just like you couldn't save her."

THIRTEEN

Auden

The sound of my alarm pierces my skull as each beep grows louder. I roll over and slam my hand against the off switch, shielding my eyes from the sun with my arm.

The memory of last night comes back to me. What I said to Asher comes back to me, filling me with regret over how selfish and cruel I was.

He flew all the way across the country with no idea how to find me, just so he could make sure his sister's last words were given to the person she meant them for. He spent the day helping me grocery shop, dealing with my heavy emotions, and not getting the answers he wants and frankly deserves. He even had a moment of vulnerability with me by sharing his experience finding Taylor. And I selfishly didn't give him anything but a shitty guilt trip and blamed him for not saving her life. I'm the only person who can give him the truth, or at least my part of Taylor's truth, and I refused. God, I'm a piece of shit.

I sit up and look over toward the windowsill where I left the shattered mess last night, but it's already cleaned. Asher must've stayed and taken care of it after I passed out, filling me with even more remorse.

A sweatshirt on my floor catches my eye and I reach down to grab it, pulling it over my head and lifting my aching body off my bed to head toward the living room. I know I owe Asher an apology and probably an explanation.

The smell of coffee fills my nostrils as I turn the corner out of my room. Dec is sitting at the island with his iPad and a steaming mug in front of him.

"Woof, long night?" he asks.

"Something like that," I respond, scanning the room for Asher and finding the apartment empty.

"Where's Asher?" I ask.

Dec takes a sip of his coffee before closing his iPad and turning to face me. I look over at the clock on the stove and realize it's already past 10:00 am.

"He left earlier this morning." Dec watches me for a moment and must notice the shock on my face.

Of course, he left. I'm surprised he stayed in this apartment through the night after what I put him through. He didn't deserve a second of what I gave him, and I didn't deserve him going out of his way for me.

"You didn't know he was leaving?" he asks, his tone tinged with concern.

I shake my head, taking a seat next to him at the island and lowering my throbbing head down onto my arms.

He left without saying goodbye and without the apology I desperately owe him.

Dec lowers his head down onto his own arms so that his face is level with mine.

"Did something happen, Auden?" he asks.

I close my eyes, unable to look at him or anywhere with lights on for that matter.

"I fucked up, Dec. I think I made things worse for Asher and doubt I'll ever get the opportunity to fix it."

Dec sits up and takes another sip of his coffee before standing up. I can hear his footsteps trailing over toward the living room.

"He did tell me that he left you a letter," he says, his steps coming back in my direction.

I sit up, faster than my head appreciates, and turn to see another white envelope, this time my name written in much smaller handwriting.

I rip the white seal open and pull out the piece of paper folded inside.

Auden,

Don't worry, this letter isn't another ending, or maybe it can be a part of a good ending.

I don't know what happened between you and Taylor, but I do know that you have the same pain behind your eyes that I saw in her eyes for the last six years. I have to return home, not for Brad, but for Taylor.

You're right, I didn't save her, and I probably could have. That's something I'll have to live with for the rest of my life.

I doubt I'd ever be able to save you, not because you're unsavable or because I wouldn't want to try, but because you are so strong that you don't need anyone to rescue you.

Taylor told you the answers you're seeking are back home in Monroe, and I will be waiting there for you.

It's never too late to trust, Auden, and I hope I've shown you in the day we spent together that you really can trust me.

You aren't alone,

Asher

A smaller piece of paper falls from inside of the ripped envelope. Dec reaches down and picks it up for me, his eyes widening as he scans it before handing it over to me.

I take the slip of paper and turn it over in my hand, reading the departure date to Monroe Regional Airport for tomorrow afternoon.

He bought me a plane ticket home. Nausea overcomes me and I race to the sink, unwilling to risk making it to the toilet, and empty the vodka from my stomach.

I clean myself up and start to head to the bathroom, hoping a shower will help make this day a little more bearable or at least enough to clear the fog from my mind.

Before I can close the bathroom door, Dec appears behind me in the doorway.

"So, are you going?" he asks.

I shake my head, something I'm instantly reminded isn't the best way to currently communicate.

"I can't, Dec. You know I can't ever go back there."

Dec takes a step closer into the bathroom as I lean down and turn on the shower.

"You couldn't go back there before, but it's not the same situation now, Auden. Asher came, and he clearly . . ."

Before he gets the chance to finish, I interrupt, my hangover helping my anger peek its ugly head.

"He clearly believes Brad is a good person, just like Taylor did. And that's another perfect example why I closed the door on Monroe, and why I will never allow it to reopen."

I take a step forward, forcing Dec to walk backwards until he's no longer in the bathroom.

"I came here and started my own life, and I did a damn good job. It's not my responsibility to make anyone else feel better because of their own decisions. Asher left, and if he didn't want to leave, he wouldn't have. Besides, I have my interview tomorrow, and you of all people should know how hard I've worked to get this opportunity."

I shut the door and start to undress, the steam filling the room as my clothes fall to the tile floor.

"Auden, you know they would be willing to postpone the interview if they knew you were attending a funeral," Dec says softly through the door.

"I won't allow Monroe to take this from me too," I say to myself as I pull the curtain closed.

FOURTEEN

Auden

I let go of Jane's hand and take a seat across from her in a plush, blue chair, matching three others in the room. The walls are painted with soft, muted tones, bringing a sense of calmness to the room. My eyes are drawn to a small nametag on Jane's black blouse with the title of Executive Director written under her name.

"Well, let's jump right in Auden," Jane says, holding a pen above her clipboard.

I straighten my posture, hoping she doesn't see me for the nervous fraud I feel I am. She has no idea that I've spent the last 26 hours grieving the death of a person I had already grieved losing once before.

"What experience makes you want to work for the Minnesota Coalition Against Sexual Assault?"

The question sends me into an instant panic. I didn't realize we'd be going straight into the hard questions on the first interview. Besides, I'm not applying to be the new therapist or to interact with any clients that may walk through those doors. I'm a background person. My job is to make sure everyone and everything runs smoothly by incorporating new systems, nothing more.

She's asking me why I want to work for an organization that helps victims of sexual assault find justice and learn how to heal. But she has no idea that I haven't healed myself, and that I'm still running away six years later with an opportunity to try and face my past burning a hole in my purse. I'm not right for this job. I fit in more as a client than an employee.

I break eye contact, looking down at my fingers and trying to keep myself from bringing them up to my teeth. My throat feels like I've been stuck in the desert, unable to swallow with the absence of saliva.

The intercom beeps and a voice interrupts us to inform Jane that she has a call on line one. Jane apologizes and excuses herself to take the call privately in another room.

The moment the door shuts behind her, I stand up and quickly walk to the water cooler in the corner of the room and pour myself a cup. I finish it in one gulp before pouring myself a second, and walking over to the window, I notice two teen girls crossing the street below me. They laugh as the wind blows through their hair. One girl pauses as the other pulls a hair tie off her wrist and hands it to her. The girl smiles back at her friend, pulling her hair into a bun as they continue down the sidewalk together.

My heart starts to ache as I watch the two of them, reminding me of the years of laughter Taylor and I had shared. Even though she broke my heart, I always secretly hoped that one day we could laugh together again.

I turn away from the window and walk over to my chair, leaning down and grabbing my purse. It takes a few seconds for my phone to turn back on, but when it does, I notice a text.

Dec: I'm in my car in parking garage B if you change your mind.

The door opens and Jane returns from her phone call.

"I apologize, we had a small emergency, but now it's all taken care of," she says with a big smile before reaching her arm out and inviting me to join her in returning to our seats.

Without a second thought, I bring my phone down to my side and give Jane my full attention, deciding not to retake my seat.

"Jane, I've been working day and night for many different companies and nonprofits for the last few years in hopes of building a resumé that I felt was worthy of finally applying here at MCASA. And I wouldn't be standing here today if I didn't believe I finally did just that."

Jane puts her hand down, her face still but intrigued.

"And five minutes ago, when you asked me what experiences I've had that make me want to work here, I froze and couldn't come up with a reason to save my life."

I walk back toward the window and look down at the sidewalk where I watched the two girls moments before, then return my attention to Jane.

"But standing in this room, waiting for you to return, I realized that I haven't been honest. I haven't been honest with you or myself."

Jane's eyebrows furrow as she shifts her feet, probably wondering where I could be going with this. I'm not even sure where I'm going at this point.

"I was sexually assaulted when I was seventeen, and not only did he get away with it, forcing me to abandon the only home I've ever known, but my best friend didn't even believe me." I want to break eye contact with Jane, but I need her to see the empowerment that's growing inside me every second. She's the third person who I've ever spoken to about my assault.

"And I want to be the badass who helps you make sure no one has to feel unheard or unbelieved again." I take a breath, watching as Jane's eyes lower, her mouth still straight as a pencil. "But, right now, I need to be the badass that saves herself and heals before I can even begin to consider how to help you and your organization grow to help more victims like myself." I swallow, taking a deep breath as my hands tremble picking up my purse. "I've wanted this job for years now, and I promise when I'm done getting myself the closure that I need, I'll continue to fight for a position here. But right now, there's a plane I need to catch so I can start earning a place here." I give her the best smile I can force, and walk toward the door, heading for parking garage B.

FIFTEEN

Brad

Most people start their days with a cup of coffee, a morning run, or, shit, I don't know, maybe even yoga. But I sure as hell am anyone but most people. The way I like to start most mornings is exactly like I'm starting this one, throat deep in my newest side piece. I like to make some know-it-all's daughter my bitch before my day continues. Nothing makes me harder than knowing one of my father's colleague's daughters is the one servicing me. The high it provides me cannot be matched by a simple man's cup of caffeine.

I open my email on my computer while Millie tongue bathes me below my desk. I can feel her head tilting so she can try to peek up and see if I'm enjoying myself or watching her, but I never look down and give a bitch that satisfaction. Women are like dogs, the more unearned attention you give them, the less they work for.

Millie works at the golf club teaching tennis. She's got a sexy little figure, a head full of tight curls and a face that screams money. Her daddy's got it, but, unfortunately for her, he cut her off two years ago, hence why she's working at the club.

    Millie's dad owns both of the two private prisons in Louisiana. He cut her off when she started snorting away her college tuition, and she spiraled from there. A coaching position at a high-end golf clubhouse pays well, but not well enough to supply high-end cocaine. But when you're willing to drop to your knees whenever I call, you can afford whatever you need. Plus, as much as I pride myself on making sure my girls are only mine when they're in rotation, I know she earns extra tips from the club members for batting those long eyelashes before bending over in her tiny white skirt. She's definitely shit at tennis, so only a fool would assume she's there for any other reason than to be objectified for rent money.

    Millie used to be my Tuesday and Thursday girl, but ever since Kelly Anne gained fifteen pounds, ten in her ass and five in her face, I dropped her, and Millie's been picking up the slack. The town can see me out with any woman I'm willing to give my time to, but they'll never catch me out with a whale. Don't get me wrong, Taylor was beautiful, but Brad Montgomery has needs and a girl like Taylor could never meet those demands. Taylor filled me with the love and devotion a Montgomery man needs. She was a good wife, she cooked, she kept the house clean, and she was always home when I arrived. She knew not to ask too many questions and accepted that her place was always going to be in the home. After all, I didn't need her in town catching up with people and possibly hearing gossip about something she shouldn't.

    Taylor's loyalty clearly wasn't as strong as I had thought, or she wouldn't have left me in this position of trying to find her replacement. Selfish wasn't a word I would've used for my wife, until she decided to abandon her duties to me all together. Till death do us part, I guess.

There're two knocks at my door, and then it swings open, my assistant Catherine storming in behind it.

I don't understand that. Knocking and then just entering without giving the person a chance to grant you permission. The entitlement. Especially in my damn office.

I look at the time on my screen, 8:43 am. Catherine knows better than to come in before 9:00 am if she doesn't want to see my pants around my ankles with a Southern belle in between. I used to get angry and allow her interruptions to stop me from finishing, but then I came to the conclusion that if she wants to walk in, she can learn to accept what happens in my damn office before 9:00. She's not going to ruin my morning and prolong my little men from diving deep down this whore's guzzle.

Catherine rolls her eyes when she notices the size 7 Sperry's sticking out from under my desk, causing me to lean back in my chair, arms tucked behind my head. My climax seems to be even better when Catherine is staring at me with those disgusted brown eyes. Her disappointment over my behavior, and having no power to scold me, always sends me over the edge almost instantly.

"We heard back from the tech department, and Jason believes he found who Asher was visiting in Minneapolis," she says as she slams down a stack of papers onto my desk.

I sit up immediately, spreading my legs further apart so Millie can keep working as I lift the papers in my hands.

Asher disappearing the day after Taylor kills herself was suspicious enough, the guy was glued to her damn hip any chance he got. Leaving Louisiana for the first time in his life not even twenty-four hours later just didn't sit right with me.

When I found out that his parents didn't even know where he ran off to, I knew something had to be up.

I remembered when I was digging through Taylor's phone that she and Asher shared their locations with one another, so I checked to see where he was running off to. Of course, the dumbass didn't think to turn his location off, but Asher has never been the smartest croc in the swamp. When I saw he was all the way in Minneapolis, I gave him a call to see if he'd fess up to whatever he's doing, but he made it pretty obvious that he didn't want to share that with me either. The guy hasn't gone more than 100 miles outside of Monroe in his life. What or who could be so important at a time like this?

So, I had Catherine call Jason from the tech department and told him to do some digging. I said he needed to figure out if there's anyone who lived in or visited Monroe or the Landry household that now lives in Minneapolis, and it seems it didn't take him long to come back with answers.

Before I get the chance to start reading Jason's report, Catherine interrupts.

"Do you know a girl named Auden Sterling?" she says, one eyebrow stuck up almost as far as the stick clearly hiding in her ass.

I immediately push my chair back and shove Millie's mouth off me, pulling my pants up as I bring myself to a stance.

"Get the fuck out," I demand to Millie, slamming the papers back down on my desk.

"Fucking rat," I mumble to myself.

SIXTEEN

Asher

I pull the shower door open and reach for a towel that isn't there, realizing I never finished my laundry before I took off to Minneapolis. The floor starts to fill with small droplets of water as I search my cabinets for something to help dry myself, and now the floor, off. The hand towel that's tucked in the back corner of a drawer will have to do.

After five minutes of patting myself dry, I head for my bedroom, covering my front and back with my hands even though I live alone. I'll never understand how people can be so comfortable fully naked. I don't like the feeling of air moving against my naked ass.

It's almost 5:00 pm and all I've done today is clean up a few random areas in my house and try not to check my phone more than every ten minutes. Auden never reached out after I left. She never texted or called about whether she would return to Monroe, or that she even got the plane ticket I left her. Dec seemed sincere and trustworthy, but maybe it wasn't the smartest idea for me to assume I know the guy just twenty-four hours after meeting him. Maybe he never gave the letter to Auden at all. I doubt he would withhold that from her though.

But before I left this morning, he sat down and had a cup of coffee with me. I don't know what it is about him, but he has this way of making me be honest even though I really don't know a thing about the guy. We started talking about Auden, and he told me about when he first moved in and they really didn't know one another. He said that she had this appeal to her, like she was broken and had built a protective shell around herself. He felt determined to break it wide open and find her true self within. I had no idea that she hadn't seen her parents in six years, and that she didn't know anyone when she moved there. He talked about how close she's become to his family, and how, as much as his family loves her, there's always a moment during holidays where she gets this look in her eye that breaks his heart, knowing there's an entire family back in Louisiana that she isn't surrounded by. It broke my heart a little hearing that, but I'm glad she at least has Dec and his family in those hard moments. I just wish she could see how much her parents miss her. Looking back at all my interactions with Mr. and Mrs. Sterling over the last few years, they seem to have the same look in their own eyes as Dec described in Auden's.

I've debated texting or calling her multiple times, but I have to be at my parents' house for dinner with my uncles in forty-five minutes, and this evening is going to be draining enough. Besides, if she did use the ticket, she won't be landing for another two hours. I think I'll be able to give my family more of my attention if I don't have the hard news of her decision not to come home before I go.

When I arrived in Minneapolis, all I wanted was to come back home, I felt like I was intruding, and I was definitely unannounced. But as the day went on, I found myself unable to stop staring at her. Her smile seemed to light up the room, and her laughter seemed to dim the darkness surrounding my heart just a bit. Every little detail about her seemed to captivate me, and I can't shake the feeling that she was something special.

But what does this mean? Am I starting to have feelings for her? Am I even allowed to feel the first spark I've felt other than just lust for a girl while I'm simultaneously trying to grieve my sister's death? Or am I somehow just as bad as Brad for finding a bit of happiness during this absolute nightmare?

I've been running every memory I have of Brad through my mind all day. He's always been too smooth, too charming. And the way he talked to my sister was almost too perfect, too rehearsed. I can't help but feel like he's constantly manipulating everyone, playing some kind of game that we're not even aware of. I want to confront him, to expose him for who he really is, but I have to tread carefully. I can't risk alienating myself or causing any unnecessary drama. But mark my words, I'll be keeping a close watch over him.

I now see the little boy who didn't want to give my sister flowers, and I shouldn't have ever allowed myself to lose sight of that moment. Maybe if I had watched him closer, my sister would still be here. Whether Auden shows up or not, I have to be on my A game until I figure him out myself. I owe it to Taylor.

Before I can make it to my room, I hear a knock at my door, causing me to jump into my room and shut the door behind me to cover my nakedness. I scramble through my room looking for a pair of jeans and throw them on quickly, hearing my front door opening before I can even get a leg in.

Laughter fills my home before the front door even shuts followed by a male voice I instantly recognize.

"I can't believe we've been brothers for over five years, and I haven't seen your white ass until now," Brad yells.

My stomach turns as I pull on my blue, button-up shirt and begin to fasten it. Why the hell is he here? My hands start to shake as the pressure of acting calm and unaware of who he is starts to set in. I quickly run to my backpack and pull out my pill bottle, throwing one in my mouth before exiting my bedroom.

"What's up Brad? I wasn't expecting you."

He smiles, walking toward me and wrapping his arms around me in a tight hug.

"It's good to see you, brother," he says, pulling his arms tighter and giving me a big squeeze.

I hadn't known a side of him that wasn't kind or helpful over the recent years, but I must not forget that he is not to be trusted. If I think about the pain in Auden's eyes every time his name is mentioned, I just might get through this interaction without Brad knowing I'm aware of his truth.

"It's good to see you too," I say, giving him a smile as I pull away from his embrace.

"I thought it'd be nice to drive together to your parents, that way we can catch up, and you can tell me all about where you ran off to," he says, his eyes looking directly at mine without breaking his stare.

I try not to show the concern on my face with his suggestion, unaware that he was invited this evening. I feel a drip of sweat tracing my hairline and running down my temple.

*

It's much darker than normal for this time of night due to the rain clouds, making it hard to see. They're also making it harder to see Brad's facial expressions, which hopefully means he can't see mine well either. He passes the faster route to my parents' house, forcing us to take the road that goes right past Auden's parents.

"So where have you been?" he asks, his face still turned to the road.

My stomach still feels uneasy knowing I have no way of getting away from him or out of this conversation. I keep my head facing forward, but my eyes are peeking over to be ready for any reactions.

"I was just visiting an old friend, nothing exciting."

His face looks forward, facing the road. He must not have a clue where I was. I'm not sure why I feel so uneasy right now. There isn't any way he could've known where I was anyways, and even if he did know I was in Minneapolis, how on earth could he know who I was with? My jaw unclenches as I talk myself into relaxing.

The car turns again, and I recognize the dirt road. It's the same one the Sterlings live on. The car slows down just a little as we start to come up to Auden's parents' driveway. I can feel my heart rate increasing as I see their white mailbox coming up. I knew we were going to have to drive by to get to dinner, but why the hell is the car slowing down?

"Since when do you have friends in Minneapolis?" he asks the moment we pass her driveway, this time his head turning to face me. He knows.

How the hell does he know?

I shift my body in my seat, turning slightly so it looks as if I don't recognize whose house we're passing.

I'm a terrible liar. I can run into a thirty-story building fire and save everyone inside, but I couldn't save my own ass if it involved lying. I get extra antsy when I'm under pressure, and Taylor learned at a young age not to trust me with anything she was worried our parents would find out about. I took a pill less than an hour ago, but I haven't been struggling with this many emotions plus the pressure Brad's presence has caused in who knows how long.

"What makes you think I was in Minneapolis?"

Nice Asher. Don't even give him an answer, then it won't end up biting you in the ass later when you forget what you said. If I could high five myself right now, I would.

"Well, you were, weren't you?"

I turn and face him, spotting the whites of his teeth and noticing his smile as he turns his head back towards the road.

"Come on, Ash, did you forget who your brother is? There's nothing I don't know or can't figure out if I want to know."

I try to swallow but my throat is too dry. I don't have a fucking answer and I desperately need one.

"So, who were you visiting up there?" he asks again.

"Just a friend from the fire department," I blurt out quickly, turning my head back towards my window so he can't recognize one of my many tells.

We pull up to my parents' driveway before he gets a chance to respond. I open my door before the car comes to a complete stop, knowing it isn't helping my case but staying in his proximity a moment longer might land me in more trouble.

As soon as my feet hit the gravel, I realize there's two dark figures talking by the bushes on the side of the house. Unable to make out who they are, I overhear one of them speaking.

"If you don't want your sales to plummet, you'll find a new shop to bring your business to."

As soon as I shut my car door the two figures realize they're no longer alone and start to walk over toward Brad and me. Once they get close enough, I make out who they are—my father and Brad's father.

"Finally!" Mr. Montgomery yells in a much more upbeat tone than moments before. My dad walks right up to me and wraps both arms around my shoulders. "Hi, son, how are you?" he asks, still holding me in his embrace.

We start to walk toward the front steps, one of each of our arms still wrapped around the other's shoulder when the reality of the interaction I just witnessed sets in. Mr. Sterling's shop is the only auto shop my dad has used for his car dealership since I was a kid. Why the hell does Mr. Montgomery want to hurt Mr. Sterling's business?

"How was Minneapolis?" my dad asks.

SEVENTEEN

Auden

It's taking everything in me not to bite my nails down to raw nubs as the cab driver pulls down my street. It's been six years since I walked away from the only home I had ever known, and here I am returning in the dark like the day I left, only myself aware of my destination.

My mom's been calling nonstop since the news of Taylor's death. I feel guilty for not answering her, but I'm not ready to hear her crying through the phone about how perfect Taylor always was, followed by more questions as to why we never stayed in touch. I needed some time to prepare and, honestly, I still don't think I'm ready to face the situation now.

We pull in my driveway and the headlights flash across the small white house, providing enough light for me to notice how different their home looks now. Different but also the same.

I pay the driver and grab my one bag that Dec packed for me, shutting the door behind me. I slowly walk toward the front steps, noticing the weeds starting to outgrow my mom's mass amount of dahlias and zinnias she's spent years tending. The light above the kitchen sink is all I can make out inside of the house, making me wonder if my parents are already asleep.

The first step creaks underneath me, something it had never done before as I reach my hand out for the railing, noticing how chipped the white paint is under my fingertips. I turn around before knocking and notice that my dad's pickup truck isn't in the driveway, making me feel uneasy. My dad always made sure he was home for dinner each night when I was growing up and seeing he's still not home well after dark is not like him. Or at least not like the "him" I always knew. I lift my hand toward the front door, feeling like a stranger on my own porch.

I knock on the door and don't hear anyone inside. The window is open, so I peek inside, hoping to see my mom.

"Mama, it's me, Auden," I yell into the screen, knocking on the frame of the window.

I can hear footsteps inside and see my mom rounding the corner into the kitchen, her hair up in a scarf, as always, to protect her curls. The door flies open, and she steps out onto the porch, pulling me into her embrace the moment her feet reach the wooden porch.

"Auden, my sweet girl!" she cries out, squeezing me tightly.

"What on earth are you doing here?" she asks, pushing me from her and scanning my body up and down "And when was the last time you've eaten? You're skin and bones."

She pulls me inside behind her and puts me in one of the old kitchen chairs, reaching for the fridge before taking another breath.

"Where's Dad?" I ask, confused as to why my mom would already be in bed without my dad being home.

"Oh, he's still at the shop. He's got a lot more work these days and not enough employees to help."

Her positive tone of voice sounds forced, making me wonder why she isn't telling me the whole truth as to why my dad isn't home. I always know when she's sugar coating something, and the words coming from her are a little too sweet to be the full truth.

"He should be home anytime now, and you being here will make his whole year."

She pulls a casserole dish out of the refrigerator and turns on the oven, cleaning the counters as she goes, forcing the smell of gas and lemon into the air.

"I'm sorry the house is such a pigsty. I really wish you gave me the courtesy of telling me you were coming home."

Normally, I would resist taking the blame for why her house is so messy, but I'm too occupied with watching her as she moves. It's only been six years since I saw my mom in person, but it feels like it might as well have been fifty, especially with how slow my mom is moving. She's still wearing the nightgown that I got her for her birthday when I was thirteen to bed. I notice how the purple coloring has faded and how snug the waistline is around her body now. She has her old, tan house slippers on. One has a big tear in the side of it, exposing how swollen her ankles have become.

My mom has never looked like most of the women in Louisiana. She has deep red hair that flows down in big natural curls and green eyes just like mine. I used to hate how different my mom looked from other moms, but now that I've stepped out of this small town and noticed other different people in the world, I can appreciate how beautiful her uniqueness makes her.

"How are you, Mama?" I ask, hoping the answer is more put-together than she seems to be.

She leans down and sets the casserole in the oven before turning to take a seat across from me, wiping the sweat off her forehead as she scooches herself into the table.

"Oh, the Lord is still providing and that's all I can ask for," she answers, smiling to convince me that she really is okay.

Mom has a special relationship with God. Most of the people I've met through church seem like they're just playing the role that they were raised to play. But mom truly loves Jesus, and there's no way you can deny that if you've witnessed her in church. It's like she's with her favorite person in the world, passing love back and forth through music.

She graduated college with a degree in education before she and my dad got married. She was going to be a school teacher but felt her calling was to be in the church as much as possible, so she took a part-time position there instead. We could have had a much bigger home and been able to afford a lot more had she followed her original career path. But dad never complained, and even loved her more for her choice to follow God instead. He always said that my mama picking Jesus over her love for shopping was the best testament of faith he'd ever witnessed.

I look around at the yellow walls of the kitchen, taking in the old signs, family photos, and whimsical decor. Even though we don't live on a farm, my mom definitely has a farmhouse style, and she has always had it fully displayed in the kitchen. I think the cluttered walls may be the reason my own home is cleaner and more minimalistic.

"You haven't answered my calls in days. I began to worry more than usual," she says, reaching one hand out and placing it on top of mine. "How are you doing with the news of Taylor?"

I inhale slowly through my nose, not wanting to have this conversation but knowing it's more than overdue.

"I'm doing alright, Mama. I hadn't talked to Taylor in years."

She squeezes my hand, letting me know in her own way that she's here for me.

"The years apart never matter when you hold them against the years you two were attached at the hip." She lets out a soft laugh through her nose. "I remember yelling at you two every day in the summer for running through this house with your muddy feet, always too occupied with your newest adventures to notice the trails you left behind."

The way she mentions that I have a right to feel the loss of Taylor, even though I walked away from her years ago, makes my heart flutter. My mom hasn't always been the most comforting, not by choice, but because I was always closer to my dad and didn't really like physical affection. But hearing her acknowledge how close she knew Taylor and I were, and hearing her memories of us together, is exactly what I needed in this moment.

"Thanks, Mama," I reply, squeezing her hand back.

She stands up from her chair and turns back to the oven, grabbing a rag from the cherrywood cabinet next to it before bending over and pulling the dish out.

"Now, I already stopped by Daddy's shop to drop off his dinner, something I've been doing more and more these days. So, it's just you and me eating the rest. I knew the Lord had me make too much for a reason. I just didn't realize how good the reason would turn out to be."

I watch as she takes out the same white ceramic plates that she used when I was growing up, my nostrils filling with the buttery smell of biscuits mixed with beef and veggies. My stomach starts to growl as my mouth starts to water. I forgot how much I love mama's cooking.

I haven't eaten anything today except a small bag of pretzels on the plane. Between the interview, my anxiety about flying home, and the endless thoughts of Asher, I haven't had much of an appetite.

"Do you remember Taylor's brother, Mama?" I ask.

She leans over and reaches for the fresh basil growing on the windowsill, breaks a leaf off, crushes it in her hand, and garnishes each of our plates before turning around and setting them in front of us.

"How could I forget?" she asks, her cheeks creasing like she's holding back a happy secret.

I feel my eyebrows furrow as I become suspicious about what's so funny about Asher.

"What are you smiling about?" I ask, waiting for the steam to cool on my plate and, of course, for mama to say grace.

She smooths her napkin into her lap, shaking her head as she continues to smile.

"Well, he works here in town for the fire department, so I still see him quite a bit. But I can't help but laugh at how much you loved running into him as a kid."

I loved running into him!? What is she talking about? I saw him a lot at the Landry home, he was Taylor's older brother' but I feel like she's implying something that I'm just not catching on to.

"Why?" she asks, "Are you nervous about running into him at the funeral on Friday? I'm assuming you are planning to attend."

Nervous is an understatement. On the flight here, all I could do was rerun our interactions through my head over and over again. I kept catching him staring at me when he thought I wasn't paying attention. At first, it was a little uncomfortable, but now I seem to find myself missing his eyes on me and wondering what he was thinking. And that isn't even touching on the fear that he'll never want to see me again after the last thing I said to him. I sure wouldn't want to see me again.

"I think I'm going to attend. Are you and Daddy going?" I ask.

She nods her head, her smile fading away.

"We wouldn't miss it. We loved that girl like our own," she replies. "We might as well go together now that you're home."

I smile slightly, moving my fork an inch from my plate and twirling it in a circle with my finger.

"Why were you asking about Asher? Is something making you excited to see him again?" she asks, sending a wink in my direction.

The last time I was in my mom's presence, I was barely eighteen, and my mom didn't want anything to do with the idea of me being interested in boys. Now that I'm twenty-four, she's showing me a whole different side of her that I had yet to experience. I kind of like it.

"I was just wondering," I reply, feeling my cheeks blushing red.

She laughs again and gives me another nod of her head. "Your cheeks are turning the same color that they did anytime that boy came around. I used to be nervous about it, but he seemed to turn out just fine. Not that you were looking for my opinion."

She reaches her hand out toward mine, bowing her head and waiting to hold my hand before saying grace.

EIGHTEEN

Auden

The smell of sausage and grits wakes me before the hot sun gets a chance to. The sound of mama clanging pots and pans around in the kitchen spreads a smile across my face as I pull the sheet off me and sit on the edge of my childhood bed. Mom and I went to bed before dad came home last night. We were both exhausted, and I needed to shut my mind off.

My parents haven't touched a thing in my old room, sending me tumbling back six years into the past. My walls are still covered with drawings of trees and flowers that Taylor had gifted me over the years and quotes on napkins and backs of receipts that I enjoyed and wrote down. My smile grows bigger when I read one from my grams, "A woman's place is wherever she wants to be. I just happen to love being in this kitchen."

A knock at the door pulls me out of my trip down memory lane. My dad slowly opens the door.

"I heard there was a little fish that swam her way home."

My feet can't make their way over to him fast enough. I leap right into my dad's arms and grip on like my life depends on it.

"Oh, Dad, I have missed you so much," I mumble into his chest.

When I finally let go, I take a step back and we both take a look at one another, noting all of the changes the last six years have created.

His hair isn't as dark as it used to be and now has a mixture of white sprinkled in, matching his eyebrows that have lost almost all their darker color. His eyes and cheeks are sunken like he hasn't slept well since I left, and his posture is so slumped he may have shrunk two inches.

"You look tired, Dad," I start to say, walking with him toward the kitchen. "Mama said work's been very busy, and you don't make it home on time much anymore."

He pulls a chair out for me at the old, wooden table and takes the seat directly next to me. He doesn't answer, instead he just stares at me with the slightest grin.

Mama plates our breakfast and sets it down in front of us, setting her own plate down last and joining us at the table.

"Now, Auden, I may be mistaken but didn't you leave here six years ago with an accent?" my dad asks.

I roll my eyes at his playful comment. I didn't realize how much I truly missed being around my dad. He's a quiet man, the exact opposite of my mama. He doesn't speak unless he has something to say, and he makes sure to take his time and really weigh out all sides of any situation before making a decision. I've never heard him raise his voice, and you'd swear the man didn't know how to complain. He could fix anything you ask him to, and I have yet to find something he's afraid of. He's always been there for me, especially when Mama would get on me about whatever I was doing wrong that day. Dad didn't judge me or want me to be anything I'm not, and I've lost sight of the value in that over the last six years.

Dad and I were like two peas in a pod while I was growing up. I was with him any chance I could get. He's called me his little fish since I was four years old and learned how to cast my own line without getting hooked on a tree, or worse, Daddy's leg. I loved fishing with my dad more than anything else. My heart sinks at the realization of how distant our relationship has become. Ever since that night with Brad, I felt like I didn't have a place in my dad's life as his little girl anymore. And for that, I hate Brad even more.

"Alright you two, let's pray and eat so Daddy can get to work on time," Mom says as she bows her head and reaches her hands out toward Dad and me.

"Oh, dear Lord, thank you for blessing us with another day here on earth. Thank you for blessing us with this wonderful meal and for giving me the strength to get up and cook it over this hot stove all morning."

My dad's hand squeezes mine when my mama mentions her hard work, forcing me to use all my self-control to hold back my giggle.

"And, dear Lord, thank you from the bottom of my heart for this sweet surprise. You have answered my prayers once again and returned our baby home to us where she belongs. You are so good to us, Lord. In your name we pray, Amen."

Before we let go of our hands, Dad mumbles to Mama and she starts up again.

"Oh, and Lord, please hold the Landry family close. Let the Landrys feel your goodness and love in this time and help guide us so that we can support them in any way that we can.

Please give Taylor the peace she so clearly needed. In your name we pray, Amen."

I keep my eyes shut a moment longer, holding back the tears before reopening them. I was always able to hold my emotions in when I was around my mom but sitting here next to my dad is making it much harder. He was always the one to wipe away my tears.

Dad hurries through his breakfast and excuses himself from the table before washing his hands in the old ceramic sink. He hums a little tune along the way like he always had. I swear the man hums more than he speaks.

"Now, Auden, you won't be swimming on back to that new pond before I get out of work, will you?" he asks, leaning down and kissing me on top of my head.

"I'm not sure when I'm returning home yet, Dad, but I'll make sure it's not before you're home tonight," I reply, noticing my mom's head swing back in my direction.

He gives me a wink before walking over to Mama and kissing her on the cheek as she starts to wash the dishes. He's never once left for work without saying goodbye to her. He slowly bends over to fasten his work boots, his back cracking, sending my heart a little pang as I notice how much they've aged over the past six years.

I've always thought my dad was a handsome man, and by the way all the wives would find any excuse to talk to him at church, makes me think I wasn't the only one who noticed. He didn't smile very often, but when he did, it was always kind and genuine.

As soon as the door shuts behind him, Mama starts to talk, keeping her back to me as she continues scrubbing the dishes.

"So, I called Tucker this morning, and he's available for lunch today. I was thinking you and I could go down to the church to see some of the ladies so they can catch up with you before you join him at the Crow's Nest for lunch."

Nausea overcomes me instantly. The fact that she completely ignored what I said last weekend about Tucker and not moving home doesn't even phase me. I'm used to her ignoring my wants over hers. The fact that she has already announced my return to Monroe makes me want to find the closest well and jump in.

"Mama, tell me you haven't told anyone besides Tucker that I'm home," I ask, praying silently that her answer isn't as bad as I'm assuming.

She stops washing dishes and turns to face me, curious as to why I sound so flustered.

"Am I not allowed to tell my friends that my daughter has finally returned home?" she asks, crossing her arms and lifting one eyebrow.

I stand and shove my chair underneath the table, the legs scraping against the old, wooden floors. I had a great time with her last night, and I hate how angry I feel already this morning.

"I didn't want anyone to know I was here. I haven't even been here a full day, and you've already filled my schedule with people I don't even know anymore." I try not to yell and fail miserably.

She pulls the drying rag off her shoulder and throws it down onto the counter, shaking her head in disappointment from my tone.

"This is exactly why communication is so important, Auden. If I had known you didn't want anyone to know you were home, I wouldn't have made the plans."

I shake my head, closing my eyes and trying to figure out how to reply without blowing up over her ignorance.

"Mama, I told you that I didn't want to date anyone here and have no plans to move home, so why would you even entertain the idea of Tucker and me?"

She turns her back to me, lifting the towel off the counter and waving it over her shoulder.

"Fine, Auden, you win. I'll call Tucker and tell him I made a mistake and tell the church ladies that you're just too busy to find time for them. It doesn't make sense why you'd even bother coming home if you hate it here so much."

She starts to wash the last of the dishes, moving slower as she processes our talk.

"I came home for Taylor, Mama," I say, my voice softer as the truth settles in.

"Well, I'll sure pray your daddy and I get to see you again," she replies, "before we too are dead."

NINETEEN

Asher

    I park my jeep in the back of my parents' property line. It's closer to the tree Auden told me to meet her at, and I have a better chance at keeping my parents out of our meeting if they don't know I'm here.

    The sound of Auden's dad's old pickup chugging down the dirt road heightens the nerves in my stomach. I know I just saw her a few days ago, but we didn't part on the best of terms. This time, I want to make sure we do.

    I love that she found the courage to come here, but I hate that now I have to tell her Brad somehow knows I was in Minneapolis. Not only that, but also the fact that Mr. Montgomery may have it out for her dad as well. I still haven't figured out why. I avoided Brad and Mr. Montgomery for the rest of the evening last night. But my gut is telling me Brad knows more than just what city I flew to. His knowledge of my location is meant to intimidate me, I know that. I just wish he wasn't succeeding. I ended up admitting to my dad that I was visiting Auden and expected that to come as a surprise. But he was unphased, so it seems he had already figured that out as well. He seemed happy by the idea of Auden attending Taylor's funeral, but I didn't confirm that she was coming back home. If I was the only one involved, I wouldn't think twice about Brad snooping on what I'm doing in my spare time, but something tells me that the only reason he's so interested in me is because I'm now the only connection he has to Auden.

Auden parks the truck, opening the door and dropping down into the gust of dust the truck's tires kicked up. Her hair is pulled back in a clip, showing off her long neck and defined collarbones. She has on short jean shorts with the pockets hanging down past the distressed hemline and a green, graphic t-shirt with a cut going down from the top to expose some of her chest. I can't help but smile when I notice the low top, snakeskin cowboy boots. She looks like she's stepped foot in the South for the first time in her life. As ridiculous as she looks, the sight of her takes my breath away.

"You skin that snake yourself?" I ask, holding back my laughter.

She kicks some dirt up at me and pushes my shoulder when she gets close enough. I can tell she's trying her hardest to hold back a laugh.

"Don't say another word. Dec packed my bag for me, and I'm not sure if I should be more upset that I didn't check the bag before leaving or because we wear the same shoe size," she replies.

Her smile makes any of the nerves I was feeling a few moments ago float away. Everything in me wants to reach out and pull her close to me. I want to swoop her up into my arms and tell her I never should've left without saying goodbye, and that the last few days have been hell not calling to beg her to come home and get through this with me. I want her to know how thankful I am to have her here with me.

She rubs the tip of her boot into the dirt, her eyes glued to the ground as if she's lost in her mind searching for the words to say next. I could watch her think all day if she'd let me. I'm sure that'd be more fun than what I need to tell her. "Asher," she says, still keeping her eyes on the ground. "I need to apologize for what I said. It was cruel, and I didn't mean it."

She looks up at me finally, her face covered in fear which sends a rock to my gut. I don't want her to ever feel scared around me. I want her to feel like she can tell me anything, and that I truly want to hear it all. I want to tell her that I'm starting to feel a way for her that I can't quite explain yet, but I know I haven't felt it with anyone else before.

My body reacts to her scared expression before my mind gets the chance to catch up. I find myself pulling her into my chest, wrapping my arms around her and squeezing her tightly as the smell of her floral perfume swirls around us.

"I'm so thankful you're here," I whisper to her, unable to find any other words and shocking myself by the impulsive truth I just admitted.

Her body relaxes into me, and I feel as if I've taken my first breath of air in days. I want to bring her comfort, but the truth is that's exactly what she has become for me.

When she releases me, she takes a step back. She turns her body to the side, holding her hand to her forehead to shield her eyes from the sun and pointing toward the oldest weeping willow on our property.

"That's where she left the letters," she says.

I turn and face the tree with her, taking one of her hands and starting to make my way in the direction of the tree.

"I remember y'all always running back in this direction, but I didn't realize you had anything interesting going on," I joke.

When we reach the tree, we stop, and I watch as she runs her hand along the tree's bark as a piece of hair falls out of her clip and frames her jawline perfectly.

"We left an old sketchbook in here and whenever one of us was away or too busy to hang out, we would leave each other a letter so the other always knew what was on our mind."

A glimpse of a smile flashes across her lips for just a moment with that memory before she reaches up and pulls out an old tin box from inside the tree's hollow. I watch as she stares at it in her hands, rubbing her fingers across the front and brushing the dust off it.

"I never realized how beautiful it is back here," I say, trying to ease the tension.

Auden stops and turns to look over the wetlands lining the bayou that starts at the back of the property, the sun turning the mucky water a tint of gold between the cattails growing along it.

"We'd spend hours out here just watching the animals and birds coming and going at all times of day and night, catching crawfish any chance we had. Not a single person bothered us in all the years we met out here, so it always felt like just ours."

I run my hand across her back and watch as two herons dance together before flying off. After a few seconds, she turns and gives me a smile before leaning down and sitting against the tree trunk's wide base. She sets the tin in her lap but doesn't open it just yet, her hands resting flat on the top.

I crouch down and take a seat next to her. We're close enough that our arms rub against one another. Whenever our skin touches, it sends a jolt of electricity through my body, and my skin starts to tingle with anticipation. She looks up at me and her eyes are full of nerves again, prompting me to reach my arm over her shoulders and pull her into my side. I want to protect her, to keep her safe and shield her from any harm. I feel a warmth in my chest and a sense of fierce loyalty and devotion toward her, a desire to be the one who makes her happy and brings a smile to her face.

"It's going to be okay, Auden. I'm right here with you," I say, forcing a smile to try and mask my own nerves intertwined with sadness.

As much as I love being in this moment with Auden, the reality of what we're here to do is overwhelming. If we open this tin and Taylor has left more letters like she mentioned, then the contents inside could determine how the memory of Taylor might be for the rest of my life. If she wrote about me in them, she could've blamed me for not being there enough for her. She could've decided that I was just as selfish as Brad, and she didn't want to live in a world with the two of us. I hate how the fact that I'm so drawn to Auden has convinced me that I may be more like Brad than I ever realized, allowing my wants to coexist alongside my grief. Either way, if she mentioned me, she will be telling Auden how she felt about me and how I impacted her life. That will be stuck in my mind for the rest of my life.

But Auden needs me to be the strong one right now. Her presence in Monroe is brave enough, I want to help take away any added fear or pain from her. So, I'll continue to push these fears out of my mind when I'm around her.

She opens the tin, and silence overtakes us. I can't hear our breath anymore, and I swear the wildlife around us is holding its breath as well. She was right. There's six envelopes tucked inside next to an old, dirty sketchbook, a few old pencils and pens, friendship necklaces with halves of a heart, a gold dollar coin, some Dr. Pepper lip balm, and the back side of a Polaroid photo.

 I reach in and pull the Polaroid out, turning it over and laughing as soon as I see the memory it captured. Auden's face flushes as she peeks over to look at it. The sight of Auden and Taylor in elementary school wearing nothing but my mom's bras and their underwear brings us both to an uncontrollable laughter.

 Once we finally get a hold of ourselves, Auden turns back to the box as I set the photo back inside. She pulls out the first letter dated over six years ago, her name written on the front in pen with a heart drawn next to it.

 "This must be the first letter she wrote me," she says, holding it like the most fragile thing in the world.

 I give her shoulder a squeeze as she carefully rips the top of the envelope open, her hands starting to shake as she pulls the papers out. She leans back into my chest and unfolds the letter, holding it high enough that I can read along with her.

5/12/2018

Auden,

I can't believe it's been a full year since you left Monroe. I found myself wandering out in the back of my parents' property and at our old willow tree. I reached inside and found the sketchbook and here I am, carrying on the tradition with no idea if you'll ever return and reach inside yourself.

Life hasn't been the same since you left. The air feels stiff, and I can't seem to get a grip on where my place is anymore. You took a piece of me with you when you left, and I still don't know if that's my fault or yours. I never hated you. I doubt I'd ever be able to do that, and I pray each night that you haven't hated me.

Brad asked me to marry him shortly after graduation and I said yes. He was adamant about the wedding happening right away. He said we had spent so long together already that there was no reason to wait. Mom and Dad sure were excited, not that that's a surprise.

I wish you gave Brad the opportunity to show you who he really is—his kind side and the big amount of love he has for me, Auden. He even asked if I wanted to invite your parents before I could even ask. They both attended. They have been like second parents to me my whole life.

He makes me happy, and he takes good care of me.

His dad bought us a house right down the road from the school. It's got a big backyard like I always wanted and a covered wraparound porch that I filled with flowers this summer. Brad even bought me a set of rocking chairs. He thinks they're for us when we get old together, but I still secretly dream of the day where you and I sit and rock, watching the birds on a hot afternoon like your grandparents did.

Some days while I'm tending to my flowers, I make up stories in my mind of what you could be up to. Whatever it is, I bet you're a rockstar like you've always been.

Brad thought it was a good idea that I focus on our wedding and then our new home, learning how to take care of it while he's in college instead of both of us going to school this year. He's currently at LSU, which is a little over 3 hours away, so he spends his weekends here at home and is gone all week long. It's not easy being apart, but I know the distance is just as hard on him. Some days he doesn't even call home because he says it hurts to hear my voice.

I pray every night that life is bringing you happiness and one day I can be a part of that again.
Happy (late) 19th Birthday.
Until we meet again,
Taylor

Auden lays the open letter on her lap and looks out over the wetlands without saying a word. I slowly take the letter from her lap and carefully fold it up, tucking it back inside of its original envelope before setting it back inside the tin.

"Are you okay?" I ask, removing my arm from her shoulder and leaning forward so I can see her face. I haven't quite figured out how to read her yet, but her facial expressions I feel pretty confident about.

She nods her head before looking back at the tin box.

"She blamed me for leaving her. She felt just as empty as I did and still believed Brad's lies," she answers.

Brad's lies. Another clue to the connection between Auden and Brad that she isn't ready to share with me yet. What could he have lied about that made Auden and Taylor end their lifelong friendship?

"Do you want to stop for the day? We don't have to keep reading them," I suggest, trying to ease as much of her pain as I can. As badly as I want to know what happened between them, between the three of them, I'd rather save Auden from more heartbreak.

"No," she replies, shaking her head again as if she's attempting to snap out of something. "I want to keep reading so we can understand her more. I need to know why five years later she was so . . ."

She pauses, looking at me as if she doesn't want to say anything that will offend me. Before she gets the chance to continue, I take the pressure off her and start to list off potential endings.

"Broken, hurt, sad," I suggest. "Lonely."

Auden reaches back into the tin and finds the second letter addressed to her. She starts to lean back but stops, her eyes trailing from my left arm that's now in my lap and then back toward the tree. I smile the moment I realize that she's silently asking me to put my arm back around her shoulder.

I lift my arm up over her head and wrap it back around her before she nuzzles her body back into me, this time resting her head on my chest. She leans into me, as if she's seeking comfort or solace, causing me to feel a surge of tenderness and compassion welling up inside.

"Will you read it out loud to me?" she asks, giving me a look that could convince me to break my own arm for her.

I take the letter from her and lift it above her head so I can make out Taylor's writing before starting to read aloud.

5/12/2019

Auden,

Well I found myself here again at our tree. Two years feels awfully unbelievable. I finally got the nerve to ask your mama how you were last Thanksgiving, hoping she'd mention that you'd be returning for Christmas. She didn't mention anything about you returning, but your dad mentioned you were succeeding in every way possible, like he knew you would, and that small town girls really can conquer big cities. I knew you would too. I just hate not knowing what city you ended up in.

If I was a betting girl, my money would be on Chicago or New York. I remember how badly you wanted to see a real snowfall, and I hear those two get a lot of it. I tried to look you up in both cities but came up short, although it was disappointing to find out you're not the only Auden in the world.

I still haven't started college yet, but Brad likes to remind me that life doesn't go as we plan.

He's still at LSU. He never made it home for the summer last year and is staying again this summer. His commitment to getting into law school early is admirable, and I appreciate all his hard work for our future, but it sure does get lonely in this big house.

I'm hoping this weekend when he's home I can talk him into the idea of me taking online classes in the fall. I really want to start leaving my mark on the kids of Monroe. Sometimes I take a walk by Monroe Elementary just to listen to their little laughs on the playground. Their joy reminds me of how your mama must feel when she sees people praising Jesus in church.

Do you remember Dawson Sanders from junior high? His little sister Reba moved back a year ago and works at Dr. Delacroix's clinic as a nurse aid. When I was there a few months ago, she hinted at the fact that she was getting close to Brad. When I brought it up to him, he told me he'd never met a Reba in his life and didn't even remember the Sanders family. I don't know what to believe anymore because I remember Brad and his brothers staying at the Sanders' house for two weeks when their parents had to go take care of Brad's grandma the summer of 4th grade. That's the same summer he and DJ didn't attend swimming lessons. Brad's never lied to me before, so I want to keep my faith in him. He's a good man.

Happy (late) 20th Birthday. I continue to pray for your happiness and for us to one day be together again.

Until we meet again,
Taylor

My heart starts to ache as I sense Taylor's loneliness. I was so busy at that time trying to get the fire chief to notice me that I had neglected to see how alone my own sister had become. I knew that Brad wasn't living at home, and the thought of her having no one regrettably never crossed my mind.

I set the letter down, leaning forward and removing my arm from Auden before bringing myself to a stance.

"Are you okay, Asher?" Auden asks as she sits up, folding and returning the letter to the box. My feet keep pacing back and forth as the memories of that time start to flood my mind.

"I just wish I paid more attention and put Taylor higher on my priority list," I answer, wrapping my hands behind my head.

Auden stands and walks closer to me, reaching up and grabbing one of my wrists to bring my pacing to a stop.

"I remember her asking me about Reba and I thought nothing of it. I didn't remember Reba or Dawson and didn't even consider why she could be asking about that."

Auden grabs both of my hands and holds them in hers, staring up at me with her shimmering green eyes, each second of her stare takes away a small piece of my building anger.

"You are so good, Asher. Please don't regret making a life for yourself. She was so proud of you."

She tucks her arms around me and pulls me into her, holding me tightly as I wrap myself around her as well, resting my cheek on top of her head. Her hair feels soft against my cheek and the scent of her floral perfume is lingering in the air. My body can't help but be acutely aware of her presence.

Suddenly I feel something wet touching my ankle and immediately break away from Auden, pulling her out of the way of whatever was trying to touch us.

"Sandy?" Auden yells before dropping to her knees and scooping up my parents' fluffy, blonde dog in her arms.

"Oh, Sandy, I have missed you so much," she says in between her own kisses and hugs.

The joy consuming Auden's face with Sandy in her arms feels contagious. I had forgotten how much Sandy loved Auden, and the sight of the two of them reuniting would bring a tear to anyone's eye. Sandy clearly remembers Auden. Suddenly, I hear a voice behind us start to speak, bringing an eerie shiver down my spine.

"Well, what do we have here, Sandy?" he asks.

TWENTY

Brad

I would pay an obnoxious amount of money to freeze this moment in time and relive it whenever I want to. The look on Asher's and Auden's faces when they saw me was a thousand times better than I could have anticipated.

I've been tracking Asher's location since Minneapolis. When it showed he was at his parents' house, I called Helen to inquire if she was home as well. When she said no, I offered to stop by her house and take Sandy out for a walk. Helen and Charles have been everywhere except home this last week dealing with everything for Taylor's funeral, and I knew taking care of Sandy was an offer they couldn't pass up.

Sandy's basically half-dead. In fact, that bitch is nearly twenty years old. She's a Bolognese whose eyesight is failing and teeth are all gone, but her sense of smell is better than ever. I knew she'd smell Asher out here, and she'd lead me directly to them. It's almost funny how easy this has all been.

Asher turns to face me, moving his body so he's standing between Auden and me. He's clearly attempting to show his dominance and that he'll try to keep us apart if I make any moves. But now I wonder what exactly Auden has been telling him that makes him feel the need to put himself between us. I watch as Auden stays behind him, reaching down and grabbing an old tin box that's sitting on the grass between them.

"What's going on Asher?" I ask, trying my damnedest to seem oblivious.

Asher tucks one arm behind him, silently instructing Auden to stay behind him before he takes a step forward in my direction.

"Why are you here, Brad?" he asks.

What the hell is this, a fucking joke? I'm clearly walking his parents' shit-ass dog, and he has the audacity to act like I'm somewhere I shouldn't be.

"Why am I here? Isn't it obvious? I'm helping your parents by taking care of Sandy," I reply, keeping my tone calm and collected with a pinch of annoyance at the preoccupied son I'm standing in front of. "Maybe I should be asking you why you're here and not offering to help with
Sandy yourself."

I scoop the bitch up into my arms and nuzzle her close to my face so she can lick me. I can't stand dogs unless they're doing something useful. But people don't like when you admit that, so I keep it to myself. I want to take a fucking bow for the acting I'm doing. These idiots have no idea what I still have up my sleeve, and if there's any intelligent brain cells inside of them, they won't take this any further and have to find out.

"Anyways," I continue, setting Sandy back in the grass beside me, "what are you doing all the way back here?"

I take a step to the side where Asher isn't blocking me from viewing Auden.

"Or, what exactly are you doing here, Auden?" I ask, pointing my finger in her direction.

My view is once again taken by Asher's shoulder before he replies for her. He's really starting to piss me off with this protector bullshit. She must've sucked him off and made him fall in love because this is just pathetic even for him. But what irks me the most is how obedient Auden is behaving for him. She's always been such a stubborn little cunt, and I hated her and loved her for it. She's been one of my biggest challenges since we were kids, never listening to others or participating in things she didn't want to. I've never been as patient in my life as I was waiting for the opportunity to be in a position where I could take control of her, to make her listen to me and have no way of refusing. So when I finally got the chance, on my eighteenth birthday of all days, it was more satisfying than I had ever dreamed of. If I said I haven't thought about that night many times since then, I'd be bullshitting through my teeth.

"She's here because Taylor left some things for her, and we came to collect them," Asher replies.

My eyes dart to the tin box and my curiosity peaks. What the hell could Taylor have left her? Taylor didn't even leave a note or anything for me, her fucking husband.

"Is that true or did Taylor just have proof of more of your lies that you didn't want to get out?"

I know I'm grasping at straws now, but I want to make sure Auden knows that Taylor still hated her. I know this because Taylor hated anything that I hated, and I have to hate the girl that accused me of rape. And now I want Asher to feel a small seed of doubt as well. It doesn't matter if he knows my side of the story yet, a tiny bit of wonder is all a person needs not to fully commit to the other side's version.

I spot Auden's fist balling up, and I realize she's become easier to crack than I remember. Maybe the city has made her weaker and she can't handle as much as she used to.

"Even in her fucking death, you won't allow her peace!" I shout, making sure to look like the angry, protective widower.

Asher takes another step toward me, his neck stiffening like he's done listening to me speak to her and I take a step back in response.

"Brad, you have no idea what you're talking about, and you need to leave," Asher says, his tone attempting authority.

His stare doesn't break and, as badly as I want to show him what it feels like to be rocked in the face by Brad Mallehan Montgomery, I know I have to play the scared and conflicted brother-in-law for now.

I put my hands up in front of me so he knows I mean him no harm and don't want any trouble.

"I don't mean to upset you, brother. It just breaks my heart knowing how much damage that girl caused my sweet Taylor, and I'm worried and concerned about why she's suddenly here now that Taylor's . . ." I pause, wiping a fake tear from my eye, "gone."

My hand smacks against my thigh, and I whistle for Sandy to follow me, waving my goodbye as I start to walk back in the direction of the house.

"Be careful, brother," I call out behind me before walking out of sight.

Asher has no idea how big of a mistake he just made by showing how much he clearly cares for that rat whore. It's like the guy is completely unaware at all times. What I just became aware of is how much I dislike seeing Auden giving attention to him. She acts like the idea of being with me was laughable, and yet she's out in the back of Asher Landry's parents' property. They don't own half the land my family does, and I bet if I hadn't interrupted, she would've been down on her back in a dirty-ass bayou. Pathetic.

TWENTY-ONE

Asher

The moment Brad is out of sight, I pull Auden to me, trying to calm my own nerves as well as hers. I feel her body stiffen in my arms and pull her back away from me, just far enough that I can see her face and make sure she's okay. She looks up at me and I see the tears filling her blank stare, prompting me to pull her back into me.

We stand there for a few moments before Auden lets go, starting to walk in circles, her hands flapping around like she doesn't like the feeling of her own skin, or maybe it's the Louisiana heat she's no longer accustomed to.

She finally stops and turns to face me, her hands raised and holding both sides of her head. "How the hell did that just happen?" she asks, looking directly at me as if I have the answers.

Well, I kind of do have the answers. Or at least some of them. I don't know what the hell to do or how I got here, but I know I was trying and planning on telling her that Brad somehow knew I was in Minneapolis. I was going to tell her about how he showed up and drove me past her parents' house and the conversation I overheard my dad and Mr. Montgomery having, and then before I knew it, it was too late. The opportunity had already passed. It doesn't matter what my intentions were, right now I know something. I knew something, and I didn't tell her. She trusted me enough to finally return home and the first chance we get to meet up, I end up finding a way to seem like a damn liar.

I pull my arm back behind me and aim it at the trunk of the willow tree, stopping myself mid-punch and releasing a grunt before walking away from it.

"What's wrong, Asher? What aren't you telling me?" she asks.

I watch as her eyebrows narrow and she takes a step forward, waiting for the answer that I still don't know how to give. I take a step forward so I'm close enough to reach her, taking both of her hands in mine and looking directly into her eyes. Fear starts to grip at my chest knowing that what happens next could take her away from me again.

"I was going to tell you, Auden. I swear that I was going to tell you today. I really was. But I didn't want to scare you."

She lets go of my hands and starts to back away from me, her expression changing from confusion to what looks like fear. My heart starts to ache as I watch all of the good she sees in me start to evaporate.

"Auden, please, let me explain."

I take a step forward and realize that's the last thing I should do at this moment. She begins to back away quicker, forcing me to retreat and put both of my hands in my pockets.

"He knew we were together, and you didn't fucking tell me?" she starts to yell, turning her back to me and walking closer to the wetlands. "What the hell could have ever made you think this is okay? Like this isn't something you should've told me before even buying that fucking plane ticket for me!"

I try to speak up, but she won't give me the opportunity. She just keeps going and when she finally turns around, I can see all of the rage that's building has forced the blood straight to her face.

"Is this some sick kind of plan the two of you concocted together? Are you just as absolutely insane as he is? Is this why you are constantly popping those pills? Because they help you come off as a decent human being?"

Her words cut deep like a knife straight to my heart. I close my eyes and try to process what she's saying but can't seem to move past the fact that she thinks I'm insane because of my ADHD medication. It's not like I haven't been contemplating the same question about myself, I absolutely have. But hearing her agree makes the fears feel more like a tragic reality.

She stays silent, and I wonder if it's because she's noticed my silence or if she's already walked away. I open my eyes, and see she's brought her hands up to her face, cradling her cheeks as if she's worried her head may explode if she doesn't hold it together.

"Auden, please give me one chance to explain," I plead, my voice softer as I try to hold myself back from any unwanted explosive emotions.

She stays silent, bringing her arms back down and crossing them against her chest. I take that as a yes and continue speaking.

"Brad showed up at my house last night and asked me to ride with him to my parents' house for dinner. I didn't have an excuse not to and didn't want to make him suspicious, especially not knowing if you were going to come home or not.

I still don't really understand what Brad's done to you or Taylor. But my gut and my heart," I take one hand out of my pocket and rest it over my chest, "have been telling me to trust you since I flew to Minneapolis."

Auden takes a step closer, keeping her arms firm against her chest.

"So, how did he know I was here?" she asks.

I look back in the direction of my parents' home.

"I don't know, Auden. But he mentioned that he knew I was in Minneapolis when I was in the car with him. I think he wanted me to know that he knew."

I look back at her, and she's tapping her finger against her teeth, her eyes swirling around over the grass like she's following an invisible map.

"Of course, he wanted you to know. Did you tell anyone where you were going? This doesn't add up."

I take a step closer to her slowly and watch her body to make sure she doesn't take another step back.

"Auden, there's more," I say, bracing myself for another harsh interaction. "When we were driving, he took a weird way to my parents. I didn't recognize where we were right away because it was dark and raining, but then I saw the driveway right as we passed and realized he made us drive past your parents' house."

She brings one hand up and covers her mouth, her eyes still and motionless for a moment. She bends over and grabs the tin box, tucking it under her arm and turning in the direction of her dad's truck.

"I have to go. I need to leave Louisiana before my parents get dragged into this mess," she mumbles through her hand.

I move after her, grabbing a hold of her shoulder gently.

"Auden, please stop for a moment," I plead, "You're right, you shouldn't go back to your parents' house. He could show up there and cause a big scene. But you can't leave Louisiana. At least not yet. You came here for a reason, and I told you that you can trust me, and I promise you still can"

Her eyebrows are so close they almost touch as she stands still, contemplating my words.

"Your parents may already be dragged into it," I say solemnly. Her eyes dart to mine with my last truth I need to reveal to her. "This is the last thing I know that you don't. When I got to my parents' house last night, I overheard two men talking and realized it was my dad and Brad's dad. Mr. Montgomery was threatening my dad and told him that he needed to stop using your dad's auto shop for the dealership."

Her lower lip starts to quiver, and I can't help but bring my hand up and rub the inside of my thumb across it.

"I'm so sorry, Auden," I say, unable to pull my eyes and thumb off her bottom lip. "Let me help you get through this."

"How?" she asks, my hand sliding down to her cheek as she begins to speak. "How the hell can anyone help me? I came back here thinking that maybe I could get some closure or help figure out what happened that caused Taylor to . . ."

I pull my hand away from her, taking a long, deep breath and look over her head at the bayou for a moment, searching for the answer. She doesn't finish her sentence and she knows that she doesn't need to.

"I'll rent a room at the Red Roof Inn."

She looks up at me with confusion. "What?"

"I'll rent us a room for the next few days. I'll be there too, so you won't need to be afraid, and Brad will have no reason to go bother your parents. But we can tell them where you are just in case he asks. We'll just have them call us immediately to give us a heads up."

I watch as her eyes start to move like she's contemplating what I just said and weighing her options.

"I mean I can stay if that's what you want, unless you prefer that I don't," I add.

"Asher, why are you still here?" she asks.

Her question catches me off guard. I'm not exactly sure what she's getting at, but I suddenly feel stupid for a million reasons.

"Why are you being so kind to me and still trying to help me after I've been so mean to you, twice now," she asks.

I sigh in relief because she's mad at herself this time, something I feel more confident in my capabilities of fixing than I do if I was the one that she was angry with.

"You are worth fighting for, Auden, and I have a feeling you may be owed a few free passes," I respond, taking one arm from her chest until I'm able to lace her fingers in mine.

"I shouldn't have said that I think you're crazy, Asher, and bringing something so personal into an argument like someone's medication is never okay."

She's right. What she said did hurt, and it was embarrassing and not something anyone should ever do. But I can move on from that if I choose to, and everything in me is telling me that she truly does understand what she said and feels remorseful. So, I'm choosing her and not holding onto bad feelings that could stop that.

"I have ADHD," I say, knowing I don't have to give her an explanation but wanting to. "I don't talk about it, but I was diagnosed when we were kids and have been on and off different medications since then. The pills just help me focus sometimes and keep me calm while also helping me with my impulses and high emotions."

She starts to smile, and it warms my heart immediately. I tug her arm and pull her into my chest, wrapping both of my arms around her.

"I'll forgive you under one condition," I say, laying my cheek on the top of her head. "You stay in Louisiana until we figure this out."

She brings both hands up between us, cupping her hands around her face. I let go of her and lean back, giving her some space. I watch as she drags her hands down her cheeks, standing up taller and inhaling a deep breath of courage.

"Okay," she says, trying to convince us both.

"Okay?" I ask, making sure that she's sure.

"Okay," she repeats, this time nodding her head as well before heading back towards her truck, "Can you follow me home first?"

TWENTY-TWO

Auden

Asher unlocks the door to our room, and we walk in. The door creaks loudly as he shuts it behind us, securing the dead bolt. The walls are coated with old, gold-floral wallpaper, and the carpet clearly hasn't been replaced since they stopped allowing you to smoke in the rooms.

The first thing we both notice is that there's only one bed, one that I'm not sure is big enough to be called a queen. Asher sets his backpack down on the small wooden desk and turns to face me.

"Well, it's not a Hilton but it's all we have available. I'll sleep on the floor, and you take the bed," he says.

We decided it was best for Asher to stay in the room with me. It wasn't worth risking any potential interactions while being alone.

He walks over to the closet and opens the door, pulling out a thick wool blanket and an extra pillow, setting it down on the small, patterned accent chair that matches the gold and maroon walls.

I set my bag down on the bed and take a seat on the edge beside it, looking around the room and soaking up the idea that this is where I'll be spending however many days I have left in Monroe. The carpet has stains all over it, and the smell continues to become more pungent the longer we're in here.

"I don't really feel like going anywhere for dinner tonight, but I doubt we can cook anything good in that miniature microwave," I say, pointing at the yellow microwave on top of the desk.

Asher opens the drawer of the nightstand and pulls out a single take-out menu.

"Options are limited, but Steve's does have a great Hawaiian pizza."

"Steve's it is," I reply.

I unzip my backpack and start to dig through the clothing options Dec packed me, praying I'll find anything that resembles a t-shirt and sweatpants. The dim lighting makes it hard for me to tell what I have, so I stand up and pour all the contents out on the bed. I'm officially convinced Dec thought I was going to Coachella and not a funeral in a small Southern town because everything is either bright, silk, or covered in sequins.

"Damn it, Declan," I mutter under my breath.

Asher hangs up the phone after putting in our order and walks over to the bed, sitting down next to the pile of clothes.

"Who's Declan?" he asks.

Letting a laugh escape me, I take a seat back on the bed next to him, feeling defeated by my limited options. "Dec. his real name is Declan," I reply.

"That's pretty funny for someone with such bright, red curls," Asher replies, smiling like anyone who knows Dec does.

"That's exactly why he goes by Dec, but that's short for his middle name. His full name is so much more exciting."

Asher's eyes widen and he tilts his forehead toward me, waiting for me to reveal the full name of the wonderful Dec. "Finnegan Declan Lindell."

Asher slaps his hand down on his knee, and his face fills with pure happiness, almost like a child on Christmas.

"I don't think I've ever heard such an amazing name," he replies before turning toward my mess of clothes sprawled out.

He reaches his hand down and starts to shuffle the clothes around until he finds a piece of silk and pulls it out from underneath the rest of the pile. He uses both of his hands to spread it out in front of him so he can see what type of clothing he may have found. His face pauses when he realizes it's a small, white nightgown, causing his face to flush, mine shortly behind.

"I don't know what he was thinking, but he sure as hell didn't pack me any suitable pajamas," I say, ripping the nightgown back from him and shoving it in my bag.

Asher stands up and walks over to the desk, reaching inside of his own bag and pulling out a grey t-shirt.

"I didn't pack much, but feel free to wear this if you'd prefer," he says, throwing the shirt into the pile on the bed.

I pick the t-shirt up off the bed, holding it out in front of me and trying my hardest not to allow my face to show the excitement I'm suddenly feeling over the idea of wearing his tshirt. "Thank you. I'm going to shower quickly if you don't mind before the pizza arrives."

*

The well water feels like tennis shoes snagging on a hot slide going through my hair. I didn't expect so many things I grew up with to remind me of how much I love city living.

I start to cry into the stream of water, thinking about how much easier it would've been if I stayed home with Dec and never stepped foot back in Louisiana. I've never been a crier, but these last few days have brought me back to the worst moments of my life and for some stupid reason, I continue to push myself into more situations that dig even deeper. Crying into a stream of water is the closest I can get to convincing myself that I'm not crying. I lean down and start to scrub the hotel soap off my skin, trying not to miss a spot and risk leaving a layer of residue on me before turning off the water and stepping out.

It takes me a minute to figure out which towel is for your hands and which is for your body as both options are so tiny. I finally settle on the longer of the two in hopes that I can stretch it far enough to dry off my back. There's no hair dryer, of course, and the towel is now soaked from drying off my body. The only towel left would never fit around my head. This day has been so bad all around that I'm convinced if one more mishap happens, no matter how small, I may need to be committed.

Is it my luck, or do normal people feel like, when they decide to face their biggest fears, life keeps sending more and more challenges their way? Asher mentioned that Mr. Montgomery had threatened his family and would force them to withhold referrals to my dad's business. Asher's location is somehow being tracked, and it feels like my life is a game that the Montgomery family will do anything to win. For God's sake, I'm hiding out in a shitty motel in a small town when I was interviewing for my dream job in my favorite city just yesterday.

    I lift the t-shirt to my nose and smell Asher's scent on it, causing goosebumps on my chest. I drop the towel and pull on my underwear, lifting the shirt over my head and down my almost naked body. The shirt falls just below my butt, and the rest of me is swimming in it. I look in the mirror, loving the image of myself wearing it.

    Danny was a great first romance, but I'd be crazy if I recognized it as anything other than a childish love filled with sneaking around and taking any chance we could to be alone. I never got to experience the first crush moments like in all the movies and books. I know most of it doesn't really happen in real life, but the small things, like the girl sleeping in the boy's t-shirt, definitely do. My cheeks feel hot as I smooth the shirt down my body. I deserve a small movie moment. Asher makes me feel like the love interest in a movie when the character realizes who they want to spend the rest of their life with.

    When I crack open the bathroom door, Asher's back is turned to me as he flips through the channels on the TV. I quickly run out and dive into the bed, pulling the covers over me as quickly as possible so he doesn't see I'm pants-less. Something inside of me wants him to see me in his shirt, but I'm suddenly very nervous in his presence.

    "The pizza just got here, there's a piece on the nightstand for you. What do you feel like watching?" he asks.

    I lift the plate off the nightstand and shove the pizza in my mouth, my stomach guiding my actions.

    "Whatever you want," I mumble through a mouthful of cheese.

"You can never go wrong with a comedy," he replies, before walking over to the chair and sitting down next to his own plate.

*

After we both finish our pizza, I find myself looking anywhere but at the TV. Time seems to be moving so slowly, and I can't stop myself from wondering how the hell Brad figured out where Asher was and how he found me too. It just doesn't add up, and the timing is even more suspicious.

I look over at Asher and he's staring at the wallpaper, probably finding it hard to watch the movie as well. I sit up in bed and put my plate back on the nightstand.

"I can't take this anymore," I admit.

Asher looks over at me and then reaches for the remote, clicking the TV off and turning to face me.

"Me either," he replies.

I slowly pull the covers off my legs so I can slip out from the bed without flashing Asher my underwear and walk over to my bag. I pull the tin box out and open it up.

"Should we read the next letter?" I ask, staring down at the small pile we have left.

"I'm ready to do whatever you want," he replies.

I tuck myself back into the bed and set the box on my lap.

"Will you read it aloud again?" I ask, patting the bed next to me.

The calmness that Asher's voice brings me reminds me so much of Taylor's. When we were under the willow tree while he read to me, his heartbeat was calming against my cheek, making hearing her last words a little less painful.

He slides into the bed next to me but stops, leaving a few inches between us. He's clearly wanting to make sure I'm comfortable and that he's not crossing a boundary with me, leaving the decision up to me. I can't help but smile about his simple gesture and scooch closer to close the gap, handing him the third letter and starting to lean in toward his chest. He notices where I'm heading and lifts his arm up over my head before wrapping it around me.

He unfolds the letter and clears his throat, squeezing me a little tighter as he begins to read.

5/12/20

Auden,

Three darn years. I haven't been feeling the happiest over the last few months. If I'm telling the truth, I'd say I may have replaced my happiness with anger.

You're probably the last person I should be telling this to, but I have no one else. My parents love Brad so much that I sometimes wonder if they'd pick him over me. I feel so lucky to have Asher still here. Whenever he isn't busy at the fire station, he comes by while Brad's away. We still laugh like kids, but sometimes I feel like I'm holding him back from going out and finding a nice girl to marry. It'd be really nice to have a sister one day. Do you remember when I used to pray that you and Asher would grow up and get married? I still wouldn't mind if you two found your way together somehow.

But I can't talk about this with Asher, he just wouldn't understand, and he'd hate Brad forever.

Brad's got less than a year left at LSU until he gets his Bachelors, then he can take the LSAT and move on to law school. He still hasn't moved home, and his weekend visits aren't as often as they used to be.

He didn't think me going back to school this past fall was a good idea. We compromised on me giving piano lessons to kids through the church. I do enjoy my time there and feeling useful for once, but I wish I could do something full time. I even offered to go work at the library, but Brad said it was beneath me. He wouldn't want the townsfolk gossiping about how his wife needed to get a job to help him through school.

    I bet you're off working some cool internship or maybe you already started in a field you love. I hope whatever you're doing it's cool enough to make up for what potential I seem to have thrown away.

    Happy late 21st. It's not that exciting once you can do it legally, but I bet you have a big group of friends who made it extra fun for you. Brad sent me flowers three weeks ago for mine and Asher was nice enough to take me to The Shop for my first legal drink. I chose gin and tonic and am praying you didn't make the same mistake.

    My prayers continue for your happiness and that one day you feel my heart tugging at yours and follow it home.

    Until we meet then,
    Taylor

TWENTY-THREE

Brad

    I pour myself and Millie a scotch, turning around and admiring her naked body still sprawled out across the bed. After such an exciting and successful day dealing with Auden and Asher, I felt like celebrating and getting my cock sucked.

    I look around the green painted walls in the guest room. I never liked the way Taylor painted this room, so I always avoided it. But since it's only been a few days since Taylor decided her privileged life was too hard to handle, I decided to keep my sexual adventures to our guest room, instead of in the master suite. See, I'm not a monster.

    She sits up, her perfect perky tits staying in place in the process. She knows better than to put her clothes back on until I tell her it's time to leave. And the amount of pent-up anger and adrenaline I have running through my body still means she'll be keeping her clothes off for quite a while tonight.

    I lay down on the bed and take a sip of scotch, resting it on my bare stomach, nodding toward my cock with my head. Millie does as she's told and starts to crawl over, reaching for me and getting ready to swallow me for the third time tonight when a knock at the front door interrupts.

"Who the hell is bothering me at this time of night?" I mutter.

I make my way over to the bathroom and grab my robe, wrapping it around me when a second set of knocks start.

"I'm coming, calm down!" I yell as I make way toward the front of the house.

I reach for the lock and the moment I open it, the door swings back at me knocking my knee in the process.

"What the hell do you think you're doing?" my father asks, his voice full of rage.

Before I get the chance to ask him what's going on, he grabs me by my robe and slams me into the wall, his face inches from mine.

"You just can't help but cause problems wherever the hell you go, can you?"

I can smell the liquored heat from his breath on my cheeks as I try to wiggle my way out of his grip.

The bedroom door creaks open, and I see Millie in the corner of my eye, fully dressed thankfully.

"Are you fucking kidding me Millie?" my father asks, letting go of me and heading into the bedroom.

He walks past Millie and whips the bedroom door open, looking around and taking in all the evidence of what I was just doing in there. He walks to the nightstand and grabs my scotch, downing the entire glass before picking up Millie's and turning back in our direction.

"Well, you were clearly smart enough to get dressed when I barged in. Now let's see if you're smart enough to know when to leave," he says to Millie.

Millie grabs her purse off the kitchen counter without saying a word or looking in either of our directions before heading out the front door. I notice tears on her cheek as she leaves, but if I'm being honest, the last thing I'm concerned with right now is Millie and her hurt feelings. Grow up, at least he's not *your* father.

He walks over toward me again and it takes everything in me not to flinch. My father has a temper that could scare Satan himself, and I've learned that if you show your fear, it makes it much worse in the long run.

"What the hell is going on, Dad?" I ask.

He sets his second glass down on the counter and points at the kitchen table.

"Sit the fuck down Brad."

I do as I'm told and take a seat, trying my hardest to put two and two together as to why he's here and so angry.

"I'm so fucking tired of cleaning up your damn messes. You're supposed to be the oldest and the wisest, making my life easier, and so far, all you've accomplished is being the oldest and even that I did for you."

He loves to remind me that I have never lived up to his expectations and that my brothers are so much better than I am. He even named my brother DJ after himself. He loves to remind me that he knew before I was even born that I wouldn't amount to anything worthy of his name. He's the reason I fucking hate my little brothers, especially Dale fucking Junior. DJ is Daddy's golden child, and they can go fuck themselves to hell for all I care.

"I got a call that Asher was out driving around with that girl Auden. You gonna tell me what the hell's going on Brad?"

My father is the king of knowing what's going on and who's doing what in this town, and I wish the old bastard could see how much I resemble him in that aspect. DJ sure as shit never knows his head from his ass, let alone what's going on around him.

"Don't worry about it. I'm taking care of it," I answer.

I try to stand up, and he immediately lunges forward and pushes me back into the seat.

"How exactly are you taking care of it, Brad? The same way you took care of it back in high school when you fucked her and sent her running to Taylor?"

His comment sends daggers of hatred through my veins with the memory of that day years ago, bringing my hand to my neck as my throat feels like it's starting to close.

I wasn't as solid with my emotions back then and made the mistake of breaking down to my mother. She knew something was off and asked me what was wrong after dinner one night. I told her I was worried Taylor was going to leave me. When she asked me why, I told her about cheating with Auden, something I knew she'd understand after being married to my father for so long. When my father came home from work and saw me teary eyed on the couch, he immediately dragged me by my collar out to the pool. He slammed my chest down onto the edge and leaned down, holding my head under water, and screaming about how if I wanted to wet my face, I should go swimming instead of being such a weak little bitch. I haven't shed a real tear since.

"Taylor didn't believe her, and no one else will either. Besides, she's been hiding for so long that I doubt she'd have the balls to speak up now," I reply, straightening my posture and trying to hold eye contact.

"Are you really this stupid?" he says, walking back to the bottle of scotch and refilling the glass.

"Why the hell would she return, Brad? You sure she doesn't have bigger balls than you and isn't back to get her revenge?" he asks, taking another swig of my scotch.

"You are such a narrow-minded thinker. You only care about how things benefit or effect you and not the world around you. You think my employees don't call me the second you tell them to do anything outside of the company?" He lets out a laugh as if he thinks I couldn't be more of an idiot. "Jason called me the second you sent in your request, and he called me first with the information you were seeking. You have me compromising my relationships with the town, and I even had to go as far as letting the Landrys know that we may need to pressure Scott Sterling into taming his daughter. You make us all look weak when you show your ignorance."

He turns his wrist, checking the time on his watch. "This is the last mess I clean up for you."

He finishes his third glass, leans back down to my eye level, and sets the glass next to me.

"Keep your damn mouth shut and act like the heartbroken husband you're supposed to be."

He grabs the bottle of scotch and opens the door, turning around once more.

"Keep yourself sober, and stay the hell away from your groupie whores until I say so."

TWENTY-FOUR

Asher

I set the letter down back into the box and turn to Auden, both of us silent as we take in the newest letter from Taylor.

I knew Brad was hours away at school, and the thought that maybe my sister needed some more support back home never popped in my head. What could that say about me, other than the simple fact that I'm clearly more selfish than I ever realized or intended to be.

"I should've known how lonely she was," I say, breaking the silence and staring down at my feet.

Auden sits up, reaching over and taking my hand in hers.

"Taylor wanted you to have your own life, Asher. She loved you so much and loved every second with you, but she knew you needed to have a life outside of her."

She's right. I would've never allowed Taylor to spend her life making sure I wasn't lonely. I enjoy my solitude. I need breaks from life's stimulation. Taylor thrived from it. She loved being around as many people as she could and genuinely enjoyed getting to know everyone. The only person I've ever felt the need or desire to be around was Taylor. And now I think Auden may be the second.

The realization that Auden has a big hold on my life brings a flutter back to my stomach, and I find myself staring at her again. Her soft skin lining her jaw, her nose that others may see as a little long, but I think fits perfectly on her face, and her plump, perfect lips that always seem to be frowning when she's lost in thought, like she is at this moment. I can't help but smile like a goof anytime I take a moment to soak in the sight of her.

"You're right. I know you're right. I just need to find a way to accept that I can't go back and be better."

Auden reaches over me and pulls out the fourth letter, setting it in my lap and sitting back so her feet are tucked beneath her.

"Do we just keep going or should we take a break?" she asks.

I look down at the letter and contemplate what could come next. I want to know everything Taylor was feeling, but I selfishly hate the way her past pain is making me feel. This week has been full of heartbreaking and eye-opening truths from my sister, but it's also been wonderful in the sense of reconnecting with Auden and getting to know her as someone other than Taylor's friend. The happiness Auden has brought back to my life feels so wrong in a sense. There's so much going on, and I feel overwhelmed by how drawn I am to time with Auden. But Taylor said herself that she wouldn't mind if Auden and I had something special, whether the timing is right or not.

"What did you end up doing for your twenty-first birthday?" I ask Auden, trying to distract myself from allowing the pain to flood back in.

She tilts her head to the side and looks up at me with a confused look, as if the question popped out of nowhere. It did, that's the point. I'm holding onto every random thought that pops in my mind and has nothing to do with my current painful situation.

"Dec begged me to wear a birthday banner and brought me club hopping. It was pretty terrible. I spent most of the evening trying not to puke from the many different free drinks he scored me throughout the night." She rolls her knuckles along the comforter and watches as the imprints form on it. "We had just moved in together, and he didn't know yet how much I hate being the center of attention," she laughs.

"Well, then, how do you feel about walking to The Shop and seeing your first Louisiana bar since turning twentyone? It's only a block down the street so we can walk. And I promise there'll be no one there that will make you the center of their attention," I say, hoping a drink will make these letters a little less damaging.

She looks down at the letter still in my lap before looking back up at me.

"Sure. I could use a drink after the day we've had. I'll go change."

She grabs the letter from my lap and sets it on top of her copy of the room key before grabbing her backpack and heading into the bathroom.

TWENTY-FIVE

Auden

Asher orders a Guinness for himself, and I decide to stick with a White Claw seltzer instead of a vodka soda, in the hope of not making another foolish comment like I did the last time we decided to have a drink together.

The dim lighting in the bar makes me feel more relaxed, knowing if anyone walks in, they'd have to get pretty close to recognize who we are. Asher takes a sip of his beer and twists on his wooden bar stool so his whole body is facing me.

"Alright, we've spent a few days now getting to know Taylor through one another, but you still remain quite a mystery," he says.

I have never enjoyed the "get to know you" questions in any situation, but Asher's eyes when he smiles could potentially get me to do anything he asks.

"Are you asking me to play 21 Questions, Asher?"

His smile becomes even bigger before he takes another sip of his beer and sets it down onto the counter. My heart may be melting as I speak. I've stared at him enough lately to notice one side of his mouth creases a little higher than the other when he smiles, and it makes me want to kiss the shorter side until it's equal.

"What have you missed the most about Monroe?" he asks.

Of course, his first question isn't something simple like my favorite color or my lucky number, which is blue, like Taylor's, and five. He wants to dive right into the thinkers, and I'm not sure how exactly to answer this one. I turn myself to face the bar and take a long swig of my seltzer, giving myself a second longer to think. I already know the answer is Taylor, but she's no longer here to say I miss her, and we're clearly playing the game to get away from the sorrow her death has brought us both.

"The magnolia trees and my mama's flower beds," I answer, the image of how sorry her flower beds currently look flashing in my mind.

Asher nods his head, his lips pressed together as if my answer was acceptable and made a lot of sense, making me feel like I passed the first test.

"My turn," I say before turning back to face him. "What's the scariest moment you've had being a firefighter?"

Asher turns his head away, and he lets out a big breath, staring down at the rim of his beer bottle.

"Every time the alarm goes off, my heart sinks to my stomach. I can't pin down exactly what call has been the scariest, but whenever it involves a child, I feel a different kind of fear than other calls."

He lifts the bottle to his lips and finishes it before waving at the bartender and asking for a second.

"Watching a child in distress or seeing them take their last breath is an image you never forget."

He shakes his head as if he's trying to erase the memory from his mind, sending guilt directly to my stomach as I realize how foolish it was of me to ask that question.

"I'm going to cheat and ask a second question. What's the best call you've been on?" I ask, hoping to undo the mood buster I just caused.

His lips curl to a smile before he turns back to me and starts to answer.

"That's an easy one. It was during my first year on the job, and I was in a pattern of multiple hard calls back to back. I was ready to quit and felt like firefighting might not be something I could handle forever. I still don't know if it's something I can handle forever, but I often think back on this call when I want to give up."

I lift my glass up and take a drink, watching Asher's mouth as he speaks. Everything about his face seems to fit so perfectly together, and the passion growing in his eyes as he talks about his job makes him even more appealing.

"The call was for a house fire, and when we got there, the whole main floor was already in flames. We got to work on the fire immediately, and when I was checking with the family that everyone was out of the house, I noticed the six-year-old daughter was pretty distraught. I knelt and told her it was going to be okay, but she explained that it wasn't because she left her stuffed orangutan up in her bedroom."

He pauses to take another drink and starts to let out a little laugh before the bottle leaves his lips.

"I'm willing to go out of my way for anyone I can, but I don't usually risk being engulfed by flames for inanimate items. But the look in this little girl's eyes made me run straight in and up the stairs. I acted before thinking, and I realized that quickly when I got up the stairs and didn't know which room was hers. Luckily, it was the first room I walked into, and the orangutan was right on her bed. I unzipped my suit and threw him inside before hightailing it out."

 I realize my mouth is wide open and quickly grab my drink to close it.

 "You are such a hero for her. I bet she marries a firefighter one day," I say before taking a drink.

 What the hell was that? I sound like a total fangirl, and I may even be a little jealous that wasn't my orangutan Asher saved from a burning building. Having kids has never been appealing to me, but I'm pretty sure my ovaries are swelling as I listen to Asher excitedly talk about them.

 "I don't think it was me she cared so much about. She gripped onto that stuffed monkey like it was the only thing that mattered in the world to her. Once she stopped squeezing, she told me that her brother had died of leukemia a month before, and he had given her that orangutan before he passed. I'm not sure why that call is the one that stuck with me the most, but it is. And I love whenever I get the chance to run into her today." I finish my drink and flag the bartender over for a refill.

 "I kind of love that story too," I reply.

 Asher looks over at me, and I notice his gaze is a little different than normal. He looks like he's lost in something, but not distraction. He may be happy because his lips are curved up just the slightest. I find myself smiling back at him until the bartender sets down a fresh seltzer onto the bar top, freeing me from my trance.

 "Your turn," I remind him.

 "Did Taylor really pray for us to end up together one day?" he asks, his smile growing across his face while he tries to keep it hidden by biting his bottom lip.

My cheeks immediately grow hot, and I turn my body further away to hide them.

"Yes," I say into my seltzer before tilting my head back and finishing it.

Why do I feel like a schoolgirl passing a note to my crush, asking if he likes me or not? I wouldn't go as far as to say that I hate men or marriage, but if the last six years have taught me anything, it's that I have lost interest in spending the rest of my life with anyone other than Dec. If I'm being honest, there's been a few moments where I've pictured the house that we'll end up in on one of the many lakes in Minnesota. It will be in the middle of nowhere, and for some reason, we always have a black cat, even though I'm very allergic.

I imagined marriage once before, the only time I had a real relationship. If you can even call a high school relationship real. Danny Faucett. Danny is the only guy I have actually trusted, and he's also the guy I lost my virginity to as well. Danny captured my heart junior year, and his parents ripped it from my chest when they packed up their house and moved out of Louisiana with Danny packed along with them.

Danny was gentle, and he didn't ask me to do anything. In fact, he was so shy that I always had to make the first move. After four months of dating and a lot of make-out sessions in the back of my dad's pickup truck, I'm the one who suggested we lose our virginities. It was sweet and well thought out, and extremely quick. I wouldn't say I really enjoyed it, but I did enjoy losing the anxiety over wondering when I would finally lose it.

And the reality is that if Danny and I had never made that decision, knowing the next person who put himself inside me could've stole my innocence, makes me extra thankful. Brad took away all hope for me to have a normal relationship.

He killed every butterfly that ever lived in my stomach, and I can always be thankful that Danny didn't allow him to steal that first from me as well.

"So did you pray for that too?" Asher asks.

I think these drinks may be pushing us down a conversation path that we have no way of returning from. The truth is, Asher has always been attractive. I can't sit here and lie that a small part of me hasn't always loved those prayers from Taylor. They didn't just score me a hot future husband, but it meant I also won my best friend as a sister.

The way Danny looked at me would always send flutters through my heart, but the way Asher looks at me makes me feel like we could fly away together. The way Asher's eyes light up when something excites him, or the way his lips curl into a playful grin when he's teasing me help to distract me from the dark cloud that has been hovering above me for far too long. His happiness is infectious, just being around him makes me feel lighter, happier. The crinkle around his eyes when he laughs and the furrow in his brow when he's concentrating are images I want permanently painted into my mind. But it's the way he looks at me that makes him so much different than Danny. It's soft and makes me feel adored in a way I've never felt before. It's as if his look alone can keep me safe and ready to face any obstacles ahead.

"Hey, you already asked your question. It's my turn now," I reply, noticing the letter sticking out of my bag.

Asher rolls his eyes and gives me that playful grin, waiting for my question to be over already. But my impulses mixed with fear and two quickly emptied seltzers send me down the wrong path.

"Will you read the next letter?" I ask, pulling it from my bag.

He looks at it and then back at me, his expression blank as he contemplates allowing this moment to potentially go dark.

"Sure," he says before reaching out and grabbing it.

He scooches his barstool closer to mine until our elbows touch and starts to unfold the fourth letter.

5/12/21

Auden,

I've been a fool for the last four years, maybe even longer.

Brad finished his bachelor's degree and came home for a few weeks before taking the LSAT. Everything felt like it was going to be okay again. He paraded me around town with fancy dinners like when we first got engaged and he couldn't keep his hands off me.

But as soon as he got accepted back to LSU for law school, he was off and purchasing a new apartment in Baton Rouge.

I missed him more than I ever had after those sweet, wonderful weeks together, and the thought of him moving away for a few more years left my heart in shatters. So I drove to Baton Rouge a few weeks ago and decided I'd surprise him. To make it even more embarrassing, I did my hair and makeup before I left and was wearing a long coat with only a tiny black slip underneath as a surprise for him like in the movies. When I got there, his roommate said he wasn't home and had no idea where he went. I tried to call him, but he didn't answer me either. It was too late for me to drive all the way home, so I stayed the night, expecting him to wake me up when he made it back. But he never made it home, and I didn't hear from him until the next evening when I was already back in Monroe.

He said he was out drinking with a professor and didn't have his phone on because he didn't want to be rude. He told me I didn't understand how the world of law works, and that I needed to trust him. He never gave me an explanation as to why he never made it home.

I brought up the idea of me moving into his apartment. It makes so much sense to me since I don't have a job anyways, but he immediately shut the whole idea down.

My parents think I'm selfish for not appreciating all that Brad has done for me and our future, and that I shouldn't be distracting him from his studies. But I feel trapped, and I don't want to keep feeling so lonely.

Brad turned on my location on my phone so he can see where I go. He said he wants to make sure that when I'm out running, he knows when I get home safe. I haven't run in two years, and I think that may have been his way of telling me I should start again.

I think I may have signed away my freedom when I became a Montgomery wife.

Congratulations on your graduation, Auden. Your mama shared at church that you graduated with a degree in Enterprise Architecture. I have to be honest; I had to look that up, and I'm not sure if I still understand what that is, but I do know that I'm so proud of you.

Happy (late) 22nd Birthday.

I hope one day I get the chance to say that to you in person. Hopefully before I write another letter.

Until we meet again,
Taylor

As soon as he finishes reading, he tucks the letter back in its envelope and waves the bartender down, realizing we both could use a third drink.

That bastard was cheating on her and barely tried to hide it. The thought of Taylor spending the last few years of her life with a real-life monster makes me want to burn this entire town down. But the thought that he didn't even attempt to be good to her seems to break a bigger piece of my heart.

We both grab our drinks the second they hit the bar top. I really know how to ruin a good moment by snapping myself and everyone around me back to reality.

"My turn," Asher says before setting his bottle down and standing up from the stool. "Will you dance with me?"

I let out an obnoxious laugh with his question, not realizing how serious he is. I hate dancing. I can't dance, and now that I think about it, I've never danced with a guy in my life, other than Dec. But does he even count? I shake my head.

"I don't dance."

He leans down against the bar so that his face is inches from mine and flashes me a smile that grips my heart.

"Please," he says, sending electricity through my entire body.

TWENTY-SIX

Asher

The way she looks at me with such seriousness about not dancing makes it hard not to smile. I don't think Auden has allowed herself much time in the last few years to let loose, and that's a side of her I really want to see. She set out on her own into a big city and seems to have conquered it, but now I want to see her conquer happiness just as easily.

I don't give her the opportunity to deny me again. Instead, I reach down and take her hand, pulling it over her head and spinning her around in her barstool until her back is to the bar. Before she gets the chance to protest, I pull her hand even higher until she's standing and begin to lead her to the middle of the floor.

Shania Twain isn't my go-to for any occasion, but when she says, "Let's go, girls," I always find myself running to the dance floor with almost every girl in the bar. Fortunately for us, Auden seems to be the only girl in the bar tonight, so she'll have to make up for the ones that are missing.

She crosses her arms against her chest and stares at me like I'm the most annoying man she's ever met, but I won't let that discourage me. I start to turn in a circle, tapping one foot around me as I pretend to play the guitar. By the third solo turn, I notice a smile start to creep in the corner of her mouth and take that opportunity to pull her into me.

"Oh, no, Asher," she says as I wrap one arm around her back and hold her other hand out in front of us.

"Oh, yes, Auden," I reply, before spinning her in a circle and bringing her back to my chest.

She begins to laugh, and it's a laugh I haven't heard from her before. She's clearly trying to hold it in, but her smile is too big to mask any sounds. Her entire being seems to radiate happiness, from the twinkle in her eyes to the way her body seems to move with a newly found lightness and grace. It's as if a weight has been lifted off her shoulders, allowing her to finally breathe freely and embrace the moment of pure, unbridled joy. She's intoxicating.

We laugh and twirl, stomping our feet and becoming feral idiots until the song finally finishes. Her face is probably just as sore as mine from all the giggling. I wonder if she has any idea how beautiful she looks when she isn't running from the pain of the world.

When the song ends, we stop and stare at one another before the next song starts to play. A slow melody on a guitar starts coming from the speakers. She starts to turn away, but I take hold of her and pull her close to me, wrapping my arms around her waist.

"Stay," I whisper.

She freezes for a moment, then rests her head on my chest, starting to sway along with me to the song If I Die Young by The Band Perry.

The irony of the song and Taylor's death isn't lost on either of us as we grip tighter onto one another. We slowly sway back and forth as if there isn't anyone else in the bar.

A few moments in, I start to feel Auden's shoulders softly shaking. I look to see her eyes shut, tears slowly making their way down her face. I pull her back to me and squeeze her tightly, ending our swaying and allowing her to let it all out while we're in this moment.

When the song ends, I hold her face in my hands and wipe away her tears. She looks up at me, and I see the pain she is experiencing. I still don't know about her past, a past that is somehow connected to Taylor's last few years of life. But in this moment of silence, I dare hope that maybe, just maybe, Auden can see me for who I truly am—flawed, imperfect, but willing to fight for her.

I grab her hand and take her back toward the bar, waving down the bartender and picking up her bag.

"Let's get out of here."

*

The walk back to the hotel is quiet. All you can hear are the crickets putting themselves to sleep and the occasional rustling of another creature not quite ready for bed.

The silence feels like it's suffocating me. I keep falling a step behind Auden as I get lost in my thoughts. The moment we had sitting at the bar—laughing, dancing, and feeling light for the first time in days—is exactly how I want to spend every day with her. But I need to understand her internal battles to figure out how to help her. I don't want to face Brad and the Montgomery family tomorrow without understanding more about what they're capable of, what Brad is capable of.

I can't shake it anymore, and I find myself stopping and my feet unwilling to take another step. *I need to know what happened.* She turns around when she realizes I'm no longer beside her and tilts her head with a confused look on her face.

"What's wrong?" she asks.

I look around us and spot a bench in the middle of a cemetery we're about to pass and start to head in its direction. "Can we sit for a moment?" I ask, assuming she's following me.

She does. She joins me on the bench, both of us looking at the tombstones surrounding us.

"Auden, I don't want to make anything harder for you. I really don't want to lose your trust. I already risked that once, and I don't want to give you a reason not to trust me again."

I try to swallow, but my throat feels like there's a rock stuck in it. I keep going, not sure where I'm headed. "But I have to ask you something, and I hope you're willing to tell me."

She turns her head away and leans forward as if she's getting ready to run. I reach my hand out and set it on her knee in hopes of calming her. Her tension is palpable. I can't bear the thought of her suffering alone. I need to know her secret to understand her completely.

"I need to know what happened that made you and Taylor stop talking."

She looks down at my hand on her knee and pauses for a moment, searching for how she wants to reply.

"I don't want to ruin your memory of Taylor." She looks up at me, her eyes full of pain as if the thought of telling me feels like torture. "And I don't want you to look at me any differently."

I shake my head. I can't imagine anything she could tell me that would make me look at her differently. I'm starting to realize she may be the piece in my life that I never knew was missing. I can sense her struggle, the internal battle she's fighting. I want to be her rock, her confidante.

"Auden, you can't keep allowing this pain to hold you back. Trust me when I say that you can tell me anything, I want to hear your everything."

She stands up from the bench and takes a step forward, putting her hands up over her eyes and dragging them down her cheeks while she slowly inhales.

"Taylor was everything to me. She could make any day brighter," she starts to say, turning to face me as I stay seated on the bench. "I believe she was that to you too."

She was. Taylor was the only person who I could say was *my person* in this world.

"The day after Brad's birthday party, I went to Taylor's house and told her about Brad." She looks down at the ground as if the memory is flowing back to her. "She broke my heart that day because . . . she . . . she didn't believe me."

I watch as she brings her fingers up to her mouth and slowly taps them on her teeth.

"The walk back down your parents' driveway felt like hot coals under my feet, sending burns all the way up to my heart. I remember slowing my pace as I got closer to my dad's truck, waiting for her to run up behind me and tell me that she did believe me, no matter how hard it was to hear."

She reaches down and brushes a leaf off a grave marker near her feet.

"But she never did, and I never spoke to her again."

I take a deep breath before standing, walking over to her and taking one of her hands in mine.

"What did you tell her about?" I ask, the anticipation killing me.

She closes her eyes tightly as if the painful image won't leave her mind and tightens her grip on my hand.

TWENTY-SEVEN

Auden

My hand feels as if I'm holding onto Asher for dear life, and I start to feel dizzy. The pressure of admitting what happened between Taylor and me feels as if it's sending all the blood straight to my brain, cutting off my ability to speak.

I don't want Asher to know the ways Brad hurt me. As badly as I wanted everyone to know and believe me six years ago, I've learned how easily life can still go on for others once the truth is out. But not for me. What if Asher doesn't believe me either? It feels like we've been close forever after these last few days, but we haven't. Taylor and I spent almost eighteen years being inseparable, and she still didn't believe me when I needed her most. How can I trust Asher?

I try to breathe but my airways feel like they're closing, so I stumble back over to the bench and sit down. Asher follows and sits close me.

The sound of Brad's laughter booms into my mind, and I reach out and grip Asher's leg, squeezing my eyes shut again as I try to gain control. My mind is racing as I try to find the right words, but I can feel them making their way up my throat about to explode all over the place.

"I just needed to fucking pee. All I wanted to do was fucking pee!" I hear myself yell.

Asher stands and starts to grab my elbow, "Okay, let's go find a bathroom," he says urgently.

I pull my elbow from him and grab his hand, pulling him back down onto the bench beside me.

"No, not now. Then," I start to say, keeping my eyes on the ground.

"I was at Brad's birthday party. Taylor wasn't there. I couldn't wait any longer in line for the bathroom."

I feel Asher settling back down into the bench, his eyes focused on me.

"Brad told me that he'd help me. He took me outside to a quiet place in the back of his dad's property." I swallow hard and reach my hand up, grazing it along my scar.

"He stole my keys and my phone. I was only at his stupid party because Taylor begged me to go. She never even showed up."

I can't hear Asher breathing even though he's so close to me.

Damn it. I want to be able to say the fucking word "rape" without feeling scared and ashamed.

Why the hell am I even the one who's ashamed? I didn't pretend to be helping a so-called friend out. I didn't steal *his* keys and phone. I didn't force *him* to answer personal and uncomfortable questions. I didn't physically pin *him* down. I didn't laugh in *his* face when *he* attempted to fight me off. I didn't ignore *his* pleas for me to stop. I didn't rip *his* clothes off while *he* cried. I didn't shove *his* body so hard into the dirt that a fallen branch cut *his* neck. I didn't rape *him*.

> I didn't rape him.
> I didn't rape him.
> I didn't rape him.
> I didn't fucking rape him.
> HE RAPED ME.
> Rape.
> Rape.
> Rape.
> Brad *raped* me.
> And *he's* the one who should be ashamed.

"He raped me," I say quietly. "He shoved my face into the ground, and he raped me."

I look up at Asher and his eyes are full of emotion, but I can't tell what's going through his mind. It looks as if maybe he's at a loss for words or is contemplating whether he believes me or not. Maybe he's wondering what I did to make Brad think he could have me. I know I've asked myself that same question too many times to count. I feel like I need to convince him so I keep going. I need to fight my shame.

"I swear I begged him to stop. I tried my hardest to fight him off, but he was so strong and the anger in his eyes was no match to my fear. I was scared of what would happen if I made him any angrier than he already was. So, eventually, my body gave up. I just laid there waiting for him to finish."

Asher stands up and starts to pace back and forth. He laces his hands behind his head. I know I've upset him. I stand up and take a step toward the cemetery entrance then turn my body back to face him.

"I'm sorry, Asher. I should've fought harder," I say, starting to cry and half-turning to leave. "If I fought harder than maybe it would've never happened. Or maybe if I stayed, I could have tried to convince Taylor not to marry him."

My lips are quivering as I try to hold back more tears, walking back toward the motel. I don't want to fucking cry anymore. I want to go home to Minneapolis, snuggled up on my couch with Dec, laughing about whatever nonsense he's been up to. I should've never come here. I should've never opened my mouth about Brad.

My shoulders feel the weight of hands on them, and Asher's suddenly turning my body back around. He wraps his arms around me and pulls me close in his embrace.

"Don't ever apologize for what he did again," he says, kissing my forehead. "I believe you, Auden. And I'm so damn sorry that Taylor didn't."

I shake my head, unable to process what he's saying and still feeling so much blame. He pulls away and takes my face in his hands.

"Listen to me, Auden," he says, looking directly into my eyes with such seriousness. "Brad made his own choice to violate you. He's a monster, and I won't allow him to get away with this." He leans down and kisses the tip of my nose.

"Taylor was a big girl. She made a horrible choice not believing you, and she had to live with that."

I notice a single tear fall from the corner of his eye and feel his hands starting to shake just the slightest.

"She shut you out when she decided to pick Brad over you and she left you with no other choice than to go on with your life." He shakes my head gently to make sure I'm paying attention. "I need you to hear me when I say this. None of this is your fault. Do you understand? I don't blame you, and I won't allow you to blame yourself."

He lets go of my face and wipes a tear off his before taking both of my hands in his.

"Do you understand, Auden?" he asks, his tone still filled with such seriousness.

I nod my head, and he wraps me tightly in his arms. My new favorite place to be.

"I am so damn thankful you are strong enough to still be here," he says, pulling one of my hands up to his lips and kissing it. "So damn thankful."

TWENTY-EIGHT

Asher

Auden's in the bathroom changing back into my t-shirt and getting ready for bed. I pull my grey sweatpants out and slip them on, folding my jeans and setting them on top of my bag. I take a seat in the chair and listen to the faucet running in the bathroom, unable to get my knees to stop bouncing as I think about what to do next.

My body feels restless with so many emotions flooding in. I want to hop in my car and find Brad, drag him by his neck into the woods, and beat him with my fists until he's almost dead, fear in his eyes as he begs me to stop. I shake my head trying to get the image out of my mind. But then there's the image of Auden laying there helpless that snaps me right back to my bloody knuckles. I want Brad to admit what he did to Auden. And then I want to hear his side of what he put my sister through as well.

My sister. I hate that I feel such anger towards her right now. How could she ever tell Auden that she didn't believe her? Auden was the best friend Taylor could've ever had. She was there for Taylor anytime she needed her, and she was willing to fight for Taylor in any situation. How could Taylor be so naive and allow Auden to walk away like that.

Before we walked back to the motel, I held Auden, both of us ending up on our knees as I cradled her and listened to her tell me the full story of the worst night of her life. She described it so vividly that I could imagine I was there, helplessly watching her.

She told me everything.

She told me every single detail.

She told me about how she felt about Brad up until that moment. She said she had known him forever, and he was her friend for a long time. But over the last year or so before the assault, he was changing. His presence started making her feel like a dark cloud was always over her when he was around.

She told me about how he took her outside and seemed like he was actually being a friend, trying to help her.

She told me how long it took for her to realize what was going on, and that Brad wasn't just drunk and emotional like she originally assumed.

She told me that Brad started laughing when she tried to fight back.

She told me that at one point she blacked out, trying to listen to the wind instead of the sounds of his lips on her skin.

She told me how the sound of his zipper snapped her out of it.

She told me she felt embarrassed, pathetic, and terrified, but at the same time, she couldn't stop running the reasons of how she ended up there through her mind.

She told me it felt like he was ripping her open with a hot knife over and over again.

She told me that he moaned each time she screamed out in pain.

She told me that he shoved her to the ground so hard, she cut her throat on a stick underneath her.

She told me when she quieted down.

She told me that a switch inside her turned everything off and turned survival mode on.

She told me he left her there, laying on the ground, covered in dirt and blood, trembling as reality slowly set back in.

Auden takes a seat on the edge of the bed, and I'm so lost in thought that I didn't even hear her leave the bathroom. I turn and look at her, sitting there in my t-shirt, her hair pulled back in a messy bun, and her eyes still puffy from our conversation earlier. She looks so damn beautiful. It feels wrong to think that at this moment, but I can't help noticing how perfect she truly is. I am in awe at the way my shirt is like a blanket around her, defining her shoulders and the tips of her breasts.

"Are you okay?" she asks, looking down at my hands that, I'm realizing now, are gripping the arms of my chair so tightly that my knuckles are white.

Of course, she's the one asking me if I'm okay, even though she just revealed her biggest secret less than an hour ago. I turn my chair so I'm positioned close enough that I can reach out and take both of her hands.

"I'm okay, but how are you?" I ask.

She gives me a small smile as if she's trying to convince us both and squeezes my hands.

"I think I'm OK," she replies. "But I'm wondering what's going through your mind."

I inhale slowly. I have so many questions, but I don't know if I should even ask them. She just spoke her truth for the first time in who knows how long, and I am so grateful for that. But I don't want to make another mistake that may make her lose her trust in me again. But if I lie and say that nothing is going through my head, she'll know it's a lie. She clearly knows me well enough to know when I'm lost in thought, and I'd rather be honest than lose her.

"I'm just thinking about how I want to strangle Brad," I reply.

It's not a lie. I have been thinking about the many ways my fist could pummel Brad's jaw, and how good the pain would feel as my bones smash against his. He may be an inch taller than me, but that won't be much of a match against the strength of my arms, that I have no doubt about.

I don't want to admit how I'm feeling about Taylor right now because I'm not sure if I even understand it myself. I've loved her more than I've even loved myself. I can't help but wonder if she had listened to Auden and made better choices, a lot of pain would've been spared for others. Or maybe if she really knew that she could tell me anything, I could've helped her in more ways than just delivering her final letters.

I watch Auden roll her bottom lip in and bite down on it, a small smile curving at the corners of her mouth and my anger subsides just a bit.

"What?" I ask wondering what I said that could've caused a smile.

She shakes her head.

"Nothing. It's just nice having someone believe me, and I kind of like your protective side."

She turns her head away, and I notice her cheeks flushing just the slightest as if I embarrassed her. I'm not sure if it's the alcohol's influence, but I have the strongest urge to reach out and grab her face and fill her mouth with the sweetest kisses. I want to wrap my arms around her and make her feel the safest she's ever felt. She's clearly never had anyone make her feel that way, and she's probably spent her life being the one to protect others, like Taylor.

"You deserve to feel safe all the time, Auden," I say, reaching my hand out and touching the side of her cheek.

She looks down at her feet and rubs her toes together.

"He took so much more from me that night than I ever realized," she starts to say, tapping her finger against her teeth.

I inch my chair even closer and place her hands back in mine, showing her that I'm here and want her to share anything and everything she is willing to share with me.

"I haven't been able to have a real relationship since that day. I lost all hope in humanity. I've tried a few times to go on dates, and the guys were always kind. I've even tried to . . ." She stops talking suddenly.

I stand up and sit next to her on the edge of the bed, putting my arm around her shoulder and a hand on her knee.

"It's okay, Auden. You can tell me anything. Judgment isn't my job," I tell her, sounding exactly like my mother.

She keeps looking down at her toes.

"I've even tried to force myself to be . . . intimate with them, but it never works. I always freeze up, or I convince myself that they're going to hurt me and won't want me because I'm used up." Her tone starts to rise, and she starts talking faster. "I screamed 'no' so many times, how am I ever supposed to trust that someone else is going to listen if I say it again? He broke me. No man could ever truly want a broken girl. A girl who flinches at his touch. A girl who may start crying if you go too fast because her skin feels like it's crawling. The truth is, long ago a man was all over me and claimed me as his even though I fought my hardest to push him off."

She turns and faces me. I notice the tears in her eyes, but they aren't sad tears that I see. They're tears filled with anger.

"I tried so fucking hard, Asher, and I wasn't strong enough. He used me up. No man will ever want me. I don't think I'll ever be able to be touched again without feeling like a dirty, used-up whore."

The pain consuming her grabs hold of my heart. I instantly reach out my arms and wrap them around her, pulling her head to my chest. She lets out an angry groan and grips hold of my t-shirt, yanking it back and forth in frustration. I don't care at all. She can smack me in the face if that brings her the slightest bit of relief.

I kiss the top of her head and stroke her hair.

"Auden, you are not broken. Or used up. Or damaged in any way at all. And you definitely aren't a whore," I say, looking down to her eyes so I know she's listening to me.

"Brad is broken, damaged, and a garbage excuse for a man."

She's looking at me with such desperation as if she's waiting for me to give her the answers on how to turn back time. If there was any way possible for me to do that for her, I would sacrifice it all and do it in a heartbeat.

"You are strong, amazing, beautiful, intelligent." I continue, "You are so lovable and precious and any man who has the opportunity to be in your light is the luckiest man on earth."

I find myself lowering my hand from her back down to her waist and I scoop her up until she's sitting in my lap, pulling her in tighter while she nestles into my chest.

"If I could go back and stop it all, I would." I kiss the top of her head. "If I could make him feel the fear that you felt, I would." I lay a second kiss on her head. "And if I can help you heal your heart and show you that you can still trust, I will."

I kiss the back of her head, leaving my lips there and holding her as tightly as I can. The fact that my touch has never made her flinch warms my heart a bit.

She sits up until she's facing me, still sitting in my lap but now only inches from my face. Her gaze fills me with a desire to kiss her the way she deserves. I want to show her what it feels like to feel safe and wanted in a way she hasn't felt before. My heart starts to beat faster, and I hear her breathing start to quicken. My eyes move down to her mouth for a moment, and I notice her biting her lip again.

"I trust you with everything in me, Asher," she says, her breath sending chills down my neck.

"I want . . ." She pauses and looks down behind us onto the bed but doesn't continue speaking.

I reach my hand up and graze her cheek, down over her neck and her scar. She doesn't stop me. She doesn't raise her own hand to the scar and doesn't flinch.

"You want what, Auden?" I ask.

She shakes her head as if she regrets starting to say that. But I can't let her run from this. If she's feeling anything like the connection that I've been feeling this week with her, if she feels the intensity that is growing inside of me every second she sits here on my lap, then I need her to say it.

She runs one hand along my shoulder, outlining the frame of my arm and stopping once her hand rests on mine.

"I want to trust your touch," she whispers, still looking down at the bed.

I stare at her for a moment, processing what she just said and contemplating how I can give her exactly what she's asking for. My hands reach around her waist. I pick her up, gently laying her down onto the bed. I lay down beside her, positioning myself on my side, making sure the length of my body is touching hers.

The second the words "your touch" left her mouth, it sent sparks from my chest all the way to my groin. I want to touch every inch of her. I want to kiss her perfectly defined collarbone down to her chest as it rises and falls with my touch. I want to feel her underneath me, moaning from the ecstasy I send through her body. God, I want to do everything and anything she wants, and I want to be the best at it all.

I've been with many women before, and I've made sure each one of them felt comfortable and satisfied once we were finished. But this intense need I feel for Auden is something so much more. I want to connect with her soul and feel her emotions flowing inside of her along with the pleasure that I imagine only I can provide.

She turns and rolls her upper body so she's facing in my direction and rests one hand on my cheek, staring up into my eyes. I look back at her and reach out my hand, resting it on her cheek, mimicking her movements.

I slowly lower my head closer until our lips are only inches away from one another, so close that when she exhales, I breathe it directly in. The sweetness of her taste sends electricity through my chest. I look down at her lips then back at her eyes, feeling the desperation of needing to be closer to her. When I notice the hunger in her eyes, I lean even closer until my top lip is just barely brushing against hers, pausing for a moment and making sure this is what she truly wants.

    Once I notice her chest has stopped moving and her eyes starting to close, I take it as a sign that she wants this as badly as I do, and push my body against hers. She releases a quiet moan as her soft lips part and the tip of her tongue touches mine. My hand gently pushes my fingers up through her hair, carefully grasping onto the back of her head and guiding her down to her pillow. She tastes exactly as I expected her to, a mix of conviction and citrus. I want to consume every ounce of her, but I know my needs can never come before hers. That's a line I can't allow my selfish desires to cross. She may be as consumed by this kiss as I am, and I'm praying she is, but she may not be as eager to take it further. Her teeth grab ahold of my lower lip, and she starts to tenderly take little nibbles until she grabs on, causing my eyes to fully open. Her eyes are looking right back at me as she slowly releases my lip, pulling her face away from mine, a full smile cheek to cheek.

TWENTY-NINE

Auden

When his lips finally touch mine, I feel like my heart is bursting, but not out of fear or anxiety like it usually does when a guy touches me. I'm relaxed. I'm not nervous or anxious at all. In fact, I think I might be really excited. I haven't felt anything like this except when Danny and I made out on our second date.

But at the same time, it's different than it was with Danny. I feel as if my heart is trying to merge with Asher's where it's safe and warm, like I've felt in his presence since the moment I saw him standing in my apartment.

I feel so confused right now. I hate being here in Monroe, but I think I love being anywhere with Asher. He brings a calmness into my life that I haven't felt since Taylor. He makes me feel like I can be strong again, something I haven't felt since Brad showed me how dangerous men can be. I thought I'd never be able to be touched again, or at least not to enjoy it. But the feeling his lips and hands are giving me at this moment makes me feel a hunger for so much more. I don't know what I want, but I know I don't want him to stop kissing me, and my body is longing for him to touch me.

Usually this is when my brain shuts off.

Usually this is when my skin feels like it's turned to ice, and my mind is fighting my body, trying to break through and escape any further touch.

Usually this is where I try to tell myself that it's okay, while I'm desperately holding back tears.

And every time, I end up so overwhelmed that I ruin any chance of intimacy.

I must be broken. No matter how hard I try not to be, or how hard I try to convince myself that I'm whole, I'm still always broken.

It's like a food that you know you don't like. You can't help yourself when it's in front of you, so you continue to try it until you remember that you hate it. Like pickles. I hate pickles, but I love the idea of them. I love crunchy foods. I lived by a pickle factory growing up, and I love the smell of pickles. So, you can find me trying pickles way more often than I should because when those green, crunchy, deliciously smelling pickles are in front of me, I can't hold back. I grab one. I bite into it. I immediately regret it, and I hate it all over again.

That's exactly how it goes with men. I like one. He's earned my trust enough that I'm willing to let my guard down. He's appealing. He probably smells good. Everyone else agrees that I should try it, and so I talk myself into going for it. But the second my lips touch his, I'm reminded of how much my body hates men, and I spit him out. Just like pickles.

But right now, I want everything except to spit him out. His kiss didn't make my skin icy cold, it washed over me like a warm, heavy rain of pleasure. I still want to break through my walls. I want to grab onto him and pull him close, as close as two people can possibly get. If his kiss can make me feel this comfortable, this warm, this safe, then I want to experience everything else his body can do.

He pulls his lips away from me and stares down at me, smiling for a moment until his expression changes, almost like he needs to know he didn't cross a line.

I rise to my knees on the bed as he rests his head on the pillow, our eyes connected. My hands travel down my body, reaching for the hem of Asher's t-shirt. With a deliberate motion, I slide it over my head, letting it fall to the floor beside the bed.

Asher's eyebrows arch in surprise, yet his unwavering gaze remains fixed on mine.

"What are you doing, Auden?" he asks.

I don't reply. If I'm being honest, I'm not exactly sure what I'm doing right now or where this is going to go or how it'll affect us. But I also don't care. I'm so tired of being scared. I just know that my body craves the sensations of Asher's hands on me to erase the tainted memories of Brad's touch. I want him to show me what genuine intimacy feels like and know the warmth of someone who truly values and cares for you. Someone you don't fear.

As I reach around to undo my bra strap, Asher's eyes widen. He shifts, propping himself up on his elbows. His mouth begins to part, but before any words escape, I let the bra slip from my chest, interrupting his impending question.

He sits up further, extending his hand towards the bra lying before me, turning his head away and trying to hand it back to me.

"Auden, what are you doing?" he asks again, his tone sounding concerned.

I push his hand and the bra away from me.

"Asher, look at me," I plead. "I need you to look at me and for me to feel okay when you do. I've spent the last six years terrified of men looking at or touching me, taking my control away again. And you make me feel the complete opposite."

He shakes his head before turning back to face me, his eyes locked on mine.

"Auden, we've been drinking and I . . ."

I reach down, gently taking his hand and guiding it towards my face, placing it on my cheek.

"Please, Asher, I've spent years trying not to be seen, and now all I want is for you to keep seeing me."

His gaze holds mine as I sense the internal struggle brewing within him. Slowly, I guide his hand from my cheek, down my neck, until it rests on my scar.

"You're the only person who's ever touched my scar."

I continue to guide his hand down my collarbone, observing his reaction as his lips part in a soft gasp.

"You've never tried to control me."

I shift his hand to the side, using mine to guide his palm flat against my skin, stopping when he lightly cups the outside of my breast. He blinks, beads of sweat forming on his brow as he struggles to maintain eye contact.

Before he can speak my name, I interject once more, unwilling to hear his reasoning.

"You have given me the strength to come back and face my past, Asher."

I guide his hand lower, tracing a path down my stomach, eliciting goosebumps that rise on my skin. Asher adjusts his position, his gaze fixed on me, his brow furrowing as my hand guides his further down my body. As we near the edge of my underwear, I pause once more, feeling a surge of anticipation coursing through my body.

"I want to reclaim control of my body. That means I choose who to give it to. I choose you," I say confidently.

I guide his hand into my underwear, parting my thighs slightly to allow his fingers to slip snugly between, cupping the warmth of my core with his palm. A moan escapes my lips as I revel in his touch, only for it to abruptly vanish.

With a jerk, he withdraws his hand, rising from the bed and striding away. He retrieves his shirt from the floor, flipping it right side out before starting to walk back in my direction. I move to the middle of the bed.

"I don't want that," I say, my heart thumping so hard I can feel it in my stomach.

"Auden, please, you don't want this," he replies, trying to reach closer with the shirt.

I snatch the shirt, discarding it behind me onto the pillow. Asher averts his gaze, but I grab his face, guiding it back towards me.

"I know when I don't want something, Asher. And I want you to look at me."

I direct his face towards my breasts and hold it there until I notice his chest start to rise higher.

"If you feel the connection between us that I feel, then don't deny me again."

He lets out a small breath like he's close to surrender.

"Auden, you have no idea how strong of a connection I feel."

I lean down close to his ear and whisper, "Then touch me so good that I forget ever being touched before."

As his head leans in closer, his wet lips press a kiss to the top of my breast, a simultaneous moan escaping from both of us. His tongue swirls around my nipple before he plants gentle kisses in a trail up to my collarbone, inhaling deeply as he traces along it. The sensation of his lips moving back down towards my other breast sends shivers down my spine, his warm breath teasing over my nipple until I press myself into him, urging him to take it further.

Feeling a deep ache within me, I reach down and guide his hand to the warmth between my legs, silently encouraging him to continue. His eyes meet mine as I lean in until our lips meet, the sensation of our tongues pressing together intensifying the moment. I moan into his mouth as he begins to rub the palm of his hand against me, his other hand wrapping around me and pulling me close against his chest.

He kisses me with such passion, and I want him to feel how good he's making me feel in return. I reach down and grab ahold of him, feeling how worked up he is as well as I slowly outline him with the palm of my hand. His groans fill the room before his hands leave me, seizing my wrists and pinning them at my sides. He pulls back from our kiss, his lips hovering near my ear.

"Do you trust me?" he whispers.

In that moment, there is no fear or haunting flashbacks, only a yearning for more of him. All I can feel is my desperation for more of him.

"Yes," I moan in response.

He secures both of my wrists above my head with one hand, sliding his other hand down my arm, tenderly caressing my breast as it moves towards my side.

"Then let me take full control," he whispers.

In one swift motion, he slides his arm under my backside, lifting me up and laying me flat on the bed. Releasing his arm from beneath me, he starts to part my knees, leaning his weight onto the elbow of the hand that still holds my wrists above my head.

His gaze fixates on his hand as it gently eases apart my thighs, his fingers caressing the sensitive skin along the inside. The intensity of his stare ignites a fiery sensation within me, causing my skin to flush with heat. Time seems to stand still as he looks at me, his gaze never wavering. He could stare at me forever and it still wouldn't be long enough. The array of new sensations flooding through me is almost overwhelming, pushing me to the brink.

Desperate for more, I attempt to press myself into his touch, but he resists my efforts. Instead, he leans in and captures my lips in a passionate kiss, pressing me back onto the soft mattress. With his mouth still connected to mine, he inhales deeply, stealing the air from my lungs before his fingers delicately part my inner walls and slide inside. A sharp gasp escapes me, muffled by his kiss, as I eagerly await the path his finger will trace next.

A surge of pleasure washes over me as two of his wet fingers begin to glide up and down in a gentle swirling motion, causing me to arch my back in response. His lips meld with mine, swallowing my moans as his hand moves with increasing speed, sending shivers down my spine.

Releasing my mouth, he captures my nipple between his lips, teasing it with his tongue in a mesmerizing dance that keeps me teetering on the brink of ecstasy.

"Look at me," he whispers, lifting himself slightly to meet my gaze as he continues his tantalizing ministrations.

I tilt my chin down to meet his eyeline and it takes everything in me to hold his gaze. His eyes are intense, focused on me, forcing me to feel his concentration on my pleasure as he speeds up. Right when I'm about to lose all control, he flashes me a smile and my eyes roll to the back of my head, moaning his name as he gives me a release that devours my entire body. Every fiber of my being trembles as I collapse down onto the bed trying to catch my breath.

Releasing my wrists, he gathers my limp body into his arms, drawing me close to his chest as I struggle to regain my composure, lying there as he showers me with tender kisses all over my face.

My whole body feels as if I just ran a marathon, and I'm not convinced my legs haven't liquified during that new experience. I look up at him and take his lips in mine, eager to touch his body in the same ways he just touched me. I reach my hand down between us and start to slip my fingers into his waistline, but he stops me right at the entrance.

"Not tonight," he says, breaking away from my kiss.

I pull myself away from him and prop myself up on my elbows.

"Why not? You don't want me?" I ask.

He smirks slightly, caressing my shoulder with his hand before drawing me back into his embrace.

"Auden, I want you in every way that you'll allow me, but tonight is solely about you regaining control over your body," he explains, wrapping his arm around me and gently stroking my back.

I don't understand why he won't allow me to take this further. The confusion is starting to make me feel as if he didn't really want me. Was he just trying to calm me down? Does he not really feel the connection between us that I thought we had? He must be able to sense my hesitation because he gives me a tight squeeze and continues to explain.

"I need you to trust me when I say that laying in bed next to you with your soft, perfect body completely exposed," he trails his fingers down my bare spine, "and your sweet scent filling my nose," he kisses my shoulder, inhaling deeply as if he's savoring my smell, "is the most difficult thing I've ever had to resist. But I can wait for all of that once you're absolutely sure you're ready."

His words send more shivers down my spine and my heart swells with his sincerity. I never want to leave this bed, and I never want to leave his arms again.

I look over his shoulder and notice it's 3:00 am.

"We should get some sleep. Tomorrow is going to be a long and hard day," I say, planting a kiss on Asher's cheek and snuggling against him so that my back is nestled against his chest.

He drapes his arm over my stomach, intertwining his fingers with mine, resting his chin on my shoulder and kissing my cheek.

"Goodnight, Auden," he whispers softly, "thank you for trusting me and sharing your truth."

His words initially make my heart flutter, but then a wave of guilt washes over me as I realize that I haven't been entirely truthful with Asher at all.

THIRTY

Auden

The sun peeking in from the maroon window curtains and the smell of bagels wakes me. I stretch my legs out and turn to my side when I hear the bathroom door opening. Asher walks out in a pair of dark khaki pants and a green button up shirt, the short sleeves lining the muscles on his arms perfectly.

"I didn't know what kind of bagels you liked so I got one of each from the breakfast bar," he says, pointing over at the small desk area. "I grabbed us coffee as well."

I stand up, wrapping the blanket around me and slowly walk over to the desk before taking a seat, my body still completely exhausted from last night. I look over at the clock and realize it's only 7:15.

"Why are you awake so early?" I ask, trying not to allow my annoyance for morning people to show.

I spread cream cheese over one of the cinnamon raisin bagels and start to bring it up to my mouth. He walks over and leans down, laying a kiss on my now cream cheese–covered lips. He pulls back and smiles as he licks his lips clean, reminding me that last night was definitely not a dream.

"Well, I wanted to make sure I had time to shower and grab you breakfast before I head out."

The thought of Asher leaving makes me feel queasy, and I set the bagel down. He must've noticed my quick change in demeanor because he comes and sits down on the side of the bed closest to me.

"I have to go meet my parents at the funeral home and make sure everything is set up for the visitations today. You can hang out here, or I'm happy to drop you off at your parents' house if you'd prefer."

I sit and contemplate my options for a moment, unsure of what I want to do with my morning. I really don't want to be separated from Asher, but I understand that he has plenty on his mind and shouldn't have to worry about me today.

I finish my bagel and brush my teeth before returning to the room.

"I think I'll stay here and shower. Maybe I'll take a taxi to my parents in a little bit and see if I have anything to wear for today."

Asher grabs his white sneakers and slides them on before walking over to me and taking a seat on the edge of the bed.

"Are you going to be okay?" he asks.

I give him a smile of reassurance and a nod.

"Yes, I think I am," I smile. "I'll see you later today."

He leans forward and kisses the top of my head before talking both of my hands in his.

"Please make sure you call or text me if you need me for any reason."

He heads for the door and opens it before turning around to face me. "You sure do look beautiful in the mornings," he says, giving me a wink before closing the door behind him.

The butterflies from his perfect face send me falling back into my bed. I close my eyes and try to reimagine everything about Asher and his gentle, strong hands.

*

I'm in a taxi on the way to my parents' house when my phone buzzes. I pull it out of my bag and see a text from Dec.

Dec: **Okay, I'm dying to know.**

Me: **Know what?**

Dec: **How is he?!**

Me: **Asher?**

Dec: **No. Robert Downey Jr.**

I never realized I could miss his obnoxious sarcasm so much.

Me: **He's hanging in there. He's been pretty amazing.**

I want to gush over every little detail of last night with Dec, but texting it all doesn't feel right. I'm definitely not going to explain it on the phone in front of the fifty-something cab driver that probably goes to my moms church.

Dec: **Love all of that. But what I meant was how he was in bed. Is he as great as I imagined? ;)**

Me: **We haven't had sex . . . yet. But I will say that I didn't realize firefighters were so good with their hands. No other details as of now, so don't even ask.**

Dec: **You dirty little virgin.**

I close out of my texts as soon as I spot my parents' street coming up. Dec has called me a virgin since he found out the details of how little sex I've had. He said that firsts don't count unless you're together long enough to find at least one kink you enjoy. That definitely doesn't count with Danny. And

Brad doesn't count at all. At least not according to Dec's book on sex. I love him for that. My heart loves him for that.

The taxi turns down my driveway, and I notice a black BMW parked behind my dad's pickup. It's 9:00 am on a Thursday, too late for my dad to not already be at work and too early for visitors. I hand the cash to my driver and step out of the taxi, shielding my eyes from the hot Louisiana sun as I approach the mysterious car.

When I make it up the steps of the porch, I notice three silhouettes in the kitchen and my stomach starts to turn with anticipation. Something doesn't feel right, and my body wants me to turn and run as fast as I can.

I open the door and take a step inside, holding my arm back behind me so the screen door doesn't slam.

"Do we have an understanding?" I hear an unfamiliar man's voice ask.

I turn the corner and see my mama sitting at the kitchen table, her face full of confusion and anger. She's sitting across from an older man in a tailored black suit. My Dad is standing in his work uniform leaning against the wall in the corner of the kitchen. His arms are crossed in front of his chest, and his eyes are full of sorrow.

"What's going on?" I ask, looking over at my dad. "Dad, why aren't you at work?"

The man in the suit turns and stands, reaching his hand out in my direction and waiting for me to take it.

"You must be Auden," he says cooly. "I'm Mr. Calhoun, the Montgomery family's lawyer."

I look down at his hand and take a step back, confused as to what he's doing here.

"I was just explaining to Mr. and Mrs. Sterling what defamation is and what could potentially happen if you were to be charged with that, Auden," he says, looking back down at my mama.

Mama shakes her head, unable to look up in my direction.

"Is it true, Auden?" she asks. "Is it true that you've been spreading lies about Brad Montgomery and Taylor?" I stay silent. I doubt I'd be able to move my lips even if I had the words. I feel completely frozen, and I don't know how to fix this without making the situation worse.

I can't believe the Montgomery family sent their lawyer after me, and to my parents' home of all places. I look over at my mama and then to my dad, both unable to look back at me. I haven't told them anything, and I'm not sure I ever would have if Mr. Calhoun hadn't already taken that choice away from me.

My mama stands up and her eyes shoot toward me. "Child, I asked you a question," she says, her voice stern and serious.

Her tone causes me to flinch and I take another step back, still struggling to find my voice.

Mr. Calhoun grabs a brown briefcase off the floor next to the seat across from Mama and reaches out to shake my dad's hand.

"Well, it seems like you understand what's at stake here."

My dad shakes his hand, nodding in agreement and mumbling a soft "Mhmm."

"And it seems like you can handle everything here, keeping Auden out of trouble," he says, his eyes locked on Mama's, a condescending grin on his face while reaching out and shaking her hand.

"Yessir, we will," Mama replies, shooting her eyes back in my direction.

Mr. Calhoun gives me a nod as he passes, heading for the door, allowing the screen to slam behind him.

Mama watches him walk out and waits until we hear his car door slam shut before laying into me.

"What on God's green earth have you gotten us into, child?" she asks, taking a step closer to me.

She only calls me child when she thinks I'm acting like one. I hated it back when I was an actual kid, and I hate it even more now that I'm twenty-four.

"You come home and suddenly we have a lawyer at our table threatening us. Telling us that if you decide to spread some lie you made up in high school that the whole town will stop bringing your daddy their business."

I look over at my dad, his eyes still glued to the ground, lost in his thoughts. I used to hate how long it would take for my dad to find something to say. Mama used to go in on me all the time, and I would stand there, zoning out and filling my head with silent prayers that he would learn how act faster so I wouldn't have to listen to Mama for so long. Over time, I learned to appreciate what he had to say when he said it, but I still wish it didn't have to take so long.

The sadness in his eyes makes me wonder what exactly Mr. Calhoun said I was lying about. Did he tell my parents what Brad had done to me? There's no way he'd admit that Brad broke the law, so what exactly do they think I'm lying about? I hope my dad didn't hear any details. I know he still thinks of me as his little girl, and I'm not sure I'm ready for that to change yet. It already changed in my own mind when Brad left me feeling completely broken and dirty.

"What did he tell you?" I ask, looking back at Mama.

Mama stops and brushes the front of her white daisy print apron that she must've forgotten to take off when Mr. Calhoun showed up. She turns her back to me and leans over the sink, looking out at her flower garden.

"Your daddy already had to sit through hearing it once, I don't believe he needs to hear what you did again."

What you did again.

The words hit me like a frying pan to the back of the head. She blames me. She thinks I'm the one ruining Brad Montgomery's life. And now I'm somehow going to ruin theirs as well. How could she ever believe that I'd lie about something like that? I can feel my teeth grinding together, and I want to shout at her that I WAS RAPED!

"Go on to work, Daddy," she says, keeping her gaze out the window. "I'll see you later on tonight."

He lifts himself away from the wall, his eyes still glued to the floor and walks over to Mama, leaning over her shoulder and kissing her cheek like he's done every morning. He turns in my direction and walks toward me, wrapping his arms around me and kissing me on the head.

I hug him back and want to beg him to stay so I can explain it all, but I don't even know what I should explain and if it'll change anything at all. It could change his opinion of me even more than this lie he was just told.

"Dad . . ." I start to say as he pulls back.

"I'll talk to you later, Auden," he says, turning and heading out the door.

*

As soon as my dad's truck is out of the driveway, Mama unties her apron, folding it neatly in half and hanging it on a hook next to the baking cabinet. She turns toward me and comes close enough to grab both of my hands.

"Now, I know you were younger, and you regret the decision you made, especially with a boy who God made for your best friend."

A boy God made for my best friend!? If God specifically made that piece of shit for Taylor, then he's no God of mine.

She takes a deep breath, looking up at the ceiling and whispering, "God rest her soul," before returning her attention back to me. "You tried to lie about it. But the truth always comes out, right?" she asks, but I know she isn't actually asking me.

"Well, now Taylor has gone on her way and her husband has enough grief to deal with, just like her family does. None of them need you coming back here adding to their pain. Do you understand me?"

I know she wants a response now. I feel like such a stupid, little child in her presence. I haven't missed this part of her in the last six years.

"That lawyer explained very clearly this morning that you'd be owing a lot more than that computer job probably pays you, and he reminded us that people don't like their cars worked on by the father of a liar."

She lifts one of her hands up to my chin and tilts it upward so that my eyes are staring straight into hers.

"Do you understand me?" she asks again, her eyebrows lifted anticipating my answer and showing me how serious she is.

I pull my chin from her grasp and turn in the direction of my bedroom, nodding my head.

"I understand, Mama," I say as I round the corner.

*

The clock reads 9:40 am and the first visitation starts in a little more than an hour. I open my wooden closet doors and start to look for something appropriate to wear. The many pink and purple items Mama bought me over the years make me laugh inside now. I was always afraid to tell her how much I hated those colors, and you wouldn't be able to find a speck of them in my apartment now. Unless of course, you went searching in Dec's closet.

I see a box up on the top shelf and reach for it, remembering that I had worn a black dress for my gram's funeral. The box is covered in dust, and I brush it off with my hand before opening. Inside is the solid black dress with a thin black belt. I pull it out and hold it up in front of me, praying that it'll still fit.

I pull the dress down over my head and turn toward my mirror before zipping it up. It fits, thankfully. I stare at myself in the mirror and remember the day that I wore it last, wishing more than anything that my grams was still here to remind me of how strong I am and how worthy of happiness I am.

My backpack catches my eye, and something inside of me tells me to read the next letter. Asher isn't here to read it with me, but I doubt he'll mind if I read ahead. Besides, he has enough to deal with today. I feel guilty for taking his attention so often when he has his own grief that he should be making a priority. I want to read all her letters before the funeral tomorrow, and now feels as good of a time as any to read the next one.

I rummage through my bag until I find the final two letters, checking the dates and making sure to grab the fifth. I take a seat on the edge of my bed, taking in a deep breath as I start to unfold it.

"Please give me something that'll guide me on what to do next," I whisper to Taylor under my breath.

5/12/22

Auden,

Half a decade and I'm still praying every day that it'll be the last.

I miss you.

I feel so foggy most days. Brad called a doctor three weeks ago and told him to prescribe me some anxiety medication. He said he couldn't concentrate on school with me crying so much around him. I don't like the pills. They make me feel foggy and tired all the time. He's right, they take away the anxiety, but they also take away all other feelings.

On Valentine's Day, I decided to drive up and surprise Brad again. I was so excited to see him that I mistakenly left my phone behind at home. I didn't realize I had been so foolish until I was halfway there and pulled over to fill up on gas. I decided to just head over and deal with the phone issue once I was with him.

I heard slow jazz music playing in the hallway and waited a few moments before knocking. I didn't want to interrupt what I assumed was his roommate romancing someone. I finally got the courage to interrupt once I remembered that I had no other way of reaching Brad.

The door opened, but the chain was still fastened when Brad opened the door in his birthday suit. Before he got the chance to slam the door and hide what he was up to, the tall brunette he was with walked past in the same lingerie that he sent me for Valentine's Day.

I ran to my car as fast as I could and drove home in tears.

I couldn't tell my family. I couldn't tell Asher.

Brad came home and begged me not to leave him. He moved back to Monroe and has been doing his classes online. I want to forgive him and move on with my life, as silly as that sounds.

If I leave Brad, I'll lose my family too. Asher wouldn't leave me, and I can't allow him to risk his relationship with our parents for me.

I still can't stop crying, and I feel sick when Brad touches me now. I think he hates me for that.

He got drunk last weekend and crawled into bed trying to start something with me. I flinched when he touched me, and he didn't appreciate that. He left in an angry fit. I still don't know where he went, but he told me that he has needs and Montgomery men deserve to have those needs filled whenever they want.

I don't really leave the house anymore. There's nothing but judgment and pity outside now, and I really don't think I can survive that.

I continue to pray for your happiness and like to imagine you with someone who loves you in every way, as you deserve.

Bring him home so I can meet him and tell you in person how much I have missed you.

Happy (late) 23rd Birthday.

Until we meet again,

Taylor

My heart sinks, and I feel like I'm crying but I have no tears left. She was so wrong about Asher and what he would've done or wanted for her. I fold the letter up and shove it back into my bag, wondering how Asher will react when he gets the chance to read it. He's had so much to deal with since the moment he found his sister, I don't want him to feel any more pain than he already has.

I lean forward, my elbows on my knees and rest my face in the palms of my hands as her words run through my mind again.

She caught him having an affair, and she still stayed. How could she feel so unbelievably trapped? Did she truly believe she had to stay and deal with such a horrible human being? No one in her life told her that she didn't have to stay with a man who wasn't faithful to her?

The collar on my dress starts to feel constricting, and the room begins to heat up. I stand and walk over to the window, opening it and sticking my head out, desperate for a gust of wind to cool me off. I start to fan myself with my hands and walk back and forth in front of the window. Then some words from the letter come back to me: *Brad called a doctor three weeks ago and told him.*

"Holy shit," I say under my breath, stopping dead in my tracks.

You don't call your doctor and tell them what medication to prescribe you, that's not how it works, especially not for a controlled substance. I sit down on my bed, thinking it through. Brad clearly has a lot more connections than even I had anticipated. He was able to drug his own wife. He fucking drugged her.

THIRTY-ONE

Asher

My mother walks out of the viewing room dressed in all black with a short black veil covering her eyes. My father is next to her, his arm looped through hers as he hands her another tissue. A pang of guilt overcomes me. I haven't been there enough for my parents. I haven't made sure they were okay during this loss, something no parent should ever experience. I haven't figured out how to make it all okay.

As soon as she sees me, she starts to walk toward me for a hug. She wraps her arms around my neck as if I didn't just spend all morning with her helping to set up.

"Oh, my sweet boy," she says. "God sure gave me two wonderful children."

I squeeze her extra tight, knowing she's missing out on half the hugs she deserves from this moment on.

"People should be arriving any minute, so now is your time to go see her," she says.

I look at the brown painted door my parents just exited, and my hands start to sweat knowing that Taylor is laying lifeless behind it. I shake my father's hand and he pats me on the back. I head toward the door, slowly turning the knob as my hands start to shake, a sense of emptiness washing over me.

 She's been here all morning, and so have I, except for when we all ran home to get changed. My mom couldn't keep herself from entering the viewing room every chance she had, savoring every second she has left to physically see her daughter. My father spent a few minutes alone with her when my mom was occupied with the entrance display. I haven't stepped foot in the room, and now is really my last opportunity to do so.

 When I walk into the room, it feels cold, the soft lighting on the cream painted walls gives it an eerie vibe. I look over at the wooden casket, open with white flowers surrounding it.

 I don't want to walk up to it. I already saw Taylor laying lifeless once. The only difference now is probably the makeup they caked on and the fact that her hands are no longer still holding any of her blood's warmth. I know this is one of my last chances to say goodbye to her, but I can't help but feel angry. How am I expected to say everything I want to her when all that comes to mind is asking why she didn't believe Auden.

 The sounds of my parents' voices greeting the guests fill the outside of the room, and I know my time is becoming shorter. I walk closer until I see her hands, they're crossed over one another and there's a planner placed underneath them. My dad's doing, I'm sure. I can't help but smile about the thought of her planning her eternity up in heaven. I bet God's having a fun time arguing with her over that.

 I take another step closer and notice she's wearing the blue dress that she wore the last time we had brunch together.

She made a point to show me the way it flowed when she did a twirl. She always found a way to embrace her inner child, and I always admired that. I already miss that.

Her eyes are closed. I don't know why that caught me off guard. I wish they could open and look at me one more time. Her skin is pale, and they put lipstick on her lips, something she hated to wear. I shake my head, and the anger turns into deep sorrow as I lean down and grab her hands, the coldness of them pushing tears from my eyes.

"Damn it, Taylor," I say to her. "Why the hell didn't you call me? Why did you have to leave us like this? You had so much left to give this world. Now I'm here alone, trying to put all of the pieces back together."

The tears start flowing down my cheeks, and I can't stop them.

"You were my best friend. You were the only person who truly knew the real me, every version—the good and the bad. I'm still here, and you've left me alone in this world."

She left me alone, but she left because she felt alone. Something I could've possibly prevented if I had just given her more of my attention.

"I should've known. I could've helped you leave him."

The smell of embalming fluid overcomes me as I lay a kiss on her cheek, snapping me out of my tearful moment. I squeeze her hands one last time and feel a sharp poke on my palm. It's the diamond of her wedding ring.

I close my eyes, and the image of her laying in her bed without her ring flashes through my mind, making me want to rip it off her finger. I attempt to wiggle it, but I quickly realize there's no way I can remove it.

The door opens behind me, and my father peeks his head in.

"We're going to have to open the room up now, Ash," my dad calls to me.

I nod my head and lean down one more time, giving Taylor a final kiss on the cheek and whispering in her ear, "I won't let him get away with this."

THIRTY-TWO

Brad

The trash can closes as I toss in my last piece of paper towel. I understand her daughter just died, but you'd think the woman would be smart enough to wear waterproof makeup on a day she knows she'll be blubbering like a baby. Or at least be smart enough not to hug a guy in an $800 suit.

I check myself in the bathroom mirror to make sure there are no traces of her drugstore makeup on my suit or tie, noting how damn good I look.

I check the time on my watch. The first visitation started half an hour ago, and if Auden is going to show up, she should be here by now.

The shock on her face when I interrupted her and Asher's little moment the other day has kept me on a high. I've been patiently wait for my next opportunity to see her. I tried to go to sleep once my father left last night, but the anger he left me with, and knowing Auden was somewhere close by, was too much to handle. I needed a distraction, but I also wanted to feel the same way I did that night with Auden. I picked Millie up around 4:00 am, and we drove over to my father's pole barn. I was so excited when I immediately recognized the same spot of trees where I took Auden, pulling Millie close behind me. Millie tried her best to play the role of Auden, but she didn't give me the taste of fear and adrenaline that Auden did. It took much longer for me to nut, and I left less than satisfied.

The bathroom door closes behind me, and it takes everything in me to force the smile on my face to disappear. I walk past a group of people sharing memories around a screen, playing pictures of Taylor. I give a soft nod to everyone, hoping they fall for the sadness I'm displaying on my face. The poor widower is a role I really don't enjoy playing. Pity is the last thing I want from anyone.

I step outside and take a look around, watching as more people park their cars and head inside. Right when I turn to head back in, I catch a glimpse of a girl walking up in a short, black dress and know instantly by the curve of her hips that it's Auden.

Before she gets a chance to make it to the building, I hustle over to her. I cut her off before she gets to the steps. She takes a step back when she recognizes me, the blood draining from her cheeks.

"Just the girl I was looking for." I smile, grabbing a hold of her wrist.

I pull her over to the gazebo, and it's frankly shocking that she's not attempting to resist. Maybe my father did take care of it, and she's already learned that she needs to behave in my presence. I don't, however, like the feeling that my father was the one who may have tamed her. She's not his to control, but I can't allow that to distract me. I know how risky of a move it is to be mingling with her so publicly.

"What do you want Brad?" she asks before I get a chance to turn around. "I'm not here to start any drama."

Her tone catches me off guard for a moment. It isn't what I expected. There's no fear in it. There isn't anger either. It's almost as if she has no feelings behind it at all. Almost robotic is not at all exciting for me. I need to change this immediately.

I flash her a smile and look her up and down. It kills me how fucking hot she's become over the last few years. She's always been attractive in a nontraditional way. But the way her curves have defined, and her small, perfect tits have perked up, I can't help but imagine what she looks like undressed. My teeth let go of my bottom lip, and I bring my hand up to caress the side of her arm.

"I just wanted a moment alone with you before all the craziness starts. We haven't had time to catch up yet."

Her eyebrows furrow, and she looks like she wants to slap me. But she doesn't, she doesn't even pull her arm away from my touch. The fact that she's being so obedient makes my cock start to harden, and the bit of emotion she's finally displaying takes everything in me not to throw her down right here and have my way with her again.

"I didn't realize we needed to catch up, Brad," she says, crossing her arms and looking in every direction around her except for mine.

I bet the bitch is looking for Asher. The thought of little Asher trying to play the savior makes me let out a laugh. He's so pathetic, and Auden needs to see that. She needs to see me right in front of her and start showing me some damn respect and eye contact.

"You left on bad terms, Auden," I say, trying to make my voice sound soothing and sincere. "And it feels like we're still on bad terms, and I don't want that."

One of her eyes closes slightly as if she's trying to focus harder to see what I'm playing at. Now I've got her attention.

"I know what we did was wrong now, and I wish I could take it back. But I have to admit, I don't regret our moment together."

I bring my hand up and brush the side of her cheek, hoping she'll see my gentle side. She looks down at my hand and her lips part. Fuck. I want to feel those lips all over my cock.

"I'm here for Taylor and nothing else," she starts to say. "Mr. Calhoun made his point, and you no longer need to worry about your secret being revealed. Now please, Brad, just leave me alone."

She starts to turn away as I notice Asher walking out of the building at the same moment. I reach out and grab her shoulder, turning her back to face me before she sees him. I know this may be my last chance to interact with her, especially with the look Asher is throwing in our direction.

"Auden, please," I say, sliding my hand slowly down her arm, as I watch Asher swiftly making his way over, his eyes filling with rage.

"I'm sorry. What I was trying to say was that I'm glad you're here," I say, shooting her my best smile right as Asher steps up onto the gazebo, his hands balled into fists.

THIRTY-THREE

Asher

My chest hits Brad's, pushing him to take a step back from Auden. I'm trying my hardest not to allow my rage to have its way and hold back my fists from landing on his jaw.

"What the hell do you think you're doing?" I ask, my blood boiling and my teeth clenched.

Brad takes a step back and lifts both of his hands in the air in surrender.

"Woah, brother, what's your problem?" he asks, his tone portraying confusion that I know he couldn't possibly have.

My feet take a step closer in his direction, and the fear of losing control starts to kick in. I'm fighting against every fiber of my being that wants to choke the life out of him.

"Don't you fucking touch her," I yell, feeling my arm being pulled from behind.

"Asher, stop," Auden pleads in a soft tone, trying not to attract any attention. "Asher, please. It's fine."

I turn around and face her, her eyes squinting in desperation as she holds onto my forearm.

How the hell is this fine? His hand caressing her skin is suddenly fine? Did I make up everything that happened last night in my head?

"It's okay, please," she pleads, tugging on my arm and trying to pull me out of the gazebo.

"Jesus, Asher, this is Taylor's visitation. You need to get it together, man," I hear Brad say from behind, his audacity on the verge of breaking my composure.

Before I get the chance to turn around and reply, Auden has both of her hands around my face, her eyes serious and glued to mine as they call for my attention.

"Asher, you need to follow me right now," she says, her voice stern.

We walk toward a small area of trees toward the back of the peace garden, far enough away that no one can hear us, but close enough to still make out the faces of others. She stops, turning toward me and staying silent for a moment.

"What the hell was that?" I ask, my anger now easing toward her.

Why would she even give Brad the time of day? There're so many people here. She could've easily avoided interacting with him. She could've kept walking until she found me, and none of this would've happened.

She shakes her head and looks down at my hands, noticing as blood trickles down through my fingertips. I rotate my wrist and open my palms, realizing I was gripping my car keys so tightly that it broke the skin, drawing blood.

"Asher, something happened this morning," she begins. "When I went home, there was a lawyer in my parents' kitchen."

My heart rate starts to slow as I listen to her voice, the curiosity momentarily replacing my anger. The stress in her tone has my full attention.

"It was the Montgomerys' lawyer, and he was there to put me in my place."

I watch as she takes a step over to the closest tree, running her fingertips along its bark. I can't help but notice how her beauty is a piece of art, and it takes every inch of me not to step closer and kiss her until my pain and anger subsides.

"What do you mean by he put you in your place?" I ask.

"I'm still not sure what he told my parents, but he made sure that they thought I had spread lies about Brad. And he implied that that's why I moved away to Minneapolis." She closes her eyes and takes a deep breath before continuing.

"He threatened my dad's business and said no one would want work done by a liar's father." She looks up at me, her eyes full of a million emotions. "You, yourself, already heard Mr. Montgomery threatening your dad to stop his business with my dad's shop."

I take a step forward and cup her face in my hands, kissing her on the forehead and pulling her against my chest. How can one family be so fucking cruel and so self-absorbed, willing to hurt anyone even remotely involved with their current victim, Auden.

"They can't do that. There's no way people would believe the Montgomerys over your father. Everyone knows what a good man he is," I say confidently, "especially my father."

She shakes her head and takes a step back out of my embrace.

"Even if that was true, I read Taylor's fifth letter, Asher. We have no idea how deep the Montgomery claws are dug into this community. Brad had a doctor on call and was drugging Taylor so she'd stop thinking about how he was cheating on her."

My heart stops. I crouch down, feeling dizzy as I try to comprehend what Auden just said.

"He was drugging her?" I ask.

Auden leans down and takes my hands in hers, resting her forehead against mine.

"Yes. Well, sort of. She was so upset when she found out what he was doing and she couldn't seem to find a way to forgive him, but she still didn't want to leave either. It was consuming her. So, he got his doctor to prescribe her anxiety medication so that she would calm down. But she couldn't feel anything, pain or happiness."

I shake my head, not wanting to believe what she's saying. Not wanting to hear about another thing I should have noticed that was going on with my sister. How I failed her once again. How the hell did I miss that my sister was being drugged?

"The pills she killed herself with," I whisper.

Auden pries my fingers open, and she removes my keys from my palm, even more blood trickling from it.

"Asher," she says, lifting me from my knees and kissing me on the cheek. "I know how hard this is, and I'm so sorry for adding to your pain, but we have to pretend none of this happened. My parents can't lose everything, and your family doesn't need any more heartbreak. If I can help make sure that doesn't happen, then I will."

Her eyes are full of such sadness, but she doesn't shed a tear. This isn't heartbroken Auden standing in front of me, this is selfless Auden. She's using all of the strength she has left to bottle up the pain she's been carrying again, and I can't help but love her even more.

Love her. Damn it. I think I do. She's the most amazing woman I've ever met, and I feel insane for feeling this intensely about her so soon, but I do. I love this girl. She's spent so long holding onto this secret, and she finally finds the courage to speak it. Within twelve hours, she's made the decision to silence herself again to protect her family. To protect my family. I love her for that. And I love her for returning to help me get answers about Taylor, even though it meant walking back into the fires of her own personal hell. I love her for every moment she spent defending Taylor as kids. I love her for how much she loves others, even though she isn't the best at showing it. I love her for how strong she was, going out on her own after being put through the worst moment of her life. She gave up everyone and everything she loved in the process.

I notice that she's still going on about all the reasons why she can't tell the truth and why she needs to protect her family while I'm lost in thought. I step forward and put my arm around her waist, pulling her to me while she's still talking. I cup her face before kissing her with as much passion as I feel. She kisses me back, pulling back just the slightest, her face full of confusion.

"Auden, I love you," I say, looking down at her, her face still resting in my hand.

She stays silent, looking back at me as if she can't register the words I just spoke.

"I know this is sudden and probably feels a little crazy, or a lot crazy. But I love you, and I just now realized it."

She stays silent, and I can tell that her brain is about to kick in and outshine what her heart wants, so I keep speaking before she gets the chance.

"I love you too much to allow you to be silenced again." I pull her face close to mine so she can't turn away when I say this.

"We don't have to say anything today, that's fine. We probably don't have time to deal with anything today anyways. But, Auden, you will not be silenced and neither will Taylor. I need you to trust me. I won't allow anything to happen to you or your parents."

Before she gets the chance to respond, I hear my mother's voice from behind us and footsteps approaching.

"So, this is where you've been," she says.

Auden pulls herself out of my grasp, and we both turn to face my mother.

"Auden," my mother says brightly, her face full of surprise. "Oh, Auden, it is you!"

My mother opens her arms and hugs Auden, tears flowing from her eyes as she holds her, rocking back and forth. My mom has always loved and admired Auden. She was always so proud of how intelligent and determined Auden was, and how she already had her future all mapped out. That's exactly what my mother dreamed of for her own children. It was kind of nice having Auden as a distraction for her when we were growing up.

"Oh, sweetheart, it's been way too long. I am so glad you're here," she says before letting go of her grasp, but keeping her hands on Auden's elbows.

"Hi, Mama Landry," Auden says, her smile quivering. "I'm so sorry that I . . ."

Before she gets a chance to apologize for anything, my mother pulls her back in for another hug.

"You're here now, and we are so grateful," she whispers.

The way she stopped Auden from blaming herself is a perfect example of why I love my mother. She has her moments. She pushes a little too hard sometimes, and then she surprises me by just loving me. She is so good at ignoring the things most people dwell on and choosing love instead. Not always, but when it matters the most. And I'm okay with that. I'm grateful for that.

When my mother finally lets her go, I reach out and clasp Auden's hand, lacing her fingers in mine. My mother looks down at our hands then up at me, flashing me a tiny smile of approval.

"Well, the first visitation is just about to end, and if I'm being honest, I need to rest while I can. Will I see you at the second visitation in a few hours, Auden?" she asks. "Both of you together?" she flashes us both another smile.

Auden looks up at me, then back at my mother, giving my hand a little squeeze.

"Of course, you will," Auden replies. "I'm just going to get some air myself, but you can plan on me being back for the second visitation."

"Good," my mother says, flashing Auden a wink. "Asher can you help me home, honey?"

I lean over to Auden, kissing her cheek and whispering, "I love you."

THIRTY-FOUR

Auden

    The brace-faced teen hands me my coffee and I go take a seat at an open booth. I'm not sure if you're supposed to call the high schooler working the grocery store coffee stand a barista, but I know for a fact that you can't call whatever is in this cup coffee.
    I choke down my first sip and lean back against the hard, wooden booth, closing my eyes and trying to quiet my mind.
    I replay my conversation with Asher in my head. I can't believe he told me that he loved me. Danny and I told each other we loved each other, but even then, I think I knew that wasn't what real love felt like. It was just hormones and the longing to swap saliva taking over. I graze my fingertips over my lips, still feeling the softness of his against them. I don't know if I can say that I'm in love with him, but the way he can so easily calm my mind makes me wonder if one day I can. I don't want to jump in and say that I love him if I really don't know. He deserves my honesty, even though I've already failed to give him that.

The fear of my parents losing everything flashes in my mind when Brad's putrid cologne catches my attention. I sniff my arm until I find the spot where he left a trace of it on me, making my stomach churn.

Asher seemed so confident when he told me to trust him. He's gone out of his way so many times for me to prove that I can trust him, but I'm not sure either of us know what we're about to go up against. He's also mentioned a few times that he's impulsive. What if he isn't even considering the position we could be putting our families in. "Auden?" I hear a female voice say.

I open my eyes and there's a blonde standing at my table. She's in a brown pantsuit, has short blonde hair, and a pair of black, cat eye-framed sunglasses on. She sets her shitty cup of coffee down on the table and takes a seat across from me.

"Holy shit, it is you," she says, pulling her glasses from her face.

As soon as the glasses leave her face and I see her deep blue eyes, I recognize her. Sarah Underwood.

"Sarah?" I say, my voice heightening with excitement.

I immediately pull myself out from the booth and walk over to her side, leaning down and wrapping her in a big hug.

"It's so good to see you!" I say as I take my seat back across from her.

"It's so good to see you, Auden. I was wondering if I'd see you back here for Taylor's funeral," she replies.

A moment of silence passes between us as we both remember the reason that we're in town. Sarah reaches across the table and squeezes my hand.

"How are you holding up?" she asks.

"I'm doing alright," I reply, not wanting to explain my absence.

"Tell me what you've been up to these last few years," I ask. "I've been waiting to see you on an election ballot, but you haven't reached Minnesota yet."

She laughs, bringing her coffee up to her lips and making a sour face as soon as she takes a sip.

"You and everyone else from high school." She rolls her eyes. "I actually changed my mind, a few times surprisingly, and now I'm the mayor's advisor in Shreveport while I get ready to finish up my law degree."

I nod my head in amazement, she truly is as remarkable as I always knew she'd be.

"But enough about me. I'm so glad I ran into you. I've been thinking about you more than I care to admit since our graduation."

I tilt my head and reach out for my coffee, stopping myself from lifting it off the table when I remember how horrible it is.

"I remember the last few weeks of school that you really kept to yourself. So unlike you. Then when you didn't show up to walk at graduation, something didn't sit right with me."

I lean back into the booth, curious as to where she's going with this. I honestly didn't expect many people to notice that I was absent. And even if they did, I wouldn't expect them to remember that six years later.

"After all, you were pretty close to taking my spot as class valedictorian. Not even attending graduation after all that hard work doesn't make sense to a fellow smart-ass. Do you mind if I ask what happened?" she asks, her eyes searching my face for answers.

My stomach turns, and I don't know what to tell her. I never expected to be in a position where anyone asked me what happened at graduation because I never planned on returning home. Something fighting inside of me, mixed with the honest concern in Sarah's voice, pushes me to tell her the truth.

"The truth?" I ask her.

She nods her head and reaches out her palms waiting for me to put my hands in hers. I reach out and grab them, knowing I need the emotional support she's willing to provide.

"That night at Brad Montgomery's birthday. Do you remember when we were waiting in line for the bathroom, and Brad came and offered to take me to another bathroom?"

She nods her head. "Of course. I was on the verge of peeing my pants and knew that couldn't be the legacy I left for my high school years."

I can't help but laugh. Sarah always made me laugh when I'd least expect it. I missed it more than she could ever realize.

"Well, he took me to the back of the property, and he..." I break eye contact with her, staring down at our hands.

Before I get the chance to finish, she squeezes my hands tightly.

"Please tell me he didn't do what I think he did."

A wave of relief crashes over me, thankful that Sarah caught on before I had to say it out loud. I nod my head. She lets go of my hands, shaking her own head back and forth in disappointment.

"That entitled piece of shit," she says, her tone filled with disgust. "Please tell me he didn't get away with it."

I lift my head and look in her eyes, my lips pressing together as I silently confirm that he did indeed get away with it.

"His family lawyer showed up at my parents' house today. He was threatening defamation and told my dad he'd lose every customer he still has if I spread any more so-called lies."

Sarah shakes her head, taping her fingers on the table as she ponders what to say next.

"Defamation is so hard to prove. He's just blowing smoke up your ass." She looks around the grocery store and then back at me. "And, unfortunately, the lovely state of Louisiana has a statute of limitations and . . ." She pulls her phone out and checks the date. ". . . we're about two months too late to report the fucker."

I reach my hand over and grab hers, waiting for her to meet my eye contact again.

"It's okay, Sarah. I've lived with it long enough now that I can accept it. I just worry that if I hadn't run away, maybe Taylor wouldn't have married him. And maybe she'd still be here now."

Sarah slams her other hand down onto the table, causing a loud slapping sound and drawing the attention of the customers and employees.

"Fuck that, Auden. There must be proof somewhere so that we can at least get the truth out. We may not be able to get legal justice, but if I've learned anything working in the mayor's office, it's the power of the truth. When it's in the right hands, it can bring down some sweet revenge."

She continues to tap her fingers on the table, louder and louder the longer she thinks.

"Did you tell anyone after it happened?" she asks.

I'm not close to God like I used to be. After everything that happened, I kind of left my faith in Monroe and never looked back. But right now, something or someone, I don't know if it's God or Taylor, is prompting me to tell Sarah the part of my truth that I've never spoken to anyone.

"I told Taylor, but she didn't believe me." I start.

My throat starts to feel like a ball is bunched up in it as I try to push the words out. Sarah leans in closer, trying to show that I can tell her whatever it is I'm struggling with.

"I had an abortion, Sarah," I say, looking up at her, waiting to see her eyes filling with disappointment. But they don't.

Instead, she stands from her seat and walks over to me, slides into my side of the booth, and wraps her arms around me.

"That's why I missed graduation. The second I turned eighteen, I went to a clinic out of town. I got on a plane the same afternoon and never looked back."

She squeezes me tightly and starts to rub her hand up and down my back.

"We've got to get this asshole, Auden," she says. "I don't know how, but we're going to bring that fuck face down, even if we have to use the power of the damn press."

I hear the bell on the door behind us and turn around to look. It's a guy walking out of the store in a dark blue suit, heading into the parking lot.

"Was that D. J. Montgomery?" Sarah asks.

*

A flower shop catches my eye on my walk back to the funeral home, specifically the sign in the big front windows advertising that they sell seeds. Dec has been working with our apartment manager to get permission to start a garden on our rooftop. I know he would love it if I bought him some seeds from Louisiana.

Before I even take two full steps inside, my elbow snags on something, and I almost knock over a tall, metal card display.

"Excuse the mess. I'm rearranging," a woman yells from the back wall of the store where she's currently talking with a customer.

I carefully walk over to a table that isn't covered in floral arrangements. When I get to the table, I feel a grin claiming my cheeks as I take in the many little paper packets of seeds spread across it. I don't even look at the price, I just start grabbing and collecting them in my hand. Gulf Coast Yucca, Louisiana Iris, Louisiana Phlox, Swamp Azaleas, and even Spicebush.

The woman finishes talking to the customer and walks toward the register just as I make my way over with my exciting new seeds. I set them down on the counter and pull my purse up from my arm, placing it next to the seeds while I dig inside for my wallet.

"Now that's what I like to call a Louisiana garden, right there," she says as she lifts each packet and scans the barcode on the back.

"I just want to take a piece of Monroe back home with me."

She pulls a small paper bag out from under the counter and tucks the seed packets inside. "And where is home for you?"

It's nice running into someone in Monroe who doesn't recognize me for once. But the fact that I didn't describe Monroe as my home sort of makes my stomach sink. I've spent a long time running from this place, and I almost feel angry that it kept functioning without me.

"Minneapolis," I answer, handing her my credit card.

She takes the card and swipes it before pulling it up closer to her face and reading it. The room starts to feel warmer as the anxiety that maybe my card was declined starts to flush over me. It shouldn't be declined. I make great money at my job. But after a few years of really struggling to get by when I first moved out on my own, that fear of getting declined finds a way to stick with you.

"Auden Sterling," she says aloud, handing my car back to me. "Are you related to the owner of Sterling's Auto Shop?"

I laugh in relief. Small town, easy connection, of course.

"Yes, that's my father," I reply, tucking my wallet back into my bag.

She hands me my bag of seeds, and I turn to head toward the exit when a man with a familiar face steps in front of me, reaching his arm out and lightly touching my elbow.

"Excuse me, Miss," he begins. "Did you say that your name is Auden Sterling?"

Oh God, what the hell is happening now. I take in the man, noticing his dark suit and put-together appearance, unable to remember why he seems so familiar. I really hope he isn't another lawyer about to threaten me, or worse, serve me.

"Yes," I answer reluctantly.

"Sorry, I didn't mean to eavesdrop, but I'm waiting for some flowers to be ready. I overheard your conversation."

I hate when people say that. How is eavesdropping ever an accident? I think he can tell that I'm a little annoyed and a little caught off guard, so he keeps rambling.

"I'm Scott Landry, Taylor and Asher's uncle."

Oh shit. I didn't expect that to come next. I don't know what to say or what he knows about me, so I stay silent.

"I just left their house a little bit ago and was sent to pick up another floral arrangement for the second visitation."

I keep staring at him like I'm stuck on mute. And, honestly, I might be because I still can't find the words to engage in this conversation. I'm not sure if it's because I'm still unaware of what he knows about me, or if it's because I just realized he has the same lopsided smile that Asher has.

He scratches the back of his neck like he's as uncomfortable as I am, and I'm sure the way I'm currently acting is the cause of his awkwardness.

"Nice to meet you," I finally manage to spit out, reaching my arm out and shaking his hand.

He lets out a breath as he returns my handshake, relieved that I finally said something.

"It's nice to meet you. I just happened to hear quite a lot about you during lunch actually."

His smile is genuine and inviting, but the comment he just made is making my expression the complete opposite. What the hell did he hear during lunch? And who the hell was talking about me?

"Only good things I hope?" I ask, trying my hardest to give off a playful vibe and not like I want to interrogate him in the backroom until I have every bit of information that he can provide me.

Smile, Auden. Smile.

"Yes, only good things. Although I like to believe the things that aren't said, are the things that say the most."

His name is called and the florist has a giant vase full of white baby's breath mixed with magnolia branches. He walks over and thanks her, picking up the vase and heading back towards me, or maybe he's heading for the exit. He can't leave because I need to know what the hell was said and who said what.

He's walking the short distance over in my direction and it feels as if he's in slow motion. Like God's giving me a little extra time to figure out how I'm going to stop this man from walking out that door after making a comment that has been tightening my lungs since he said it. But my mind is completely blank. It's like when I watch Jeopardy and I laugh because the question is so easy, but when I go to say the answer out loud, there's nothing in my mind but a tumbleweed of ignorance.

"Well, it was nice to put a face to the name, Auden. I'll see you at the visitation in a bit?" he says, his feet staying in motion.

Speak damn it, speak.

"You absolutely will," I reply, watching as he continues to the exit door. "Unless I should be too embarrassed by whatever some mystery person said about me at lunch today."

Oh, Auden, be embarrassed. That comment doesn't even deserve you trying to lie to yourself that it wasn't that bad. It was so bad. It was so obviously bad.

He opens the door and turns his body back to face me, keeping the door propped open with his left foot, the vase tucked in his left arm and motions with his other hand for me to walk through. I walk out in front of him, taking note of his quiet snicker.

"Sorry, I didn't think about how my comment may have affected you."

Excuse me?

He's sorry about his what?

Affecting who?

Who is this wonderful man, and is he why Asher is so considerate?

"I'm a really relaxed person, and sometimes that makes it hard for me to consider how other people may feel when I'm vague. Especially uptight individuals."

What the fuck did he just call me? My head drops to the side, and I can feel my face starting to scrunch together. He must realize that I'm not thrilled by his choice of words to describe me. Uptight? A person he doesn't know at all.

"Like my wife. My wife is uptight, and she's the one who reminds me that I'm way more relaxed than most people, and I should try to be more considerate because of that."

His explanation mixed with the sweat beads forming on his forehead forces me to let out a laugh, and it sets him at ease. He reaches in his pocket and pulls out a key fob, clicking the button to a tiny, red rental car parked in front of the shop and opening the door to the back seat.

"Anyways, before I forget again to finish what I was originally talking to you about, today at lunch you were brought up when the family was sharing stories of Taylor over the years. You were brought up quite a bit, and I didn't catch on to that at first. But then my wife pointed it out." He leans down and places the vase in the back seat, pulling the seat belt out and securing it around the flowers.

"She's good at catching things like that. But I don't pay attention to what people say that much. I like to zone the voices out most of the time and tune into their body language and reactions to the conversations." He shuts the door to the car and steps back up on the curb. "And it didn't take long for me to see that anytime your name was mentioned, Asher's eyes would light up, and his cheeks would flush just the tiniest bit."

He shoves the key fob back into his pocket then starts to make his way around the car until he's at the driver's side door. "And anytime he told a story about you, he'd get a big goofy grin on his face, just like the one on yours right now."

He opens the door, and I bring my hand up to my cheek. I'm embarrassed because I had no idea that the information he's giving me is making my feelings show all over my face.

"Anyways, you need a ride to the funeral home?" he asks.

I shake my head. "No, thank you. I suddenly feel like it's a beautiful day for a walk."

THIRTY-FIVE

Auden

The sweet scent from the Magnolia trees fills the air as I cross the street toward the funeral home parking lot. I feel so much lighter after running into Sarah and the other Mr. Landry. Although, my conversation with Mr. Landry was by far the highlight of my day. I'm not sure if telling Sarah my hardest decision will help me bring the truth to light but knowing that she's on my side has definitely brought a little hope back.

I weave through the many cars filling up the parking lot when I hear a man's voice behind me.

"A little birdie told me you were supposed to be the mother of my grandchild."

My head whips around, and I see Mr. Montgomery leaning against his '57 Corvette, still in mint condition.

I place my hand up to my forehead, shielding the sun from my eyes, watching as he uncrosses his arms and ankles and heads in my direction.

"I'm sorry?" I ask, trying not to allow him to see my fear.

He stops once he's less than a foot away from me and slowly removes his sunglasses before tucking them inside of his black suit jacket.

"Let's cut the shit," he says, looking me directly in the eyes.

"You and I should've had this conversation a long time ago. For that, I apologize."

Sweat starts dripping down my neck, and I try to hold eye contact with him.

"I have eyes and ears all over this town, and there's nothing that did or ever will happen here that I don't know about. That goes for the things my idiot son likes to do as well."

My heart is thumping so hard now that I can hear it in my ears. I'm afraid Mr. Montgomery may be able to hear it as well.

"Now, if I remember correctly, you used to be a smart girl," he says, reaching out and tucking a stray hair behind my ear.

I want to run inside and find Asher. My head turns and scans my surroundings, praying there's someone close enough to see this interaction. There's no one in sight. The feeling Mr. Montgomery gives me when he touches me is the same as when Brad violated me. Their touch makes me physically sick.

"So, I shouldn't have to explain to you what your life would be like if the town found out that you murdered my grandchild." He pulls his hand away from me as my eyes dart back to his.

"I wonder what the church would think of your devoted mama. Do you think they'd enjoy hearing that she raised such a sinner of a daughter?"

I can feel the tears trying to break the surface, but I use all my strength to hold them back.

He's right, and I hate how right he is. If anyone found out what I did, they wouldn't even care about my side of the story. They wouldn't see me as the victim that I was. They would only see Brad as the father who lost his chance at parenthood, and they would play me out to be the murderous mother. The church is my mama's lifeline. I have no doubt that she would pick them over me. I don't even want to run the scenarios through my head of how my dad would react.

"Mr. Montgomery," I start to choke out. "I don't understand why you're doing this."

He reaches into his suit pocket and pulls his sunglasses back out, holding them at his chest for a moment as he continues to speak.

"Auden, you need to remember that actions have consequences. And, sweetheart, your decision to return to Monroe will not bring you the outcome you desired."

A tear runs down my cheek, and I hate myself for not being strong enough to hold it back. He puts his sunglasses back on and reaches out to wipe the tear away with his thumb, continuing to hold his thumb against my cheek.

"Now, I'm going to head inside and continue mourning my daughter-in-law's death. If you want my advice, you'll do exactly what you did six years ago and leave. Allow your parents the chance to preserve their reputation and potentially your relationship with them. Don't ever come back."

He removes his thumb from my face and reaches back into his suit pocket, pulling out a white envelope and handing it to me.

"I took the liberty of helping to make this easy for you," he says, turning toward the funeral home.

"I hope I never see you again," he says as he walks away.

*

My eyes burn as I stare at the plane ticket in my hand, trying my hardest not to lose control in this moment. I look up at the funeral home and my heart aches knowing Asher is inside. I want to run to him and cry in his arms. I want him to fix it all, but I know he can't. There's no way that he could change the minds of everyone in Monroe, as desperately as I wish he could.

Mr. Montgomery is right, and I hate him for it.

Both Asher and I were raised here. Even if he had the strength and heart to love me after finding out what I did, I couldn't put him through that. He just lost his sister, and I've been selfishly laying more pain on him every day since. I'm not worthy of his love if I allowed him to carry more of my pain. I can't allow him to have the choice of picking me or his life, career, and family. Everyone in this town is connected to the church, his family included. If Asher chose me, his family would have to disown him or lose the support of everyone at church as well. They could never accept me after what I did. And the truth alone that Brad and I were together, no matter the situation, could tear the Landry family apart.

The church is so clear about their views on abortion. It's murder. It doesn't matter if the mother would die if she tried to carry the pregnancy to term. They would view that as God's will. It doesn't matter if I was sixty-five or nine years old. They would condemn me to hell for not giving a cell life. They don't care that if I were to have my rapist's child, I would have given up my future and been stuck raising a baby that made me want to die every time I looked at it.

The week I knew I had Brad's seed inside of me was the worst of my life. I didn't sleep, and I couldn't eat. I wanted to take a blade from my dad's tool bench and rip the damn thing out of my body myself. I was willing to risk death before I would bring another Montgomery into this world.

Nausea takes over me, and I lean behind a Ford Focus, vomiting on the paved parking lot. The tears start to stream down my sweaty cheeks as I continue to heave behind the bumper, trying to catch my breath. I lower myself to the ground and lean up against the car next to my own bile, resting my head against its hot exterior.

My mama wouldn't survive hearing this truth. And I don't think I'd survive losing her or knowing that I took away the thing she loves the most, her church. I've seen it happen many times growing up, and I know that no matter how loyal she's been to them, they would disown her the moment word got out. My dad wouldn't be able to handle watching Mama go through that, and they'd both lose everything once the town stopped using Dad as their mechanic. The destruction my truth would bring far exceeds my own pain.

I reach into my bag and find a pen, pulling the plane ticket out of its envelope and placing it carefully into my purse.

THIRTY-SIX

Asher

I shake the last guest's hand at the exit of the funeral home, looking over his shoulder into the parking lot for a final time, hoping Auden will come running toward the door with an explanation of why she never returned.

My dad starts to walk over followed by my mother, and he puts his hand on my shoulder.

"How are you holding up, Son?" he asks.

"I'm holding," I reply, giving him a closed lip grin.

This day has been so emotional. I almost let Brad get the best of me, I confessed my love to Auden, and I said my last goodbye to my sister, something you can never be prepared for.

All three of us start to head to the parking lot, and I walk my mother to the passenger side of their car, her arm linked in mine. I open her door, and she turns to me before getting in, wrapping her arms around me and holding on extra tight.

"It was so good to see Auden," she whispers to me before kissing my cheek and taking her seat.

"I love you, Mom," I say before shutting the door and heading to my Jeep.

My heart feels like it's on fire as I slowly make my way through the parking lot. Where was Auden? All kinds of possibilities run through my head. What if she got hit by a car and no one knows yet? Or she freaked out after I told her I loved her. What if Brad got ahold of her after he left an hour earlier and she's locked up in his house?

I shake my head at how ridiculous that last thought is, but is it really that crazy? I've learned so much about what Brad's capable of over the last week that it may be naive to assume he isn't willing to do such an outrageous thing.

When I reach my Jeep, I spot a ripped envelope on the windshield and reach for it, noticing my name written on it. I flip it over and see a note written to me.

Asher,

I'm sure another letter is the last thing you need at this moment, and I'm so sorry I have to be the one writing it. I need you to know that you are worthy of so much love, and I wish I could be the one to give you that. You have changed my life for the better, and for that, I will forever be grateful. You thanked me for being honest with you last night, and I wish that I was. But there's a part of me that you still don't know, and I can't bring myself to tell you. I want you to keep the good memories of us. The memories I know I will hold onto for the rest of my life. You have transformed my life in such a positive way, and I can never express how thankful I am for you. Don't ever doubt that Taylor wasn't proud of you because she was, and she still is. There's no way she couldn't be.

I have to leave before I ruin your life. I have to leave before I ruin your parents' lives and my parents' lives.

I will miss you all so much.

Thank you for giving me a chance to remember a good part of Louisiana.

And for loving me, even if it was just for a short while.

Xo, Auden

I throw the letter back onto my windshield and throw my face into the palms of my hands, pulling them down slowly as I pace around my truck.

What the hell is she doing? We talked only a few hours ago about how we were going to face all this together. She seemed so confident in us. She believed me. I told her I loved her, and within hours, she's about to leave me behind without any real explanation.

I kick my foot into the tire, and a stinging pain shoots through my leg.

"Fuck!"

I need to know what the hell happened. I need to know who got to her and what threats were made. I need to know what could've possibly torn her away from me this time, when I feel like I need her the most.

I look back at the funeral home where Taylor is still laying, cold and alone.

*

I knock on the door of the Sterling household, knowing Mr. Sterling must be home because his pickup is in the driveway. Mrs. Sterling comes to the screen door and opens it for me, her face full of surprise.

"Asher," she says, opening the door further and stepping out to give me a hug. "Is everything alright, Dear?"

"It's good to see you, Mrs. Sterling. Everything is okay. Is Auden here?" I ask.

She holds the screen door open wider, motioning for me to come in. I take a step inside, noticing Mr. Sterling at the kitchen table, a plate of roast in front of him and realize I'm interrupting their dinner.

"I apologize, I didn't mean to interrupt," I say, walking over to Mr. Sterling and reaching out my hand.
"I was just wondering if ya'll knew where Auden was."

Mr. Sterling's face has a look of sadness on it, a look I haven't seen him wear before. He wipes his mouth with his napkin before returning my handshake.

"She came home and grabbed her bag about an hour ago. She said she couldn't make it to the funeral with us tomorrow, and said she had to leave back to . . ." Mrs. Sterling pauses, not knowing if she can reveal Auden's whereabouts.

She's running again. I look at the clock and see it's already 7:15. I turn to head toward the door, prepared to race to the airport but something stops me first. I turn back and face both of them, taking in a deep breath as I contemplate how to say what needs to be said.

"Mr. and Mrs. Sterling," I start to say. "I don't ever want to be disrespectful, especially not to the parents of the girl I've found myself falling in love with." Mrs. Sterling's posture straightens, and she lets out a quiet gasp. "But I need you to know the truth, and it's going to be hard to hear."

Mrs. Sterling's eyebrows furrow, and I can tell it's becoming hard for her not to interrupt. I look down at Mr. Sterling, and he's turned his chair so he can face me, giving me his full attention.

"I know about Mr. Calhoun coming here, and I know what he said would happen if Auden continued to lie. But she wasn't lying."

I can feel my stomach tying into knots, and it takes everything in me to keep going.

"In fact, it was Mr. Calhoun and the Montgomerys who have been lying. Auden may hate me for the rest of her life for telling y'all her truth. But if that's the case, then I'll risk it if it means you both know what she's been dealing with since the day she left Monroe."

Mrs. Sterling puts one hand out as if she's trying to interrupt, but I keep talking before she gets the chance.

"Brad Montgomery took advantage of your daughter six years ago, and my sister," I pause and take a deep breath, "Taylor, didn't believe her. And she should have because it's true."

I watch as Mr. Sterling's shoulders slump with the realization of what really happened, one hand covering his mouth as if it all made sense now, the other in a fist, tapping aggressively against his knee like he's contemplating what to do next.

"Auden would never betray Taylor the way that Brad has been saying she did. And she's had to live with Taylor believing that for the last six years. And now I'm coming to find out that Taylor had a hard time living with the truth that she didn't stand by her best friend when she should have. But I have made the decision to stand by Auden, and I'm only telling y'all because I hope you can find it in your hearts to make the same decision."

I take a step back and nod my head at them both.

"Thank you for letting me into your home, and I'm sorry to leave in a rush, but the love of my life may be getting on a plane as we speak," I say, nodding my head to both of them again and racing out the door.

I get in the driver's seat and head straight to the airport, praying I'm not too late and didn't just make the worst decision for Auden's life.

THIRTY-SEVEN

Auden

When I sat waiting for my plane to Louisiana, I felt an overwhelming sense of anxiety and fear—the unknown of how my parents would react seeing me, the potential of seeing anyone from my hometown was so intense, I'm still not sure how I made it on that plane. Now as I sit here waiting to return home to Minneapolis, I can't help but feel the tugging of my heart strings telling me to stay. I didn't even call Dec to let him know I'm flying home. He would have asked too many questions knowing that the funeral is tomorrow. I don't need another person trying to talk me into staying. The truth is that my heart is trying desperately to convince my body to stay in Asher's arms and trust that he will make everything right.

My heart thinks it's fallen in love in just five days. That's absolutely insane. Isn't it? It doesn't matter if I keep looking behind me every couple of seconds as I put my items inside the security bins. It doesn't matter if my heart aches as the security guard waves me through, allowing me access to my terminal to Minneapolis. It doesn't matter if Asher's voice keeps replaying "I love you" in my mind. Each step I take brings me closer to my gate.

I pull my phone out and see Dec calling, my heart instantly tells me to answer, so I decline it, knowing I need to follow my head instead.

These are the last few moments I'll spend in the state of Louisiana. There's something telling me that I have unfinished business here. But what more do I expect myself to do? My presence clearly just causes more people pain, and I can't keep doing this.

Failure keeps coming to mind. I'm failing Taylor again by leaving without another truth being revealed. But maybe the truth isn't always meant to be told.

If the truth is told, yes, maybe there's a chance that I'm believed this time. Yes, maybe, there's a chance that Brad is held accountable for his actions, and others are spared from his future endeavors. Yes, maybe, Asher choses to love me even after he hears my full truth.

Or maybe everything Mr. Montgomery threatened all happens. My parents lose even more because of my choices, and the family I always considered my second family loses more than just their daughter. I can't and I won't be the one who takes that risk.

I hear the intercom announcing that my plane has just landed, and they'll be boarding within the hour. I'm so exhausted from this draining week. The smell of coffee catches my attention. I head over to the airport café and order myself a grande, hoping to get a grip on my thoughts once I have a little caffeine in me. When I reach into my purse and hand the cashier my card, I see the white envelope at the bottom of the bag. The last letter Taylor left.

When I take my seat back at my gate, I reach back into my bag and pull out the letter, slowly running my fingers along the envelope's edge.

"Why did you have to do this Taylor?" I whisper to myself.

I sit and stare at the envelope for a few minutes before I get the courage to open it, knowing these are the final words I will receive from my old friend.

As I unfold the letter, I notice the dried tear drops that stain it. I run my fingers along them, feeling the rough texture they created over the smooth surface of the paper. The weight of those tears feel like they linger in the air around me, reminding me of all the hard things Taylor had faced and written to me in the letters, leading up to this final one. None of the previous letters contained tear stains, not even the one she died holding. That fact alone rattles me to my bones. Fear of what made Taylor end her life, or even more, fear of what made Taylor feel relief in knowing it was the last few moments of her life.

5/12/23

Auden,

You would think the years passing would take away my longing to talk to you, but I feel I miss you the most today. I miss your level head and your forceful nature I have learned to appreciate now that it's gone. I don't know what to do.

I've been counting down the days until today so I could get this off my chest. I've even gone as low as checking your parents' mailbox when your mama's at church, hoping you sent something with a return address.

Brad still lives at home with me and has started working for his father even though he's still a year away from the bar exam. He's gone quite a bit, and I've learned to appreciate that. When he is home, he expects me to be there too. I stopped taking the anxiety medication regularly almost a year ago, but Brad doesn't know that. I hide them so he won't get suspicious. I still take them when he wants to make love because there's no love to be found with him anymore, and it's become too much to bear. I finally said again that I wanted to go to college and get a degree. He demanded that it was time to start a family, and that I won't have any time to go to school or work a job once I have children at home. You know that kids have always been a dream of mine, but now it feels like a nightmare.

    And that nightmare came true.

    Auden, I'm pregnant. And I can't have this baby.

    I think Brad may be a real-life demon. You warned me, and I would do anything to turn back time and listen. He's terrifying and cruel. I could never bring a baby into a world where he's the father.

    But I can't have an abortion. I wouldn't be able to go through with it, and I would hate myself for it. If anyone ever found out, I would be ruined for good, and maybe even lose Asher, the one good thing still in my life.

    I feel so angry, and I want to blame you for not being here. But I know now that I should've run after you in my driveway, and I should've believed you like I did everything else in our lives.

    Please pray for me as I always have for you. Please come home.

    Happy (late) 24th Birthday, Auden, and may all the Birthdays to come be just as happy.

    I'll be waiting at the gates to meet again,

    Taylor

The letter falls from my fingers onto the carpeted airport floor.

She was pregnant. Her life with him became so terrifying that the thought of making him a father was unbearable. I can't stop myself from weeping as the realization sets in. I want to find her and hold her and tell her that I understand how she feels more than anyone could. But it's too late. She's already gone. She took care of the situation in the only way she thought she could. I bury my face into my hands, my shoulders shaking uncontrollably as reality keeps crashing in.

I slide my butt off the chair and sink onto the floor next to the letter, trying my hardest to catch my breath. I don't care about anyone around me and how loudly I'm howling in this airport. If they had any idea what I had just read, the whole airport would be flooded from all our tears.

The sound of Dec's voice pops into my head, telling me to breathe. *Breathe, Auden. You're okay. Just breathe.* I try to slowly suck the oxygen in.

The intercom comes on and the attendant announces that it's time for all small children to board our plane. I stand, collect the letter, and shove it in my bag, contemplating what to do next. I see a family joining the line to board, a mother and father with two small children, one in a stroller and a little boy holding onto his mother's hand. The little boy turns around and faces me, giving me a big smile and a wave. I notice he has a tiny birthmark on the inside of his wrist just like Taylor did.

I turn away from him, trying to keep myself calm, and I shove my hands in the pockets of my black dress that I never changed out of. My left hand catches on something thin and crinkled. I pull it out, and it's a small, white piece of paper. I unroll it in my hand and flatten it in my palm so I can read it.

It's a note that Taylor must have sneaked into my pocket on the day of my gram's funeral. It's faded now, but if I hold it up to the light, I can make out what it says.

Keep this note with you forever. I will always be with you.

You are strong.
You will get through this.
Trust in yourself.

THIRTY-EIGHT

Asher

I almost ran right off the road multiple times trying to drive and simultaneously search for flights to Minneapolis. The thought of missing Auden before she takes off back to Minneapolis makes me break out in a sweat. My thoughts are all over the place, and I know I shouldn't be driving.

I exit the expressway and can see the airport towers. My right foot is pushing down on the gas, and my left won't stop bouncing as I race to the terminals.

My mind can't figure out what I've done to make her feel like she has to run instead of telling me what's going on. I tell the girl I'm falling in love with her, and she still thinks I wouldn't walk through hell for her, or at least beside her. She mentioned that she hasn't been honest, something that most people would be infuriated by. But I can't help but feel an ache in my heart knowing that she still has a secret weighing on her, a secret that is still holding her back from truly living her life. I want to take all that weight from her and put it on myself.

Taylor's passing has shown me just how untroubled my own life has been, and just how willing I am to shoulder the pain of others when they're struggling. I just need to know about it.

She said she had to leave before she ruined my life. Has she really been so blind that she can't see how much better my life is with her in it? I don't want to go back to living without her now that I've had a taste of how sweet she makes everything just by being present.

My bluetooth goes off when Dec is returning my phone call, and I quickly answer it.

"She's on Delta but sent my call to voicemail," Dec says.

"I don't understand why she's doing this, Dec. I told her that I love her and that I would move the damn mountains if that's what it takes. And within a few hours, she's left me a note on the back of a piece of trash and is trying to fly away. What am I not seeing here? What am I doing wrong?"

I hear Dec sigh, and it's taking everything in me to keep my eyes focused on the road.

"Asher, from my point of view, you haven't done anything wrong. In fact, it sounds like you're doing everything you can to help and support her. Shit, dude, you're in a high school love story right now, racing to the damn airport to stop the woman you love from flying out of your life forever."

The way he describes my current situation is somewhat comedic, and, at the same time, completely heart wrenching because the idea of not making it to her in time and losing her forever is too much for me to handle.

"Do you think she'll stay if she sees me?" I ask, my voice shaking as the fear kicks in.

"Honestly, Auden is one of the most hard-headed people I have ever met, but that's what I love about her. I love being able to witness her hard exterior being shaved away as she pushes through new challenges, and I think if anyone can get her to stay in Monroe right now, it's you."

 I hang up with Dec as soon as I drive up to the terminals and find myself in the back of a long trail of cars, taxis, and shuttles. Delta is three terminals in, and I can't find a way to weave in and out without being sent back through the line having to circle the entire airport again.

 "Damn it!" I yell, hitting my hands against the steering wheel.

 There's only twenty-five minutes until her flight takes off. If I wait in this line any longer, there's no way I'll find her in time. Especially if I have to stop and buy a ticket, pass through security, and make it to her gate. I try to call her cellphone again, but it just keeps ringing. She's making this incredibly difficult.

 A spot opens on the curb in front of Allegiant, and I whip my Jeep in, slamming it into park and stepping out with the key still in the ignition. The second I step out, a security guard points up at the sign stating "no parking," and I ignore him, passing right by and giving no shits about what he'll do in response.

 "Hey man! You can't leave your car here!" I hear him yell, followed by the static of his radio.

 There's so many people getting in and out of vehicles around me that they all blend together. In and out of the automatic doors, hugging and linking together, making my path even harder to move through.

 I accidentally knock my elbow into a short businessman and spill his coffee, ignoring as he cusses, "Jackass." He's right. I am a jackass. I'm a jackass for splashing his coffee and for never considering how unhappy my sister was. I'm a jackass for allowing Auden out of my sight, knowing that so many people in town wanted access to her. I'm a jackass for not ripping Brad out of the visitation by his throat and telling everyone what type of man he truly is.

My whole body feels like it's trembling as I frantically weave in and out of more passengers until I hear it.

"I need to head back to Monroe."

I move past a family unloading from a taxi, and I see her. She's standing on the outside of the exit doors, handing her bag to a taxi driver, and taking a step down off the curb. I yell her name. She pauses for a moment and looks back over her shoulder, her eyes looking directly at me.

"Asher?" she asks, her face filled with confusion.

I take a step down behind the taxi and gently tap the driver on the shoulder, reaching into his trunk and grabbing Auden's bag out.

"I'll take that, Sir," I say to him. "Thank you."

I step back onto the curb and take Auden's hand, pulling her out of the way and over to the side with me.

"What are you doing here?" she asks.

I shake my head. She should already know, but my heart feels nothing but relief that I found her.

"You know what I'm doing here, Auden," I say, giving her a smile so she knows I'm not upset. "I couldn't let you run away again, not without talking to you first."

She breaks eye contact and looks down at our hands, "Asher, I . . ."

I pull her into my arms and wrap myself around her, ignoring the many passengers pushing their way around us.

"Auden, I told you that I've fallen in love with you, and I meant it. I told you I would stand by you, and we would face everything together, and, damn it, Auden, I meant it."

I pull her away from me so she can see the seriousness in my eyes.

"I won't chase you again. If you truly want to leave and forget about all of this, I will let you go. But I couldn't let you get on a plane without you knowing that you have me. You have me, and I don't want to lose you if there's any chance that you feel the same way. You said I make you feel seen. Well, I see you right now. I see you trying to run away when I'm right here begging you to allow me to fight for you."

She shakes her head. "Asher, I haven't been honest with you."

I feel my shoulder being pulled back, and the security guard is standing behind me. He leans over to catch his breath, his hand still on my shoulder to keep him supported, "You're not allowed to leave your car in the unloading area, man," he says.

I turn back to Auden and take her hand again.

She looks over at the security guard, her eyes wide and her cheeks flushing with embarrassment. He looks back with eyes just as wide as he processes why I frantically pulled in here.

"None of that matters right now, if there's anything inside of you that is telling you to stay, come back with me now. Don't make this man tow my truck."

She squeezes my hand, and I apologize to the security guard as we walk back to my Jeep.

THIRTY-NINE

Auden

Asher reaches over and holds my hand as we near my parents' street. I give him a squeeze as I look out at the darkness surrounding us.

Asher told me that he couldn't handle my parents thinking so poorly of me and apologized for telling them about what Brad did to me six years ago. If you'd have asked me before how I'd feel if Asher told my parents my secret, I probably would've told you that I'd never speak to him again. Violating my trust, especially on such a personal subject, is something I thought I could never forgive. But now that he's told them, I can't help but feel a sense of relief that it was him instead of me.

My mom doesn't always listen to me, and when she does, she doesn't always take me very seriously. I doubt it could've gone any better if I had been the one to tell them. But I can't help but feel as if my dad isn't going to look at me the same again, not that he did anyways after Mr. Calhoun's visit. There's just something different about disappointing your mom versus your dad. It stings more to me, and it brings a more intense feeling of self-disappointment.

We turn down my parents' street, and Asher kisses the top of my hand to let me know he's with me no matter what.

"Are you ready for this?" he asks.

I keep my eyes focused out the window, noticing as more stars fill the sky the closer we get. That's one thing I forgot that I loved about my childhood home. There isn't another place in the world where you can see the sky so full of stars like my parents' backyard.

"No," I reply, "but no more running, right?"

Asher puts his car in park, and I notice the lights still on inside of the house. My heart skips a beat knowing I now have to face them. He gets out of his seat and goes to the back door, opening it and grabbing my bag.

Breathe, Auden. Just breathe.

Asher opens my door and offers me his hand. I take it, slowly lifting myself out of his car and heading toward my parents' steps. Each step feels like a mountain as I try to control my breathing and body, feeling like my knees could buckle and I could collapse at any moment.

Asher reaches out and opens the door, holding it for me as I take a step in.

I remove my shoes, looking into an empty kitchen. Asher is still right behind me as I take another step, passing through the kitchen and rounding the corner to the living room.

Mama and Dad are sitting in their matching, overstuffed recliners. Dad's reading the newspaper, and Mama's reading her Bible. Mama lowers it, setting it on the small wooden table next to her and removes her reading glasses.

"Auden," she says, her voice soft and empty.

I feel Asher's hand on my waist, guiding me over to the couch across from them. My dad folds up his newspaper and sets it down on the carpet next to his chair before lowering his feet from the recliner. I stop myself from taking a seat on the couch when I notice my dad coming to a stance. He walks straight for me, around the glass coffee table and grabs both of my shoulders, pulling me to his chest, his musky cologne filling my nostrils as he holds me against him.

"Baby fish, I am so sorry. We had no idea," he whispers into my hair before giving my head a kiss.

I hear Mama's recliner closing and her footsteps heading in my direction. Dad's arm opens, one still wrapped around me and the other allowing Mama's arms to come to my side, joining my dad and wrapping herself around the both of us, making me feel like I'm covered in the safest blanket.

"We're here, baby," she says, her voice choking up. "You aren't alone in this."

My heart swells as they hold me like they did when I was a child. I start to lose control, crying into them both.

They believe me. Something I never thought would happen. But here I am, listening to them apologize for not knowing what pain I was holding in. There's been a dark spot on my heart where Monroe had been for the last six years. I swear that in this moment I can feel the blood pumping through again.

They release me after a few moments, and I join Asher on the couch. I turn to Asher and put one hand on his knee, looking back and forth between all three of them as I try to muster the courage to tell them my last secret.

"I haven't been honest with you, and I don't know if you'll be able to accept this as easily as you've accepted what happened." I turn to Mama and look her in the eyes, trying to hold back my own fear of being judged.

"You may never forgive me, and I would understand that." I close my eyes and drop my head to my chest. I'm taking a moment, but I know I need to get this out before I change my mind.

People don't really talk about abortions. It's not a topic that comes up lightly unless talking about your politics or your options. But when it does, you can feel the air in the room shift. People aren't comfortable with the topic because some hate it and view it as one of the most vicious crimes you can commit—a form of murder. While others see it as basic medical care and a human right. When you don't know everyone's view on the subject, it becomes uncomfortable. And everyone feels it. This is true whether you've had an abortion or not.

Occasionally, in rare moments, you may come across someone openly sharing their personal experience with abortion. Or you see an advertisement on TV or in a magazine discussing the various emotions that can accompany the decision. In these instances, it is not uncommon to hear about feelings of regret, the emotional pain involved, or the sense of relief that some experience.

There have been a few moments when I've questioned myself, wondering why I didn't feel any sense of regret. It's understandable why some may feel that way. Often, those who undergo abortions have had to navigate through a multitude of challenging options beforehand. Sometimes, they may have even attempted to conceive that pregnancy, only to find that their bodies were unable to sustain it.

I get why people have those hard feelings. I really do. I had hard feelings walking in there too. I was alone, scared, and completely freaking out. But I was also so unbelievably relieved when it was over. I need to learn how to accept that feeling relief is okay. Even if the topic of abortion still makes the room feel heavy around me, I am allowed to feel thankful that I had one. I'm allowed to not regret it. Because I don't.

I don't regret making my future my first priority.

I don't regret not throwing myself into the category of single teen mother.

I don't regret fighting for the rest of my life.

I don't regret not allowing a piece of Brad to feed off my body for nine months.

I don't regret not bringing a child into this world who would have a father that has no moral courage and a mother who would hate them for that.

I don't regret saving my own mental health from a lifetime of what-ifs as I spiral through a hellish life.

I don't regret it at all. The only thing I regret is how often I feel scared of people finding out how I had to save my own life.

I turn to Asher, looking him in the eyes and searching for his support. He gives it. He smiles at me and pulls me closer to him, kissing the top of my head and silently telling me it'll all be okay.

I sit back up and face my parents, taking in one final breath of courage.

"After Brad assaulted me," I start to say, keeping my eyes on the old buck head hanging on the wall between my parents' heads. "I tried to go on with my life like normal. I really did. But a week before graduation, I felt off." I swallow, trying to hold back tears, tucking my hands between my legs to keep them from shaking. "I realized that I was . . . pregnant."

I turn my eyes to the floor, unable to look at anyone's reaction. I hear my mama gasp and my heart sinks. I knew she'd be the most hurt by what I have to say next. Asher puts his hands over mine, making sure I know that he's still here with me the way he promised.

"I couldn't do it. I couldn't live with a child who came from the worst day of my life. So, I made a decision. The day I turned eighteen, I got in a taxi with my bags packed, and I headed for the airport, stopping at a clinic on my way."

"Oh, Lord, no." I hear my mama say as she begins to weep.

Asher's arms wrap around me, and he pulls me closer as Mama stands from her chair.

"I need to pray," she says, heading out of the living room.

Asher lays hard kisses on the top of my head and forehead, never letting go of me while I sit in the silence. Once I steady my breath, I turn my head and look at my dad, his hand wrapped around his chin and his eyes stuck on the floor as he processes what I just said.

He stands up, and I brace myself for his exit. But instead, he joins me on the couch, grabbing hold of one of my hands and pulling me to face him.

"Auden, I love you," he says. "You had to make a decision that I could never imagine having to make."

I feel a tear stream down my cheek, followed by another.

"Mama will come to terms with this, but for now, she needs time to process."

I nod my head so that he knows I understand.

"We may not agree with the decision you made, and some others may even hate the decision you made and be cruel to you. But God loves you either way, and so do I, Auden. You know that right?" he asks.

I nod my head, and he pulls me to him, laying a kiss on my head. He lets me go a moment later and stands up from the couch, walking around the coffee table and putting out his hand to Asher.

"Thank you for not letting us go another six years in the dark with Auden," he says as Asher brings himself up from the couch to shake his hand. "You're a good man, Son, and Auden is lucky to have you in her life. We all are."

Asher gives my dad a nod and a closed lip smile, shaking his hand back.

"Sir, I would do anything for your daughter," he replies.
"Even when she doesn't want me to!"

My dad looks down at me and gives me a smile before turning back to Asher.

"She likes the stars, and they sure are shining tonight. She'll probably sleep outside in her favorite spot. We don't allow unmarried couples to stay in the same bed in this home, so I can't invite you to stay. Anyways, I'll be going to sleep now and won't be getting up until around 7:30 tomorrow morning."

He turns to me and bends down, giving me one more kiss on the cheek and a wink before he turns to head off to bed.
Did he just give Asher permission to sneak into our backyard?

"I always thought this town was too small for you, Auden, that you needed to go out and find your place in this world. You needed change that Monroe couldn't give you. I think I may have been wrong. I think maybe this town needs you so it can change, my little fish."

FORTY

Asher

    I park my Jeep around the corner from the Sterling house and sneak through a clearing of trees into their backyard. Auden is standing a few feet from the garage with a pile of blankets and sleeping bags. She's changed out of her dress and is now in just the grey t-shirt I didn't realize she still had. She's stuck in a gaze up at the sky with a smile across her face. I pause for a moment before she notices I'm there, soaking in her peacefulness for as long as I can. Seeing her so happy over such a simple thing like sleeping under the stars reminds me of how simple her wants in this world are. She's not the type of girl who needs anything fancy. She just wants to be surrounded by the beauty in the world, and that alone makes her such a precious being.
    She notices me when I finally start to walk toward her, taking her face in my hands as soon as I'm close enough, leaning down and giving her a soft but highly anticipated kiss.
    When I pull away, her eyes are still shut for a moment, and I catch a glimpse of a smile.
    "What was that for?" she asks as she opens her eyes.

It's adorable and heartbreaking that she needs to ask why I would want to kiss her.

"Because you're beautiful and brave. And I'm so happy I get to sleep under the stars with you."

My comments make her cheeks flush, and I can't help but lean in and kiss her again.

We start to head further out into the back yard. I follow her as she leads me to a spot that she clearly knows is the best in the far left corner. Once we get there, she stops, turns around, and grabs my head with both of her hands.

"Do not look up until I tell you to," she says, her voice stern and serious.

"Yes, Ma'am," I reply, pulling a blanket out and laying it flat onto the grass.

I set two pillows directly next to each other on top of the blanket. I grabbed an old gaslit lantern from my Jeep and set it next to the box of Girl Scout thin mints that Auden had stashed in her bag before laying two more blankets down for us to sleep under. I lean down and start to light the lantern, but Auden stops me, instructing me to lay down on the blanket instead.

"Keep your eyes closed," she says as she leans down and lays her head on the pillow next to me.

Both of our backs are flat against the blanket when I feel Auden's hand grab ahold of mine.

"Are you ready?" she asks.

"Ready."

She squeezes my hand and I open my eyes, looking up at the deep indigo canvas full of tiny sparkles of light.

"Isn't it the most beautiful sight you've ever laid eyes on?"

I turn and face her, watching as the sides of her mouth curve upward and her eyes twinkle with the reflection of the stars.

"This is where I would come any time I needed to escape. I liked to think that each star is another person out there that felt just as lost as I did."

She turns her body to face me and tucks both of her hands under her pillow.

"What made you feel so lost, Auden?" I ask, reaching out and tucking a hair behind her ear.

She gives me a closed lip grin, her eyes trailing the length of my arm all the way up to my shoulder and stopping just above it.

"I guess I've never really felt like I fit in here in Monroe. Everyone seems to have always had their lives planned out. They knew what they were going to be when they grew up or what their role was going to be, and there was never much change. It felt like a suffocating routine that I didn't conform to."

She reaches out and brushes her hand through my hair, causing me to close my eyes and memorize every stroke. I want to appreciate every moment where she wants to physically connect. I've been with plenty of women, and each one had their own physical experiences before me. To my knowledge, none of them had a traumatic experience that scared them off from intimacy like Auden did. I was able to touch them and be touched by them without much of a second thought. But Auden's precious. She's been underappreciated, and her body has been treated so poorly that she convinced herself that it's damaged. I want to show her how wrong she is, and how her body deserves to be worshiped. And being touched by her is a privilege.

She turns her body back so she can take in the stars again, but I stay still, soaking up every emotion she's feeling as she continues to talk.

"Taylor and I were always so close. But she never really understood why I felt so different from the rest of the people in our town. She still supported my dreams of finding my place in the world one day. She loved Monroe, and she wanted to continue to love all the kids in Monroe. She always told me that she hoped I'd run into the other lost stars someday."

I watch as a tiny tear drop slides down the side of her face, and I wipe it away.

"She was meant to teach all of the littles in this town, and she was meant to tell kids that they weren't different. They were just stars that hadn't found their universe yet."

I roll back onto the blanket and stare up at the sky, breathing in the fresh, cold air as I absorb what Auden just said.

"Maybe Taylor was meant to show you how to find your place so that you could go out and collect all the other little stars," I whisper.

We both stay silent for a few moments and take in the night and all the emotions that we've both battled and embraced the last few days. I feel Auden shift her body back so she's facing me, and I lift my arm up, inviting her to snuggle against my chest. She scooches closer and lays her head down on me, running her hand up and down my stomach. I love how perfectly she fits next to my body.

"Have you ever been in love before?" she asks.

I wrap my arm around her shoulder, keeping her snug against me.

"No, I've never had a strong enough connection to anyone to say that I loved them," I reply.

"Have you been with a lot of women?"

I pause for a moment, making sure I know what I want to say before I say it. It's easy to see a man who's been with a lot of women intimately and assume that he just wanted to use their bodies. Maybe I'm guilty of doing that to an extent. But I've never intentionally led anyone to believe that I was using them. I just never felt anything more than lust with other girls before Auden.

"I have," I answer, keeping my eyes on the sky. "I've been with a lot of women, and all of them are worthy of so much love. But, for some reason, I never felt anything close to a deep connection with them. I'd end things as soon as I realized that."

She stops trailing her fingers and rests her hand on my chest.

"I've only been with two people in my life. I doubt I'd ever be able to compare to the women you've been with in bed."

I pull her closer to me, reaching my other arm over and gently lifting her chin so she can see my face and I can see hers. Her skin is glowing in the moonlight.

"Auden, sex is easy," I reply. "Sex is when you allow your body to touch and connect with another, following the exciting feelings as they come to you and moving your body in different ways to make each other feel good."

Her eyes stare at my lips as she listens to my explanation. My heart starts to pick up its pace as I think about the difference between her and other women.

"But sex with someone you love is a totally different thing. You aren't just pleasuring each other's bodies. You're consuming them. You aren't focused on your own needs because you need to become one with the other person. You feel as if you're starving, and the only way to feed yourself is to get so close to the other person that you become one. You let that person inside of you in every way imaginable."

I run my finger along her cheek and down her neck until I reach her collarbone, pulling the collar of the t-shirt until I see it fully exposed. My eyes drop to her chest as I notice her breathing pick up, and I can feel my pants starting to tighten with her reaction.

She looks up at me, and her eyes move back and forth between mine and my lips. I watch her, using all the strength I have in me to not devour her right this second. Her hand grips my shirt and I lean down, pulling her lips to mine. Every time she kisses me back, I feel the desperation for more of her consume me. I'm not sure how much longer I can handle my need for her.

She pulls her lips away and wraps her leg around my waist, pulling herself fully on top of me as she makes her way down my neck and over to my shoulder, leaving soft kisses along the path. My breathing starts to quicken, and I take ahold of her waist with both hands, pulling her closer and closing the gap between her thighs.

Her touch becomes too much for me. I lift her lips off me, pushing her up until I can see her entire face looking back at me.

"Auden, I can't handle you touching me like that," I say to her, as I feel her weight pushing on me in resistance.

"Asher, I need you," she replies. "I want you to make me feel the way you did last night. I want you to teach me how to make you feel just as good."

She scooches her hips back so she can see the top of my jeans, reaching down and unbuttoning them. I lift myself off the ground when she starts to yank at my waistline, pulling my jeans down to my thighs. She reaches back up to my briefs and starts to pull them down slowly. I stop her, holding both of her wrists until her eyes meet mine.

"Auden, you don't have to do this," I tell her. I want to make sure we don't cross any lines we can't come back from.

She repositions herself so she's on her knees, slowly leaning her head down and planting a kiss above my waist.

"I know that I don't have to do anything when it comes to you," she says, laying another kiss against my skin, this time her tongue slipping through her lips. "I want to taste you." I let out an involuntary groan.

"I want to feel you inside my mouth, Asher." Her words make me twitch below her chin. "And then I want you to show me how hungry you are for me."

She tugs at my briefs again, and I watch as she releases me, her eyes wide as she sees how big she's made me grow.

She leans her head down until her lips are inches from the tip of me, looking back up at me and smiling. My lips part, and it takes all of my self-control not to take her. I watch her tongue slowly touch the tip, trailing her warm saliva down to the base of me.

"Fuck, Auden," I whisper.

She trails her tongue back up my shaft, and her hand grabs ahold of the base, keeping me still as her mouth wraps around me. The moment the tip of me is snug inside of her warm embrace, I feel shivers down the length of me, forcing my eyes to close as I try to hold myself back from releasing immediately.

She removes her mouth from me, still holding onto the base.

"Open your eyes," she whispers. "I want you to watch me."

I do as she asks, reaching forward and running my hands through her hair, her eyes locked on mine. She's so damn sexy, and I've never been so scared of cumming before I get the chance to pleasure her.

She brings her head back down and starts to work her mouth up and down me, allowing me to go deeper with every slow bob of her head. She lets out a small moan as her lips meet her fingers, the back of her throat clamping down on me and bringing me close to the edge.

"Auden, please," I say, leaning up gently guiding her head off me. "I don't want too yet."

She sits back on her feet, her eyes starting to fill with disappointment.

"Did I do something wrong?" she asks.

I shake my head and hold the bottom of her t-shirt, looking back at her as I slowly run the tips of my fingers along her stomach.

"You are amazing, Auden. And the feeling of your mouth on me was about to make me cum harder than I believe I ever have."

I pull her t-shirt until she's close enough for me to take her waist, lifting her and wrapping her legs around me. I take her face in my hands and kiss her with all the passion I have, our tongues twisting together until we both need to take a breath of air. I lean in until my lips are directly over her ear, and I start to whisper to her.

"The first time I cum is going to be deep inside you as I watch your body shake in pleasure."

I hear her let out a gasp, and I push my groin into her, feeling her start to grind back into me with excitement.

"I want to hear you moan my name as your eyes roll to the back of your head."

She pushes me away from her until my back is flat on the ground and crosses her arms down across her body, grabbing ahold of her t-shirt and lifting it over her head, exposing her perfectly round breasts.

She looks me in the eyes, biting her bottom lip. "I need you now, Asher," she replies, her voice full of desperation.

I sit back up, my hands running along her back as I take her left breast in my mouth, suckling harder with each moan she releases. One of my hands drags across her skin, leaving a trail of goosebumps as I work my way to the front of her, pulling her panties to the side and slipping my hand in.

As soon as my fingertips enter her panties the warmness catches my attention, and I moan into her breast before pushing my fingers further until her wetness starts to cover them. She parts her legs further, and I can tell she's desperate to feel my touch again. I rub one fingertip along her, slipping into her opening as I watch her trying to control her breathing as she rocks back and forth, grinding into me.

I remove my hand from inside of her and lift her off me, laying her down on the blanket beside me as I push myself up until I'm leaning over her, grabbing her panties with both of my hands and pulling them down as she lifts herself until I pull them off the end of her feet and toss them over my shoulder. I position myself between her ankles, reaching forward and resting my hands on her knees. She takes both of her breasts into her hands, and my eyes lock on them as I watch her twirl her nipples in her fingertips, touching herself for the first time. I spread her knees until her legs are wide open, exposing her wet perfection in front of me, causing my mouth to start to water.

"You are so damn sexy," I whisper, leaning down onto my elbows until my mouth is hovering above her glistening slit.

I close my eyes and inhale her scent, pushing my groin into the blanket as her intoxicating scent fills my nostrils.

I can't wait another moment to taste her, and I lean forward, my tongue pushing between her lips as I push deeper, trailing up and circling around her swollen little mound. She moans as she reaches forward, grabbing the back of my head and pushing herself into my face.

My tongue starts to work up and down her, licking up every drop of her sweet juices as they continue to flow out of her, my cheeks and chin slipping against her thighs as I moan into her. I reach my arms under her legs and grip ahold of her ass cheeks, lifting her up into my face and sliding my tongue deep into her hole. I start to throb uncontrollably, but I don't stop licking.

I feel her starting to swell more and more as I pick up my pace and my fingers grip tighter against her cheeks, pulling them apart and exposing her fully to the cool night air. I slide my pinky further down her exposed crack until I feel it graze against her asshole, sending a moan from her lips as I feel her juices start to trickle against my pinky, lubricating her ass for me.

She holds her breath as she feels my finger circling her hole, an area I'm sure she never realized could bring her pleasure. I push my mouth deep into her, my nose rubbing up and down her slit and pushing my pinky into her hole and forcing her to gasp for air. I study her face and know she's close to orgasm as I slowly move my pinky in and out, as she thrusts herself against my face.

Her legs start to shake, and I know she's about to lose all control. I grip her legs tighter, making it impossible for her to move away from me as I thrust my pinky in and out, licking every inch of her sweetness at the same time until her jaw drops open, her head falling backward, and her grip on my head tightens. She moans my name as she releases into my mouth. I moan back, letting her know how much I love the taste of her.

Her body goes limp, and I stay between her legs, licking up the sweet juice she rewarded me with. She lets out soft whimpers as I continue while she tries to steady her breathing.

I wait until she stops throbbing, knowing she's calmed down. Then I reach my hand back up to her, using my index and ring finger to spread her lips apart before pressing my middle finger back into her, listening as she releases another gasp.

I sit up until I'm on my knees, looking over her perfect, naked body as my finger continues to swirl around her. Her eyes watch my free hand as it trails down to my jeans and briefs, working them off the end of my body until my bottom half is just as exposed as hers.

She sits up, keeping her legs spread and allowing me to keep pleasuring her as she reaches for my shirt, pulling it up and over my head. I reposition my hand back down onto her opening as she pulls me forward to her. Our lips connect, shoving her tongue deep into my mouth as my finger continues to flick against her.

"I want you inside of me," she moans into my mouth as her hand grabs hold of my throbbing member.

I let out a gasp as she works me up and down, matching the speed of my finger.

She lets go of me and grabs both of my shoulders, pushing me to the side and guiding me to the ground until I'm flat on my back. Her hands travel down my chest, slowly trailing kisses down wherever her hands last touched. My body starts to ache with the anticipation of feeling her wetness wrapped around me, and I reach up for her, letting go of her warmth and kneading both of her soft breasts in my palms. She sits up on her knees and holds herself directly above me, using one hand to grab my base and lining it up with her opening.

She slides me between her wet lips and holds me there, dragging my tip up and down her slit, teasing me against her hole. Her head leans upward and her eyes lock onto mine as she lowers herself, the tightness of her entrance grabbing the outside of my head.

She bites her lip as she pushes herself down, swallowing me whole. Her jaw drops open and she lets out a loud gasp, followed by a whimper. Her eyes are filling with satisfaction. I sit up the moment she's taken my full length, wrapping my arms around her bare back, pulling her chest against mine and starting to kiss every inch of her neck while she moans into my hair. I grip on to her ass cheeks and guide her back and forth as I slowly thrust inside of her, feeling every inch of her tightness as she pulsates against me.

She pushes my chest away until I'm laying back down, keeping both of her palms flat against me. She works herself up and down on her own, moaning as she watches my climax building with every movement.

"You feel so fucking good," she groans. I try to lift myself back up to kiss her but she resists, holding me down to watch her as she takes control.

I've never been so turned on as I am at this moment, watching her find her own pleasure and taking control of me as she brings both of us to the edge of climax. I feel my orgasm start to build and try to lift her off me so I can't release inside of her, but she pushes herself down harder, forcing me to lean up and try to lift her again.

She wraps her arms around my shoulders and pulls me in closer, leaning down to my ear and kissing it.

"Auden, I'm too close," I plead, still trying to pull her off of me as she thrusts against me, moaning into my ear.

"It's okay," she whispers, and I don't think she realizes what I meant.

"Baby please," I try to plead, using everything in me to hold back.

Her hands take my face in them, and she pushes her lips against mine, inhaling as she parts both of our lips.

"I need to feel all of you," she whispers into my mouth. "It's safe, trust me."

Her words send me over the edge, and I grip onto her tighter, taking back control and thrusting faster into her sweetness.

"I fucking love you, Auden," I moan as I watch her eyes start to roll back.

She starts to throb and pulsate against me, and her moans become louder as she reaches the point of ecstasy, sending me over the edge as I release myself into her.

When we both finish, I fall back to ground, her chest still touching mine as we both collapse together, gasping for air.

She wraps her naked body around me, holding me close as I run my fingers up and down her back while she begins to relax. "I love you, too," she whispers into my chest.

FORTY-ONE

Auden

Falling in love has never been a part of my life plan. Even back when I was crushing on boys and writing their names inside of hearts on the notes Taylor and I left one another. I was never the girl that had my wedding or future children's names planned out. I didn't even want to be touched or looked at by another man after Brad, and that eliminated the option of marriage all together. I had accepted this, and the option just floated away as I continued to move on with my life. But here I am laying against the chest of the man I just told I love you to. And I truly mean it. I love him with everything in me.

He tilts my chin up and looks down at me, his deep brown eyes making my heart dance.

"Are you okay?" he asks.

I feel my lips curving into a smile. His genuine concern for my wellbeing is a gift I never thought I would receive. I love him even more for it.

"I'm better than I've ever been," I reply, leaning forward and kissing him softly before resting my head against his chest.

"Auden, I shouldn't have been so reckless just now. It was stupid, and I'm so sorry I didn't stop myself."

I shake my head and lean up onto one of my elbows, looking down at him and hating how easy it is for him to try and take the blame from everyone else's decisions.

"Asher, you did as I asked. I wanted you to do it, and I meant it," I reply, meaning every word I speak to him.

He brushes his hand along the back of my shoulder, taking a moment to process what I just said.

"Auden, you've been through so much. I don't ever want to be the reason why you end up in another clinic."

Each second that goes by, he shows his true colors. His giant heart makes my heart grow a little bigger, filling with more love for him.

"You don't need to worry, Asher. I'm on birth control and have been since the day I left Monroe," I answer, watching as the anguish washes away from his face.

He pulls me back to his chest and kisses the top of my head, pulling a blanket from beside us and wrapping us both up in it.

"Good, because I have so many plans for us. And a baby just doesn't fit in them quite yet."

A surge of hope travels through me as I listen to him mentioning his future with me, a feeling I haven't felt with anyone before. It feels safe.

"You plan to have kids with me one day?"

"I plan on doing everything and anything with you, Auden," he replies "Kids, one day, only if you want."

I want to spend the rest of my life right here, laying in my favorite place under the sky full of stars, dreaming of every new experience we can share together. I want forever with this man, and I wish it started years ago.

We lay in each other's arms, soaking in each other's presence and the millions of stars dancing above our heads. "Auden, we need to talk about what happens next," he says.

I hold my breath, knowing that he's right but wanting to keep us here in this moment instead of moving back to the darkness tomorrow will bring. I don't want to make any decisions. I'm sick of fighting for people to believe me, and I just want to run away from it all, with Asher running beside me.

"I'm not ready for the coldness. I feel like if I try to share what happened again, it'll all become so dark again."

He rubs his hands up and down my arm as if he's trying to warm my body.

"What do you mean?"

"My last few weeks in Monroe before graduation were torture," I begin to explain. "I walked the halls of the school and felt nothing but emptiness. Everyone who looked at me made me feel like they knew what had happened, but not my side of the story, never my experience. Just the same assumptions Brad put into Taylor's head."

I take a deep breath, the smell of Asher's sweat mixed with his cologne making me feel safe enough to keep going.

"And once I found out I was pregnant, I felt as if everyone knew that as well and disowned me. I think I may have disowned myself and even blamed myself for being so reckless. I know how irrational this all sounds, but I'm terrified that if I go to the funeral tomorrow, that same shameful feeling will come back again. I don't think I can handle that."

Asher pulls me closer and kisses my forehead, sending a warmth through my body.

"Auden, you are so damn strong. I wish I could take away every fear you have ever had. I can't do that, but I can promise you that I love you. I love you with every inch of me, and I won't let you face anything else alone. So, whatever you decide from this moment on, I will support you and love you through every second of it. You won't ever be cold and alone again, because I'll be there, ready to warm you or freeze to death by your side."

I feel a sting in my chest as I listen to him describe how he wants to love and support me. As badly as I want to stay here and savor every second of this invaluable moment, I know I have to be honest with him. I have to tell him what I learned in the last letter from Taylor. It'll tear him apart, but I realize now that loving someone means keeping nothing from them, the good and the bad. I lift myself from his chest so we can see into each other's eyes, hoping he can see how much I truly love him.

"Asher, I read Taylor's last letter. It's the reason I was leaving the airport when you arrived."

His eyes stay glued on me, and I feel his body start to stiffen as he waits for what I have to say next.

"I'm so sorry, Asher," I say, knowing I'm about to break his heart. "She was pregnant. She found out that she was pregnant, and she didn't want to bring a child into this world where Brad would be the father."

Asher closes his eyes and leans forward, lifting one hand from my back and bringing it up to his head, shielding his eyes with his hand.

I kiss his chest as he takes in the horrible truth of Taylor's suicide, silently letting him know I'm here for him.

I wrap myself around him, his head nuzzled under my chest, his shoulders starting to tremble as the reality floods in. I stroke his hair as his tears wedge between his cheek and my chest, my heart breaking for his. I feel his pain as if it were my own, and I would take every ounce of it from him if I could. "How is any of this okay?" he asks, his voice full of anguish.

The truth is that none of it is okay.

No matter what decision Taylor made, the outcome would've been heartbreaking. She could've stayed. She could've given birth to a child that she would've loved with everything in her. But that child wouldn't only get her love, they would have to live with Brad as their father. They would've been raised by a man who gets pleasure from degrading others, mentally abusing them, and sedating them when convenient. What if Brad continued to push Taylor to take medication and she became dependent, potentially having her child taken away. What would have become of that child's future?

Sometimes the unknowns of the future are too big of a risk, and not allowing yourself to travel that path seems the better of two evils. Even when that means you sacrifice yourself and your own happiness.

So, none of this is okay. But I understand why Taylor picked that path, even if it devastates me to accept it.

I lift his face up until my lips reach his forehead. I kiss him. And keep kissing his face, slowly kissing his eyes, cheeks, and mouth, tasting his salty tears as I clean them from his skin.

"She was protecting the child in the only way she knew how, Asher. And as hard as it is, I hope you can forgive her for it, as you forgave me."

He opens his eyes and pulls my lips to his. I can feel the desperation and pain inside of him through his kiss, and I hold him close.

"I am so damn thankful you were strong enough to stay here, Auden," he whispers, leaning his forehead against mine. "I love you with everything in me."

"I love you," I whisper back as he pulls me down to the ground, cradling me against his chest.

I stay awake until I know he's asleep, listening to his heartbeat between each breath. A blanket of peace starts to cover me as I realize there are no secrets left between us.

FORTY-TWO

Auden

2017
  I set my backpack down on the gravel and turn in a circle, making sure no one is around before leaning over and unzipping the outer pocket. My hand digs in until I feel the little plastic rectangle. I grab onto it and pull it out, making sure to keep it close to my body in case anyone pops up around the corner. I look down and run my thumb over the tiny screen with two pink lines, my stomach turning as I try to hold back the nausea. I'm not sure if it's the pregnancy that's been making me so sick or the fact that there's a piece of Brad trying to suck more life out of me.
  I take one more look behind me before throwing it over my head and into the giant, blue dumpster, reading the sign's big white letters: PROPERTY OF MONROE HIGH SCHOOL, before reaching down and picking up my backpack.
  I swing my bag over my shoulder and head toward the front of the school, keeping my eyes on my feet as I count how many steps it takes to get to the front doors. Fifty-seven.

Fiftyseven steps later, I reach my arm out and open the glass door into the school. I inhale a deep breath, trying to prepare for another long day of pretending my life doesn't feel like a sick joke every morning that I wake up.

    The bell rings, vibrating through the hallway as I enter my first period class. I hope Mr. Arnold doesn't draw attention to me for entering right as the bell ended. Most teachers love a good opportunity to single you out or crack a joke and being late is asking for it.

    I walk through the middle of the rows of desks, keeping my eyes on my feet as I pass my old desk and walk to the empty one in the way back. It's been four weeks since I sat at the desk that I spent all year in, and it's been four weeks since I sat next to or talked to Taylor. Every day I wonder if Taylor's heart sinks like mine does as I stroll past her, pretending like we weren't inseparable the last seventeen years of our lives.

    There's thousands of books and TV shows about kids that feel invisible, but until the moment you're the one no longer seen, you have no way of knowing how much it truly hurts. Day after day, I walk into the same building full of hundreds of students that I've known most of my life. And each day, they all pretend as if I'm not there. It's as if my skeleton, covered in skin and pumping blood, isn't standing right in front of them, full of feelings and thoughts that they no longer want to acknowledge.

    Staring at my feet so I can't make eye contact or notice the lack thereof has been oddly eye opening. If I wasn't so terrified of looking anywhere else, I never would've noticed how dirty our campus' floors are, how much trash we allow, how people's shoes really do match their personalities, or how easily precious items can fall and become forgotten. It reminds me of myself. Something that was just dropped so easily and completely forgotten about. I just wish anyone would take a moment to look down and notice that part of me.

Taylor wouldn't have told anyone about the lie Brad told her. Or I guess from her point of view, about the lie I told her. She wasn't even angry when she told me that she didn't believe me. She stood there with this blank expression and explained that Brad had already told her what I tried to do.

What I tried to do. At first, my mind didn't even register what she was implying because it was so far from the truth. I tried to explain to her what really happened, but she told me she didn't want to hear it. I couldn't stomach standing there any longer and had to walk away. The fact that she didn't even question his side told me more than anything else could. She broke my heart. And I wonder if it broke hers too.

But even if it didn't, she was never the type of person to gossip, even if she hates my guts. I would bet my life that she never said a word to anyone about what she believes happened. But Brad has been a monster with a mouth his whole life, and I'd be stupid not to assume he made sure everyone heard his side of the story first.

I don't want anyone to hear any side, but I realized quickly on the Monday after his birthday that I was the newest topic of discussion. All their eyes on me as they shared their whispers felt like fire being released around me. Yet somehow, now that my life is no longer interesting enough to be concerned with, their eyes have started seeing right past me. I wish they still cared. At least when they were disgusted by me, I still felt alive. I'm just a ghost now, roaming the halls while simultaneously being haunted, desperate for any way out.

The end of our senior year is a week and a half away, and every classroom in the building has a countdown somewhere inside of it. But my countdown ends two days before theirs, and it's filled with every emotion except excitement. My countdown is for the day I turn eighteen and leave Monroe forever.

    Saying goodbye to my parents is going to be the hardest part now that I don't even speak to Taylor. I'm going to miss my dad so much, and I think I'll even miss Mama with all of her yelling. Things have been different lately between me and my dad. He doesn't look at me the same, like he somehow knows what happened. Or maybe I just don't look at me the same anymore because I *do* know what happened. And what's about to happen.

    The class bell rings, and everyone starts to collect their things, filling the room with their mindless conversations that, for the first time in my life, I so desperately wish I was a part of. I stay seated, waiting for the class to clear out before I attempt to sneak out unnoticed. Taylor stands from her desk, and I spot her shoulders starting to turn. I hold my breath, watching her eyes as they slowly scan the room, heading in my direction.

    Please look at me, Taylor. Look at me and see how badly I need you right now. Look into my eyes and see how terrified I am of losing my future, my family, and the most precious thing of all, our friendship.

    Her eyes are inches away from meeting mine when she stops, closing them as she takes a deep breath, shaking her head before opening them again and turning back toward the classroom door. She grabs her bag and heads directly to the exit, walking out and reminding me that there's no future in Monroe for someone who's been forgotten without even dying.

FORTY-THREE

Auden

My dream last night reminded me of how sad my last few weeks in Monroe were. I can't help but wonder what would've been different if I had fallen in love with Asher back then.

The light peeking out over the horizon reminds me that the day is about to start. I roll over onto my opposite side and notice Asher is no longer beside me. I lift myself up onto my elbows and look around, seeing him nowhere and his things gone. I look back at his pillow and notice a folded-up receipt resting on it. I grab it, unfolding it, and beginning to read what's written inside.

Auden,
I wanted to sneak out before your parents woke up, and I needed a head start to get ready for the day. I wish I could've stayed and watched you longer. Seeing how peaceful you are when you're asleep is going to make it hard to get up each morning going forward.

Today is going to be hard, but I promise I am here with you every step of the way. No matter what you decide, or what you choose to share, I am here and ready to face it with you.

Just do me a favor, don't do any of this for Taylor. I know how much you love her, and how you spent most of your life protecting her. I will forever be grateful to you for that.

But you need to do this for yourself, for your own healing and truth, not for her.

Thank you for being you.

I love you.

Asher

I've always been the friend who looked out for her. She never had much of a backbone, and, in its absence, I found my place as the perfect support for her. I soon discovered that I enjoyed being her pillar of strength. And that's exactly what I became—the strongest backbone she could have wished for. I made sure that no one could disrespect her and get away with it. After I dealt with the first person who dared to push her during recess, no one ever tried again. I even took drastic measure to skip my biology class sophomore year just so I could stand outside her English class and catch a glimpse of her presentation. As soon as she was ready to begin, I confidently entered the room, interrupted Mr. Fields with a question, and gave each student a piercing stare before making my exit. No one dared to disrupt her speech after receiving that serious warning from me.

After almost eighteen years of that type of a friendship, I feel guilty knowing that her death could've been prevented if her backbone wasn't missing. Maybe if I stuck around longer, she would've been able to reach out sooner. And I could've helped her find the strength to leave.

And maybe Asher is right. Maybe I'm only back here and putting my all into helping get Taylor justice because I still feel the need to fight for her. To protect her. Or at least the memory of her. Maybe I need to really think about where my role should be in all of this. When have I ever put my own needs first?

I guess I did when I left Monroe and started my life over in Minneapolis. But was that really what I needed? Being home again has shown me that maybe I need my mom and dad more than I realized. Maybe I needed a few more magnolia trees and laughs with Sarah about how badly the world sucks. Maybe I needed Asher, much sooner than when he found me. Maybe I needed my best friend's belief in me way before she died.

But without thinking about Taylor, without putting her needs into the equation at all, what do I need? What do I need from Brad after everything he did to me?

My stomach starts to turn as I push the question to the front of my mind, forcing locked memories of that night to rip open the wounds I've worked so hard to bandage up.

I lay my head back down on my pillow, twirling my fingers in the soft grass around me.

I was almost eighteen. I had my life all planned out, and I worked my ass off for it. It took years of determination, structure, and dedication to make the grades I had. I took my future seriously when I decided my major, the one I never even ended up attempting in Minneapolis. I had the best friend in the world, and we were going to still be near one another. I had a family, and although I wasn't close to my mom, I still needed her, especially in my adult years. I had a father that could teach me a new hobby or skill in an afternoon as easily as he could take a breath. And I didn't have a fear of men. I went everywhere with confidence, and I wasn't afraid of any man crossing my path, let alone claiming my body at the drop of a hat. I definitely wasn't holding onto a dark and very deeply buried secret. I was on top of the world and full of life and excitement.

He took all of that away from me.

And I think I need him to feel as close to that feeling as he possibly can. I need him to feel like he's so close to grasping everything he's ever wanted in life that he can taste it.

And then I'm going to take it all away from him.

*

I exit the mall and walk into the parking lot, unsure of where I parked my dad's pickup. There aren't many cars in the lot with how early it is, but I was so distracted on my way in that I can't seem to remember what side of the mall I entered. The truck is old enough that the keys don't have an alarm button on them, so I start to make my way down the rows starting in alphabetical order. The Louisiana sun is starting to heat up, and I know if I don't find the truck soon, I'll end up having to race home for another shower.

When I spot the truck, I feel a wave of relief over me as I climb inside. The funeral starts in less than two hours, and I'm still not sure what my next move is. I look out the window and watch as more cars trickle in.

Today is the last chance anyone has to say their goodbyes to Taylor. It'll be the last public display of everyone's love and affection for her. After today, the only time Taylor will be mentioned is when a memory pops up from a close friend or family member. There will never be another birthday or big event where she's the center of attention. The thought makes my heart ache, and I hate knowing that Taylor will be just a memory, gone before she should have been.

   I wonder how often people thought about me after I left Monroe. I was shocked when Sarah mentioned that she'd thought about me. I bet my mama did a good job of pretending that she was more up to date with my life than she really was. I don't blame her for any of that. She's a good mother, and she's always made sure to stay in touch. She just hasn't lived anywhere besides Louisiana, and it's hard to keep up a conversation with someone who is experiencing things you never have.

   A blonde woman gets out of her minivan and heads to the backseat to unbuckle a blonde little boy from his carseat. She pulls him out and sets him on the asphalt, grabbing his hand and walking him into the mall. That could've been Taylor if she went down a different path. She could've become the mother she always dreamed of being, or the teacher she always wanted to become, or even just a friend to me again, if I had given her the opportunity to know where I had been.

   I turn the key in the ignition, and the loud rumble of my dad's truck causes me to jump. It's been so long since I was learning to drive this big, loud hunk of metal that I'm no longer used to the startling sound of the engine warming up. I guess it's been a long time since anyone in my life or Monroe has heard my loud rumble as well. It's been a long time since I turned the key in my own ignition and was ready to drive off into any situation.

    I pull out of the parking lot and head home to get changed for the funeral. I'm still not sure what to do next, but I have a feeling that by the end of the day, the town of Monroe is going to hear my rumble, along with Taylor's.

FORTY-FOUR

Brad

My father called last night and said that he took care of the Auden problem, and I won't be seeing her again.

He's such a dick. I could've taken care of her just as easily, but he had to take away all my fun.

Now I have to walk into the funeral this morning and give the performance of a lifetime. I don't even get to end the day with another interaction with the girl who drives me the craziest. The way she looked in that little, black dress at the visitation yesterday almost sent me over the edge. Her breasts have filled out so nicely. I bet my face would fit perfectly between them. And that ass, oh fuck. Her ass is so damn perfect. It took everything in me not to slap those cheeks until they were raw.

I'm not ashamed to admit I spent a few hours last night thinking about her while I slapped one off. The girl has been an addiction of mine since middle school. She used to call me Bradley after my father made it clear that he didn't want me called that. The defiance to my father is what made me realize she was someone to pay attention to. There's also something about the way she hates me that makes my cock harder than any other bitch could get it. My cock twitches in my pants at the thought of her underneath me again, but I don't have any time to spare.

My doorbell rings and the door opens before I get a chance to answer it. Millie walks in with a navy blue dress on and matching pumps. She flashes me a smile, and it takes everything in me not to roll my eyes. I know she's just trying to support me during this time, but the neediness is so damn annoying.

"I know you have to go, and I'm only dropping by for a second before I head over to the church," she says, her hands in the air as if she means no harm, or maybe she doesn't want any harm from me for showing up unannounced.

"Millie, I'm heading out the door," I reply, my voice unable to hide my annoyance.

She takes a few steps closer and reaches for my tie, adjusting it and straightening it before taking a step back.

"I know that we can't act as if we know one another as well as we do today, so I just wanted to quickly give you a small reminder that you aren't alone. I'm here whenever you need me."

She bends at her waist and reaches down to the hem of her dress, hiking it up slightly until she reaches her red thong. She pulls it down her legs, leaning down further and slowly stepping out of it with each leg. As soon as it's completely removed, she walks over to me, pushing them into the palm of my hand and leaning up to kiss me on the cheek.

"Whenever you need me," she whispers before heading back out the door and shutting it behind her.

I look down at the thong and bring it up to my nose, closing my eyes and taking in the deep scent.

"Fuck," I whisper to myself as my cock starts to grow against my pants.

I walk straight to my bathroom, the panties still in hand and rip my pants down as soon as I get inside. I grab a hold of my cock in one hand and start to stroke it as I hold the panties to my face, inhaling as deeply as I can while I continue to stroke myself.

"Fuck, you're such a nasty girl, Auden."

FORTY-FIVE

Asher

    My chest feels heavy as I wait in the hallway for the ceremony to start. All the guests are already sitting inside of the church sanctuary, and I'm anxiously waiting to see Auden. I know the sight of her in the room will make the air feel less suffocating. I've been so numb since the day I found Taylor, but today it feels as if the numbness has finally subsided, and the reality of my sister's death is finally crashing in.
    I barely slept last night thinking about the choices I've made over the last few days. I was living each day of my life in the same routine, something I felt I needed to keep my life under control. I would wake up, eat a nutritional breakfast, go for a run, high tail it to the firehouse, and work my shift. Every Saturday morning, I had brunch with Taylor. On Sundays, I would have dinner with my parents. Tomorrow will be the first Saturday I don't wake up, shower, and drive straight to Taylor's house for our weekly brunch.
    The last six days have been anything but structured, and I wonder if I have been making all the wrong decisions

because of it. I've been so consumed with figuring out how any of this could happen, and when the painful reality starts to set in, Auden has been there to escape into.

I shake my head and try to get the negative thoughts out of my mind. Auden isn't just a distraction. I know that as a fact. There hasn't been another woman in my life that's even come close to making me feel the way she does, and I'm risking my happiness and Auden's by allowing the idea to even graze my mind. She was basically forced out of Monroe and came back to risk everything for my sister. That alone is enough to recognize how important she deserves to be.

"Will Auden be joining us at the cemetery?" my mother asks, her hand gripping a ball of used tissues.

My reason for allowing myself to escape the pain has been justified, but I can't run away from the other fact that I haven't been a good son. I haven't spent more than a few hours with my parents, and their loss is just as big as mine, if not more. No parent should bury their child, and I have basically allowed mine to go through this without the only child they have left. I need to make them a bigger priority, but Taylor was always the one who was best at that. She didn't miss any big moments, and she never allowed me to forget them either.

"I haven't asked her yet, but I would like for her to come if you're both okay with it," I answer, looking at both of my parents for confirmation.

"That would be lovely," she replies.

Brad takes a step between my parents, his face completely dry with no traces of tears to be found. Typical for someone who seems to have not cared for his wife at all.

"I thought she flew home last night," Brad states. But I know he's really just inquiring if she didn't follow through with his father's instructions.

I shake my head. I don't want to give him a second of my time or energy today. I'm afraid if I give him too much thought, he'll end up on the ground, my fists flying at his smug face. He doesn't say another word. He just smiles as if he received some good news that he was anxiously waiting for.

The sick bastard seems to love any opportunity to get at Auden. I know she's worked her ass off to overcome the hold he had on her life the last six years. Today is already full of so many emotions, I worry about her and what Brad is capable of doing today in her presence.

Soft background music starts to play, giving us our cue to get ready to enter. Brad stands directly in front of the thick wooden doors, and my parents are side by side behind him. I'm standing at the end of the line, waiting to enter for all the guests to see us walk in carrying our grief.

The whole process of a funeral is kind of mortifying if you think about it. I've realized that when you lose someone, especially someone who still had their whole life ahead of them, the grief almost strips away your self-control. It's not a situation you can ever imagine yourself in. The acceptance of it alone is something your brain can barely process. And as you struggle to get your body to function and to remember to feed yourself and bathe through it all, you somehow must find a way, in less than a week, to make yourself presentable so you can be gawked at by strangers.

I take a deep breath, my throat dry and scratchy as the doors open and we start to walk in single file. The many sniffles and whispers start to mix in with the choir as we continue down the carpeted path to the front pews. A wave of sadness washes over me as the tears start to well up in my eyes.

Before we make it to the front, I feel a warm hand grab at the side of my sleeve. I turn and see Auden and her parents in a pew to the left of me. She lets go of my sleeve, giving me a smile and mouthing *I love you* as I continue walking. I needed that more than she could ever know. Just the sight of her gives me enough strength to grab ahold of my composure and continue to my seat in the front row.

    I sit next to my parents in the hard, wooden pew before Pastor Russel heads to the stage, running his hand along Taylor's casket before turning to face us. My stomach churns as I hear my mother let out a howl as she looks up at Taylor's lifeless body displayed in front of us. My father and I both wrap our arms around her, trying our hardest to calm her and keep ourselves together at the same time. I've never seen my father cry before, but lately it seems rarer to see him without a tear in his eye. Brad keeps his eyes forward as he sits on the end of the pew, symbolically representing himself as the closest person to Taylor.

    I hate him for that. The man can't even shed a tear or attempt to comfort his mother-in-law but gets to play the role as the person Taylor cherished most. I want to scream at the pastor and at every individual in this place that if Brad Montgomery had never met my sister, none of us would be here today. But that isn't my truth to tell, if it was, Taylor would've written those letters to me. I'm just the one who was trusted enough to get it into the right hands, and Auden has shown so much strength this last week, that I know Taylor chose right.

    Pastor Russel clears his throat as the music comes to an end, standing tall in his off-white robe with gold embroidery down the front. I hold my breath as I wait to hear what he could possibly say that will make Taylor's suicide mean something.

"Friends, family, and all who loved Taylor, thank you for gathering with us today to honor such a wonderful and kind woman's life. Taylor loved Jesus, and we pray that she is up in heaven, playing the piano with him as we speak."

He goes on for what feels like an hour. He doesn't even attempt to touch on the real Taylor and the struggles she went through. He doesn't attempt to encourage others to look for signs of their loved one's mental health issues or how Taylor is absolutely up in heaven. He just keeps repeating that we should pray that she is—as if there's a chance that God said she wasn't worthy of eternity with him. We weren't even worthy of the short twenty-four years we had with her. God would be more than lucky to accept her.

When his sermon ends, I wait for my father to stand up and speak about Taylor, but he doesn't. My mother had called me two days ago asking if I wanted to speak at the funeral. I declined because I'm a terrible public speaker, but Taylor, of all people, wouldn't hold that against me. The truth is that I've been so angry at her that I couldn't even begin to find the words I would want to say. I assumed when I declined that my father would take my place and say something, knowing my mother wouldn't be able to stand up there without her grief consuming her. What better second option than my father. He's a damn car salesman. He could possibly even talk Taylor into rising from the dead if he tried hard enough. The last thing that ever came to my mind is that Brad would speak. But here he is, standing up and being introduced as Taylor's loving and devoted husband. If I wasn't in complete shock of his audacity, I would probably be laughing about how ass backwards this all is.

He steps up to the podium, unfolding a piece of paper and slumping his shoulders as if his sorrow is too heavy to carry. His hair is perfectly gelled back and his face clean shaven, unlike anyone I've seen in mourning before.

"The last time I stood up here was when Taylor and I were saying our vows." He pauses for a moment, making it look as if he needed a second to collect himself. "Being loved by Taylor was one of the best things in my life. She had a smile that was contagious, and the choir can probably attest that she had the voice of an angel." He turns and gives the choir a smile, forcing them to smile and some to laugh in reaction.

The fact that he can come off as the most charming man in Monroe makes me want to vomit all over the freshly polished floors. It wasn't even a funny comment. All the women up there probably just laughed because the sight of a handsome widower sends butterflies to their stomach.

"She loved me more than anything else in this world, and she dedicated the last few years of her life to making sure I could get through law school so we could follow our dreams together. My dreams became hers, and I was so grateful for every second of that dedication." He pauses again, this time bringing his hand up to his eye and wiping a tear away. His acting is so good that I hear the sniffling behind me increasing. They have no idea how untrue all this bullshit really is.

"Taylor loved her time in this church. She loved teaching the kids how to play piano, one of her passions, and she loved Jesus with all her heart." I'll give him props for speaking one thing that was true, but that's all I can give him.

I turn and look behind me for Auden. She looks back at me, her hair pulled tightly back in a high ponytail, and gives me a soft smile and a nod of her head, silently telling me that she's thinking the same things I am and that we'll get through this together.

"I did everything I could to make her happy, and I will have to learn how to accept her decision not to be here with us anymore. I pray that all of you can remember her for her kindness, her love, and her devotion to Christ, and not her moment of weakness." He folds up his piece of paper and inserts it in his coat pocket, before turning and resting his hand on Taylor's. "I love you, Taylor, and I will miss you forever." He walks back to the pew and the choir starts to sing again as my parents and I come to a stance, getting back in single file, making our way back down the aisle to the church exit. It takes everything not to show the fury in me over Brad touching Taylor and pretending to love her, but I know that his time will come. I just wish I knew when.

We stand as a family in the same order as we entered, listening to the guests' condolences as they make their way out of the sanctuary. I shake all their hands and hug some of them back as they come filing out. I'm sure they're all saying very nice things and genuinely sorry about our loss, but I don't hear any of their words. I'm too busy waiting for Auden to make her way out. This room is continuing to suck the air right out of my lungs, and I just need her so I can take a big breath and keep moving on.

I finally spot Mrs. Sterling making her way over to me. She walks up and wraps me in her arms, holding me longer than any of the others. "She is with God. I have no doubt about that," she whispers. I know she goes by the Bible before anything else, but her comment gave me the little boost of faith I needed at this moment. Someone needed to say it.

After Mr. Sterling shakes my hand, following up with a hug, I see Auden, standing there with a smile on her face that clearly shows how proud she is of me for keeping it together. She looks so elegant with her hair slicked back and her all black jumpsuit with blue shimmering pumps that I can only assume she bought knowing it was Taylor's favorite color. Anything blue and sparkly could make Taylor squeal with joy. Auden should've been the one up there talking about Taylor. Whether they had spoken in six years or not, Auden still knew her better than any of us could've dreamed of knowing her.

She wraps her arms around me before letting go and grabbing ahold of my pinky with hers as we stand still together. "How are you in this moment?" she asks, knowing each second could bring new emotions.

"I'm standing," I reply, trying to focus on the small accomplishments.

"Are you joining us at the cemetery?" my mother asks Auden, reaching over and embracing her in her arms.

"I would love to if that's alright with you all."

Brad leans forward, gripping one of Auden's wrists and pulling her over to him. "Of course, it's alright," he says, forcing Auden into his arms and pulling her in tightly.

My face starts to crinkle as I watch Brad crossing way too big of a line. Before I get the chance to step in and pull her away from him, Mr. Sterling runs his hand along Brad's arm, pulling Auden from his grasp and back behind him.

"You should go Auden. We'll meet you at the reception," Mr. Sterling says. "Just stay with Asher until then."

He looks over at me and gives me a nod, silently telling me he's going to support us both and trusts his daughter in my care. The small gesture goes a lot further than he realizes, and by the smile on Auden's face, I believe she feels the same strength her father has just given me. I reach out and grab her hand, pulling her over to my side as we continue to thank the rest of the guests for attending.

FORTY-SIX

Auden

My insides feel shaky as I stand behind Asher, anticipating our trip to the cemetery.

I didn't even consider the idea of Brad giving a speech today. I've been so wrapped up in my own pain, Asher's, and the truth behind why Taylor ended her life that how today would actually play out never crossed my mind.

I watch as Asher continues to shake hands and receive condolences, the muscles in his jaw continuing to flex each time Brad speaks. He must've been just as shocked by the ceremony as I was. The way he looked at Brad before my dad pulled me away from him, reminded me of the rage in his eyes during our last interaction with Brad. I keep reaching my hand out and touching his back so that he knows I'm right here, ready to face the day with him like he's promised to face each day forward by my side.

Most couples, if you can even label us as that, spend months getting to know one another through adventures and doing all of the happy couple-type things. I doubt there are many that start their relationship off by grieving together the loss of their favorite person. I doubt few spent early dates at a funeral or watching their partner's sibling be buried. I wonder what that will mean for our future. Will we make it longer because we jumped straight to the supporting roles and hopefully passed each other's tests? Or will we fail at this because we're incapable of having many happy times together and only thrive when one of us needs the other deeply?

His face suddenly lights up and a smile begins to take over as he takes a step forward into the line of guests. I move my head around, trying to watch where he's headed and what could be causing his sudden burst of happiness. When I spot him, he's reaching out for a girl, maybe ten or eleven years old. She has long, straight brown hair flowing down her back, a navy blue dress with flower earrings, and a white purse hanging off her shoulder.

She smiles as he leans down and takes her into a warm embrace. Her mom and dad stand behind her. They walk back in our direction and head straight for Mr. and Mrs. Landry, being introduced to them by Asher. He takes the girl's hand and guides her over in my direction, a big smile still on his face.

"Auden, this is Lily, the girl I told you about with the orangutan stuffed animal."

I look down at the girl, reaching my hand out and shaking hers, "It's so nice to meet you."

Asher rests his hand on Lily's shoulder, "Lily, this is Auden, my girlfriend."

The word girlfriend catches me and Lily by surprise. Everything has been so fast and crazy these last few days that labeling our relationship was the last thing on my mind. Lily's eyebrows shoot up as Asher introduces me, followed by a smile.

"It's so nice to meet you too, Auden. I'm glad Asher has a girlfriend as pretty as you."

I can't help but laugh and either can Asher, followed by Lily's parents who seem used to her blunt statements. "Do you like orangutans, Auden?" she asks, reaching into her white purse.

"I don't think I've ever met anyone who doesn't," I reply, curious as to why she's asking.

Lily pulls out a small keychain, flipping it over and handing it to Asher. "I didn't know Taylor well enough to get you anything that she may have liked, but I thought maybe you could look at this keychain and remember that it's hard but possible to go on with life once your sibling dies."

Asher takes the keychain and looks closely at it. It has a small picture of an orangutan on the front enclosed in a heart. I watch as Asher's eyes well up, and it takes everything in me to hold back my own tears from this precious gesture.

Asher gives Lily another hug before thanking them for coming and saying goodbye. My heart swells as I watch the way Lily brings so much happiness to Asher in this moment. His heart is worthy of so much love, and seeing how this young girl knows how special he is makes me feel like maybe our lives can turn out alright. Maybe people will be able to see past the stigmas and see into my heart when I finally speak my truth. Maybe someone out there has their own orangutan that matches mine, and they'll show me when I show everyone mine. My truth orangutan.

Once the last of the guests exit the church, Asher and I head out to the parking lot and hop inside of his Jeep. The moment Asher's door shuts, he leans his head down against the steering wheel and closes his eyes, taking a long drawn-out breath.

He's having a moment. He's been taught his whole life not to have big moments or big emotions and he's been selfmedicating to tame that, but at what point is he allowed to have big emotions? When does he let them out?

I reach over to him and rub my hand up and down his back, trying to find a way to bring him a small bit of comfort.

He suddenly jerks his head back, slamming his fist into the grips of the steering wheel hard enough to send a swish of air in my direction.

"How the hell can he do this?" he yells, his eyes glued to the wheel. "How the fuck is it okay for him to speak at her funeral when she died to escape him?"

My heart starts to beat rapidly. I've never seen Asher show this magnitude of anger before, and I'm not sure exactly how to help him calm down. He's been the one calming me down most of this week.

"He stood up there and put on this show for everyone to see him as this sad and devoted husband, but in truth he didn't give a damn about Taylor!" His face starts to turn red and the tears start to flood out of him.

"I'm so sorry," I say to him, reaching my arm out and grabbing his fist in an attempt to stop his rage from hurting himself. "You're so right. She deserved so much more in life, and she sure deserved much better than Brad."

Asher throws his head back into the headrest, looking straight up at the plastic ceiling of his Jeep. The anger I feel about Brad's performance can't even begin to be as gut wrenching as his must be. Yes, I have my own reasons to hate Brad on top of what he did to Taylor, but the difference between my position and Asher's, is that I can still find some form of justice and closure. What does Asher really get?

I look out the back window, seeing the church again.

"We can't redo the entire service, as badly as we both wish we could. Why don't you tell me right here and right now, what you wish you could've said today during the service."

Asher lowers his chin and faces me, his eyes softening as he takes in what I just said. "What do you mean? Like if I had taken the opportunity to speak today, what I would've wanted to say?"

I brush my hand through his hair, giving him a small smile as the idea registers in his mind. "Exactly. What do you wish was said up there today? We do these funerals to honor our loved ones, and we do them to help ourselves feel better. Taylor will hear what you have to say whether it's in the church or in your Jeep right now."

He looks out the window, slowly nodding his head. He lifts his left elbow and leans it on the door, his hand covering his mouth while he takes a few moments to think of what he would've said if he chose to speak today.

After a few minutes he turns back to me, his eyes looking nervous, and I turn my body until I'm cross legged in my seat fully facing him.

"Taylor was my little sister, and the best little sister at that. She was a planner. She knew what she wanted, and she had her schedule planned out years in advance, along with the schedules of everyone she loved. Although Taylor was my little sister, sometimes I felt like she was the older one. She always knew how to break me out of my funks, encourage me to do the things I told myself I couldn't do, and she never once allowed me to shame myself. She accepted that I was quiet around others, and she allowed me to be loud when it was just us. She was so full of love, and she truly embodied the words of Jesus when she was told to love thy neighbor. She was beautiful on the outside and even more beautiful on the inside.

She gained joy by seeing others' happiness."

He pauses for a moment and looks out the front window, taking a deep breath.

"And I've come to realize over the last few days since her death, that she's one of the strongest people I have ever met, and I wish more than anything I could say that to her right now. Taylor, I love you. I'm sorry I didn't see your pain like you always saw mine, but I hope you know how proud I will always be to call you my little sister."

I watch as a single tear falls down his cheek, and I feel many more falling down my own. I wipe my own face and lean into him, reaching my arms out and wrapping him into my embrace.

"That was beautiful, Asher. Thank you for sharing that with me and with Taylor."

He doesn't say anything, he just turns to me and kisses me on my forehead, keeping his lips there against me.

"Asher, I promise he won't get away with this."

He pulls away and closes his eyes for a moment, keeping his head facing out the window and trying to control his breathing. A car beeps behind us and we notice that the hearse has started driving towards the cemetery, prompting Asher to start up the ignition and fasten his seatbelt before putting it in drive. Another distraction.

"How are we going to make this right, Auden?" he asks, his voice cracking with desperation.

I want to be able to snap my fingers and make it all better. I want to travel back in time and change every second leading up to this horrible tragedy. If I could numb every emotion inside of Asher I would, but I'm choosing to instead trust in myself and have faith that the answers will come to me. I just have to be ready for them.

"I'm still working on that part," I say, taking his hand and holding it in my lap as we follow the trail of cars in front of us.

*

The hearse pulls into the Monroe Cemetery and both of our heartbeats slow down, the sudden silence in the Jeep evidence of that. We park along the side of the grass-lined gravestones, and I notice the group of people gathering around a rectangular hole in the ground. Asher exits the Jeep and walks around to my side, opening the door and giving me his hand as I step down.

I grip onto his hand and keep it laced in mine as we make our way over to the burial spot. There isn't a cloud in the sky and the weather couldn't be more perfect, but the feeling in my heart makes the day feel cold and eerie. We don't say a word as we make our way over, the wet grass squishing under my heels with every step.

Brad and the Landrys are sitting on a bench set directly in front of the hole, Taylor's casket suspended right above it. Mrs. Landry pats the bench and motions for me to come and sit by her. I give her a smile and a nod and start to head over, stopping next to the casket on the way and running my hand along its shiny wood frame. I never got the opportunity to see Taylor at the visitation, and I was sitting so far back during the service that I couldn't see her there either. I feel so sad realizing my last image of her will always be from six years ago, when she could no longer be bothered to look in my direction. I'm not sure if that image is better than the one the rest of her loved ones will have, her body lifeless in a shiny, expensive box. But I can't help wish we all had something to remember her by that showed the brightness she brought to so many of our lives.

I take my seat next to Mrs. Landry, Asher joining on the other side of me as the pastor asks everyone to gather in close. The group here at the cemetery is much smaller than at the church. Taylor's grandparents have all already passed, and she didn't have a big extended family. It's mostly just her uncles and their wives, a handful of cousins from out of state and then the Montgomerys here to say their final goodbyes. I've been avoiding all interactions with Mr. Montgomery today. I'm not sure I'm ready to face his continued attempts at intimidation since he ordered me home to Minneapolis. I am wondering if that makes him angrier with me or if maybe he's just shocked by my disregard for his authority.

The pastor goes through another speech about how death is something we shouldn't allow to make us sad but instead we should rejoice in the truth that one day we will all be joined together again. I remember Pastor Russel giving the same speech years ago at my gram's funeral. I hated how much comfort it brought everyone besides me, just as much back then as I do now.

What exactly does God expect to happen on the days that we join Taylor up at the gates of heaven? Is she going to be terrified when she sees Brad, if he's even allowed up there? Lord knows I don't believe he is. Will she apologize to me and beg for my forgiveness? Or will she just pretend none of this ever happened? Honestly, I doubt I'd even accept an apology. I wouldn't even want it at this point after discovering the truth about everything that's happened. I just wish I could take back the time with my best friend.

Asher squeezes my hand and I try to focus my attention back on the ceremony. I look over in front of the casket and notice a white tarp resting over the headstone. It had to have been so expensive to rush a headstone in time for her burial.

"As we lower this casket into the ground, let us find comfort in the knowledge that Taylor is now in a better place, free from pain and suffering."

Asher's grip tightens on mine as he closes his eyes, bringing his fingers up to his face and pinching the bridge of his nose, trying to hold back his tears. The soft humming of the motor lowering the casket into the ground is drowned out by the sniffles and weeping of Taylor's loved ones. I lean my head against Asher's shoulder, feeling my own tears as they wet my cheeks.

Once the casket comes to a stop, the pastor walks over to the head of her grave, reaching his hand out and grabbing onto the white tarp.

"Taylor's in-laws, the Montgomerys, wanted to make sure she was laid to rest with her headstone intact. They graciously paid for it to be rushed and customized by today so everyone could be here for the revealing."

Pastor Russel lifts the white tarp and the dark, smooth, marble headstone glistens under the sunlight.

Taylor Noelle Montgomery
B. 4-22-99 D. 6-08-23
A loving wife and daughter.

My chest feels like the grip of God has captured it. I've never heard or seen Taylor's name as anything other than a Landry and nausea consumes me as I see her as a Montgomery for the first time. She will forever be remembered as a wife to Brad Montgomery, and my heart breaks that she won't be seen as the loving sister, a role she loved more than anything.

And if the wording isn't bad enough, the whole vibe that the headstone gives is nothing I would imagine. I haven't put a second of thought into how I would want it to look, but this dark and expensive hunk of rock just doesn't scream Taylor or anything remotely reflecting her personality.

    Her family starts to disperse, the sounds of their shoes clicking against the gravel pavement as they make their way back to their cars. I find the strength to stand and walk over to her headstone, running my hand along the freshly carved edges. A gust of wind blows and I close my eyes, lifting my face into the fresh air as it brushes against my cheeks.

    I take a moment to look around, observing the many other headstones. Some have aged and are now covered with so much moss and dirt they're no longer readable. Some still have fresh flowers inserted into plastic vases by them, and a few have wreaths that are already half dead. The vibrant colors of the silk flowers left at many of the graves are what stand out the most. They're the headstones that have become a burden to visit, so their families have left them with cheap reminders of how inconvenient their death had become to them.

    I look back down at Taylor's headstone, rereading the permanent phrase. I wonder if she would've wanted it to say "a loving mother" as well. She would've been the best mother this side of Louisiana had ever seen, full of so much love and laughter. She never would've been able to live with having an abortion, so I understand why she felt the need to sacrifice herself alongside her unborn child. In her own way, she did her best to protect both of them. I'll forever hold onto that.

    I spent six weeks living in the shadow of Brad's darkness. I can't imagine the strength Taylor had to possess to survive the last six years. She was so much stronger than her death could ever show.

    "Are you ready to head to the reception?" Asher asks, walking up behind me.

I nod my head, my eyes still on Taylor's headstone. "Where is it?" I ask.

Asher rests his hand on the dip of my lower back. "Evidently, it's at the Montgomery's house. I guess I really didn't pay attention to any of the planning for this."

I kiss the inside of my middle and index finger before bringing them down and resting them on the top of the headstone, leaning forward and whispering my goodbye to Taylor.

"Everyone will know how strong you are, Taylor. Rest easy knowing I will take care of that, until we all meet again."

FORTY-SEVEN

Auden

The gates open and we enter, circling the Montgomery's large driveway. The giant, white pillars remind me of the many days I spent here during my childhood running throughout the yard.

When you've known multiple versions of someone, how can you even begin to describe your feelings toward them? I hate the monster that Brad is today. I'd even go as far as to say that I wish it was him we just left buried under the cold dirt at the cemetery. The version of Brad back when he raped me can go jump off a cliff as well, or maybe something much longer, scarier, and definitely more painful. But the version of Brad that I spent summers swimming in his pool with, camping in his backyard and having every school event, birthday, and fundraiser right on this very property makes my head hurt. That Brad was still kind. He was full of life and love. If only his horrible father hadn't broken him. That version of Brad— Bradley—I grieve for because I know in my heart that Bradley would've never have allowed any of this to happen.

Asher puts the Jeep in park and unbuckles his seatbelt before turning towards me. The whole ride here was silent. The words don't need to be said. We just left Taylor in the fucking ground, and it's killing both of us.

"Are you ready for this? One last event until we're through it all," he says.

Through it all.

Are we ever going to be *through it all*? Or will we continue to grieve, maybe even harder now that our hunt for the truth has come to an end.

"I don't think I'll ever be ready for this. Even when we're done," I answer, followed by a huff of laughter. I don't think anything is funny, but this last week sure feels anything but real.

I lean forward until my forehead is leaning against Asher's and one of my hands is grabbing onto one of his.

"I have to speak the truth, Asher. I don't know what exactly I'm going to say or when I'm going to say it. And, honestly, that's the scariest part of all." I lean back in my seat, still holding his hand as my nerves continue to build. "But I know I have to speak about what Brad has really been up to, for myself and for Taylor. And I'm telling you this so that you aren't shocked and hopefully are able to support me in this."

I want to look at him, but I can't. Today has been so hard for him and everyone he loves. I really don't want to add to anyone's pain, but time feels as if it's slipping through my fingers, and I have nothing left to grasp. I need to speak my truth before it's too late. I just wish I was strong enough to have said it before. Perhaps I could have spared the pain of so many people I love.

"Just promise me you won't be anywhere alone with him."

I lift his hand up to my mouth and kiss the top of it. "I promise."

"I mean I don't want you alone with Brad, anyone from the Montgomery family, or anyone who works with them," he says, as if he's making sure he didn't forget anyone. "Or maybe I just shouldn't leave you alone."

This protective side of Asher is different from the angry side. He's thinking about all the possibilities that could happen to me when we walk in there, not about his own pain or discomfort. He's everything I never realized I wanted and that makes believing this time in my life is real, so much harder.

"Deal."

*

Asher opens my side door, giving me a hand down into the perfectly manicured lawn. I was always so amazed as a kid by how green and soft the Montgomery's grass was. Now I know that if you have enough money, you can make everything so perfect it almost doesn't seem real anymore.

We follow a big sign set upon a wooden easel saying Reception with a big arrow under Taylor's face leading to the backyard. If I didn't just come from the cemetery, I would assume I was attending a graduation open house or a wedding for one.

When we make our way around the house and into the backyard, I pause for a moment, stunned by the large number of people I didn't expect to be here. The thought of seeing so many people that I grew up with and all their families never even crossed my mind. Now that I'm walking into the thick of it, I regret not thinking through this scenario more. The tables are starting to fill with dozens of flowers people helped transport from Taylor's service, some from old classmates I dread seeing.

Flowers are my least favorite part of funerals. They have always been a big part of my life. My mama and my grams have always been known for their beautiful flower gardens. I was raised learning how to tend to them, listen to them, and appreciate their life cycles. I love flowers.

But when it comes to flowers at a funeral, I rarely have an emotion other than disappointment. Not for myself, but for the people who brought them. I know it's not always the case, but most of the time flowers are bought out of guilt. They're from the people who didn't have enough to say about the person who passed on that they could write in a card. Or they didn't know them well enough to send a gift to their loved ones with something that actually symbolized their life. Like Taylor loved music and teaching the piano. Someone who knew her well enough to know that simple fact could've sent a piece of sheet music to one of Taylor's favorite songs, maybe had it framed or written a kind memory of her on the back. But they didn't know her well enough to do that. They could've sent a basket of apples, her favorite fruit, or even a small apple tree for her parents to plant on their property. Nothing like that is here. It's just flowers because, in life when we didn't do enough for someone while we still could have, we send flowers out of guilt.

And according to Taylor's words reflecting how her life has gone in the last six years, a lot more people should've sent flowers.

The yard is scattered with giant, white tents filled with wooden tables and chairs set to help shield guests from the sweltering Louisiana sun. The large patio above us surrounding the pool is lined with azaleas and has multiple tables with pictures displayed on them. They reflect years of Taylor's life, and the first table is stacked with pamphlets with Taylor Montgomery printed on them. I can't help but cringe, flipping the pile of pamphlets over as I walk towards the second table, taking in the many photos of Taylor as a child, and me standing next to her in most of them.

    I miss her more than I ever have at this moment. I've gotten so good at pretending that I didn't have a past before Minneapolis that I might have convinced myself it was true as well. But you can't hide from your past when it's displayed in hundreds of photos right in front of you. I would do anything to be sitting under a magnolia tree, laughing with her about our future plans as we ate an apple we stole from her grandfather's garden. Those little girls had no idea what their futures had in store for them.

    "Time sure does fly. It feels like it was just yesterday that I was snapping that photo of you two," mama says, leaning in next to me and rubbing her finger along the edge of a photo of Taylor and me.

    She moves her other hand to my shoulder, giving it a little squeeze to let me know that she understands what I may be feeling.

    "She loved you so much, Auden, even after you left. I hope you know that."

    I do know that. I know it deep down, and I believe I always have because that's exactly how I've always felt. Even though we no longer fit in each other's lives, we would always fit in each other's hearts. I just wish I would've had the opportunity to tell her that before it was too late.

    "Mama," I begin to say, turning my body away from the table and facing her, "I'm so sorry if my decisions have broken your heart and put you in a position where you have to pick me or your faith."

My heart feels like it's starting to chip away at itself as I give my mama permission to leave my life. I've run the scenario through my mind many times now, and I've come to the conclusion that this time, if someone needs to remove me from their life, I want it to be on good terms. I want it to be the happiest ending I can give it.

She grabs both of my hands and pulls me closer to her.

"I need you to know that I love you, Mama, and I always will. It'll be one of the hardest challenges of my life, especially not hearing from you every Saturday. But I'll respect your wishes if you can't support who I am anymore," I say.

Mama pulls me into her arms and wraps herself around me, the smell of her sweet shampoo consuming me.

"Auden, you are my heart. I could never be whole without you in my life," she whispers between kissing the top of my head. "You may not have always done life the way I wanted you to, and maybe you aren't as close to Jesus as I had always planned. But you are my strong, sometimes sweet, and always amazing daughter. You are someone I could never give up."

I clear my throat, trying to hold back the tears and hold onto my mama a little longer and a little tighter. My daddy always talked about how mama was one of the most amazing and loving people he had ever met, but I always thought he must've been talking about someone besides my mama. She was never very affectionate with me, and it seemed like all of our conversations ended in arguments, mostly started by me. But I've never needed this side of her more than I do right now, and I am so grateful for this moment. Maybe it was me who built the wall up between us long ago, but Taylor's death has forced me to tear it down.

    She pulls me back from her chest and takes my cheeks in her hands, looking directly at me with the smallest glimpse of a smile inside of her tear-lined eyes.

    "You don't ever have to worry about losing me," she whispers. "Do you understand me?"

    The way she asked me if I understood doesn't make me want to run away and slam my bedroom door like it had in the past. This time I can't help but laugh because I truly do understand. And at this moment, I've never felt more loved and supported by my mama.

    Asher walks over, handing her a glass of lemonade and myself a martini. "I hope I'm not wrong for assuming you only wanted lemonade, Mrs. Sterling. I didn't want to walk over empty handed."

    Mama smiles, taking the lemonade from his hand. "You have grown into such a fine gentleman," she says, making her way over to the table where my dad is sitting, joining him and leaving me with a lump in my throat as I try to swallow. It's wonderful seeing my loved ones enjoying time together. It warms my heart.

    The sound of silverware clanking catches my attention and I turn in the direction of the kitchen, recognizing the smell of Miss Meg's famous crab cakes.

    Without saying a word, I make my way around the rest of the patio and up the dark, wooden stairs, ignoring the many Montgomerys sitting and standing around the poolside bar and head through the tall glass doors that lead into the kitchen.

    "Oh, eyes don't you fool me now," I hear coming from the corner of the spacious marble-floored kitchen.

I turn around and see Miss Meg. She's much older than the last time I was standing in this kitchen begging for her crab cakes. Her hair is still pulled back in a bun tight enough to straighten out her curls, but the color is no longer deep brown. It's been replaced by all silver. Her smile is still the most genuine smile in all of Louisiana, and I can't hold myself back from running to her and wrapping my arms around her.

"Miss Meg!" I say, my voice full of glee. "I knew that smell could only be your crab cakes."

She wraps her hands around my arms and pulls them down the length of me, shaking her head. "You clearly haven't had any good southern food in quite a while, Miss Auden."

Miss Meg has worked as the cook for the Montgomerys since before any of us were born. She never married or had any kids, so all of us that hung around the house sort of became like family to her. We loved her as if she was our family as well. And boy can she whip up the best seafood this part of the country has ever tasted.

The rest of the workers continue moving through the kitchen around us, stirring sauces on the extra-large gas stove, polishing silverware, and stacking hors d'oeuvres on serving trays. The smell in the air is so delicious, I swear my belly could convince myself that I haven't eaten in weeks.

My stomach starts to growl right as Mrs. Montgomery comes in, her hands on her hips before her feet even leave the patio. "Miss Meg, the guests are waiting on you to get this food plated."

Miss Meg drops her hands from my arms and gives me a small grin before turning to Mrs. Montgomery and nodding, "Yes, Ma'am, we're just about ready."

I pull Miss Meg in for one more hug before turning and walking back toward the patio, Mrs. Montgomery right behind me. As I start to descend down the steps, I hear her starting to address all of the guests.

"Food will be out in about ten minutes. Please continue to enjoy the refreshments and the music until then."

I walk past a group of three men dressed in all black, each playing a different string instrument underneath the gazebo. The music is slow and sad, enough to make your heart long for a lover you'd never met before. I spot Asher at the table with my parents, and I stop for a moment, watching his body language as he engages with them.

His hands are flailing in the air like he's telling the most exciting story anyone has ever heard, and his smile is so big I fear it may stretch off his cheeks. The sight of his happiness during such a hard moment in his life makes my heart start to race. The way my dad is starting to cackle, his hands repeatedly slapping the table in front of him while my mama wipes away tears of laughter makes me start to giggle to myself, their happiness contagious. I could get used to this sight. I could spend the rest of my life watching those three enjoying each other's company. Something inside of me wonders if Taylor is out there thinking the same thing as she watches Asher and my love for one another grow by the minute.

The smell of smoke catches my attention and I turn in the direction of the cigar bar in the furthest corner of the lawn. I notice a few older men from around town, sitting on the leather bar stools while they puff on their cigars. I think one of them may even be Judge Perry and his bailiff, but I'm not close enough to be certain. Then I spot her. She's in a striped, royal blue blazer over a crisp white shirt and trousers to match. She's absolutely iconic looking, and somehow makes the long, white cigarette in between her fingers look extremely classy. She exhales a big puff of smoke. When her eyes meet mine, she gives me a grin, waving me over in her direction.

"You are so much cooler than I could have ever imagined," I say, walking up and giving Sarah a hug. "Oh, shut up. I know I should quit the nasty things but dealing with idiots every day has become my overused excuse."

We stand quietly for a moment, both of us looking out at the yard full of the people from our past. I swear every person that has crossed paths with the Montgomerys or walked the streets of Monroe are here. Now that I'm standing next to Sarah as I take in the sight of them, I feel like this may be the opportunity I've been waiting for.

"I found some more information," I say, keeping myself standing next to Sarah, looking out at all the guests.

"Anything you can build a case on?" she asks, taking a drag on her cigarette. "Or *we* can build a case on because I'm fully invested." She turns, giving me a grin as she ashes in the grass.

"Maybe not, but it sure as hell has given me more motivation." I look over my shoulder, noticing we're a little too close to others to keep this conversation going. I point my head to the right and we both take a few steps until we're out of earshot.

"I read the final letter that Taylor wrote me and it explains why she did this."

Sarah's eyes get big and she leans down, pushing her cigarette into the grass until it's no longer lit and tossing it over her shoulder behind us, uninterested in where it lands. She crosses her arms against her chest and lifts her glass of wine up to her lips, leaning her head back and finishing the glass before waving one of the workers down with a tray of refills.

As soon as the server hands Sarah a fresh glass, she turns back to me and nods, "Go on, I'm listening."

I peek around us one more time, making sure no one is listening in. "She was pregnant."

Sarah's eyes widen again, this time to the point that I can see all the whites of her eyes as she brings a hand up to cover her gaping mouth.

"And she felt like she couldn't bring a child into this world that was a part of . . ." I turn my head and stop when my eyes fall on Brad. "Him."

Sarah shakes her head, reaching into her purse and pulling out her pack of Parliament cigarettes. She rests one in between her lips and lights it before turning in my direction, tilting the box and offering me my own. I reach out and grab one and put it between my own lips.

I've never been a smoker. But Dec is, and occasionally when I was having a bad day or going through a really stressful moment, I would sneak a drag off of one of his. I lean in as she lights it for me, taking in a small puff and coughing like a newbie.

"So, what do you want to do next? It's a little late for a biopsy," she asks.

I scan the lawn until my eyes catch another glimpse of Brad. He's back at the bar on the patio having a drink with his dad and his dad's friends, his eyes looking right back at me. He puckers his lips out in the position of a kiss and shoots me a wink, landing straight in the pit of my stomach. I look away without a reaction, knowing that's exactly what he wants from me, and he'll get it, just not quite yet.

"You said the best way to get justice can sometimes be the truth in the right hands, right?" I ask.

Sarah pauses for a moment, scanning her eyes across all the guests before turning her body so she's facing me directly, a sly smile crossing her lips. "Hands like those of local judges, sheriffs, Pastor Russel, and maybe even Mike Taylor, the newest publisher for the Monroe Daily." She points her head in the direction of the table next to my parents, the one Mike and his wife are currently sitting at.

I nod my head.

If I'm going to actually speak my truth, then I can't think of a better crowd to share it with. I know what I have to say may cause a lot of pain and embarrassment for a lot of people here today, and that's the last thing I want. But at least here, the Landrys can leave at any moment, something the Montgomerys will have a harder time running away from.

"Please find a place to take a seat so we can have a few final words in honor of our dear Taylor," Mr. Montgomery announces from the patio deck. The sound of his voice settling like a heavy weight deep in my core.

Sarah grabs my arm, her warm hand giving me a squeeze, "Go take a seat. I'm going to grab us both a refill, and I'll join you over at your parents' table"

I make my way over to the table, Asher standing when he notices me and leans in to kiss me on the cheek. "Everything going alright?" he asks.

"For now," I reply, trying to give him a smile but my trembling lips prevent me from it.

I take a seat between my dad and Asher when Sarah walks up, handing me another martini that I desperately needed.

"I noticed you didn't get a chance to hit the food table yet, so I grabbed you some of Miss Meg's crab cakes," mama says, sliding a small plate across the table in my direction.

Mr. Montgomery strolls to the patio's edge, a glass of scotch in hand, as the seated guests' murmurs gradually hush. Raising his hand to quiet them, he commands their attention. Mrs. Montgomery gracefully joins him, the epitome of the supportive wife she has always been expected to be.

"I want to thank you all for gathering here today in our home. The loss of Taylor is something that has truly broken our hearts and we couldn't be more grateful for all of you showing up and supporting us through this loss." He turns his body in the direction of the Landry's table next to us. "Charles and Helen, you raised an amazing daughter. Taylor became a daughter to us, and she was everything we ever hoped for. She was kind, loyal, and so loving. Thank you for bringing her into this world and allowing us the opportunity to love her."

He sure knows how to captivate a crowd. I'll give him that. But the sound of his voice as he pretends to give a shit about anything other than himself and his own gain makes my blood start to boil. I want to run up to him and uppercut him like Kevin had taught me, but I know I can't do anything that will give the Montgomerys the upper hand.

"There's plenty of food and even more drinks so please keep helping yourselves and stay to celebrate Taylor as long as you'd like. I want to point out that there's a guest book near the entrance for all to sign and leave a kind memory or message to Brad or the Landrys." Mrs. Montgomery adds, "Now, our son Brad would like to say a few words."

I slide the crab cakes around on my plate, unable to muster the appetite to take a bite. My knee bounces anxiously as I anticipate Brad's approach to the patio's edge, dreading what words may come next. Asher notices my agitation and gently places his hand on my knee, a gesture meant to soothe my nerves. As soon as Brad comes into sight, my whole body starts to tingle, and I begin to feel a little nauseous. I grab my martini and finish the rest of it to try and calm my nerves.

"I would also like to thank you all for coming. These last few days have been the hardest of my life. But I hate the idea that you all may leave here today with sad memories about how Taylor left this world instead of all of the beautiful things that she did to make our lives so much better."

I tug at the collar of my shirt, attempting to cool down as beads of sweat form on my forehead. Uncontrollably, my teeth clench down so hard against my lower lip, I'm surprised I haven't broken the skin yet.

"Taylor and I have known each other since we were just little kids. Our parents wanted us to spend forever together, and although Taylor was on board with the idea since grade school, it took me a little longer to hop on that wagon."

The guests all join in laughing at the cute thought of a young Brad as a boy who didn't have time for a love-stricken little girl. I force myself to swallow, knowing it was just the beginning of Taylor's end. I notice the way Asher's jaw muscles are twitching and his knee is being gripped tightly by his own hand.

"But once I did join in on the idea that Taylor and I were meant to be together, boy did my life change for the better. Taylor set her eyes on me, and I felt a love that I doubt I'll ever experience again. She knew how to make the hardest days into happy endings, and she supported me through every dream I've ever had, never allowing me to give up. The day she said yes to marrying me was the happiest day of my life and the easiest decision I've ever made."

My body starts to feel like it's spiraling out of control, like I railed a line of speed and need to run thirty miles to stop my muscles from ripping out of my skin. My dad must've noticed how fidgety I am because he rests his hand on my shoulder for a moment, leaning into my ear and whispering, "Be the change, little fish."

My dad's words go straight to my core, my nerves subsiding as I remember why I'm here and how supported I really am. Taylor isn't here to run, speak her truth, or make another decision for herself again, but I am. And I won't allow either of us to run away from a Montgomery again.

"Taylor, I wish I knew what was going on that made you feel like you had to leave the way you did. I wish I could go back and take away all your sadness and bring you the same joy that you brought so many of us. But I know you knew how much I loved you, and I will hold onto that for the rest of my life."

I look over at Sarah, and she gives me a nod as I stand, praying my knees don't buckle beneath me.

"That's a lie," I state, my voice stern and my tone just loud enough for me to steal the guests' attention. Everyone turns to face me, the sound of chairs shuffling and quiet gasps surrounding us.

I want to turn around and high tail it out of here. I want to get on the first flight home to Minneapolis and pretend the last thirty seconds of my life never happened. But here I am, standing up in front of the most important people in Monroe, and I'm about to reveal the secrets of one of the most powerful families in Louisiana. What the fuck have you done, Auden?

I glance down at the table, expecting to see my parents, Asher, and Sarah, giving me disapproving looks. To my surprise, they're all looking at me with unwavering support, ready to stand by me no matter what I say next.

"Excuse me?" Mr. Montgomery interjects, walking up and standing at Brad's side. "Miss Sterling, this is hardly the time or the place for you to be acting so outlandish."

I turn back and face both of them, looking up as they tower over me from the patio deck.

"And where is the place that I'm allowed to speak, Mr. Montgomery? Is it back home in Minneapolis where you tried to send me just yesterday so I couldn't reveal your son's dirty little secrets?"

Mrs. Montgomery walks up, whispering into Mr. Montgomery's ear, and I know my time is about to be cut short. I quickly pull my chair out and step up on it, Asher grabbing ahold of it and keeping it stable as I raise myself higher so that no one will miss what I have to say next.

"A lot of y'all may have noticed that I haven't been around the last six years, and if this town has taught me anything, it's that you have all probably formed your own theories as to why I left in the first place. I'm fine with that, I accepted that truth long ago, and as much as I missed my home, I was prepared to never return to it."

I look down and notice Sarah, along with many other guests, holding their phones out and recording my every word. I turn my head back and look directly at Brad, his face now red as a ripe apple and his nostrils flaring like a mad bull.

"But then Taylor left me a letter the day that she took her own life, and I now know that she too was running away from Brad Montgomery, but after six years, she had reached her limit."

Mrs. Landry let out a gasp that catches my attention. I turn to her, her face full of pain, and I know what I'm about to say will break her heart even more, but she needs to hear it. They all need to hear it.

"Brad Montgomery took me to the back of his father's property, and he raped me on the night of his eighteenth birthday." The words lift off of my chest, the weight of the world with it. The guests all start to gasp and share soft whispers before Brad chimes in.

"That's a damn lie," he shouts, his fists crashing down into the railing of the patio.

"You might not believe me and that's okay. Like I said, I've accepted that. The truth is that when I told Taylor six years ago what Brad had done to me, she didn't believe me either." I turn my head and look down at Asher. "But when Asher showed up at my apartment in Minneapolis a few days ago, with the letter Taylor had left for me, I realized her years being married to Brad had shown her the truth. And at the end of her life, she believed that Brad was the monster that I had warned her about."

"You need to leave immediately, Miss Sterling. You have more than overstayed your welcome," Mr. Montgomery demands, his tone deep and threatening. "How dare you speak such horrible accusations in the middle of Taylor's celebration!" He tilts his head toward a few of the workers, and they start to make their way over in my direction when Asher stands up next to me, grabbing ahold of my hand and standing tall by my side.

Mr. Landry raises his hand in the air and rises from his seat, turning to face me. "Now, hold on," he says. "I want to hear what Auden has to say."

"Charles, this is outrageous!" Mr. Montgomery shouts back at Mr. Landry, his eyes protruding as he rolls his collared sleeves up to his elbows, the staff slowly backing away as they disregard his silent instructions to remove me.

"I've listened to you and your demands for too long, Dale. This is my daughter's reception, and Auden was always the closest thing Taylor had to a sister. I've known the girl just about as long as I've known my own daughter. I have never once seen her cause a ruckus, and damn it, if she knows something about why my daughter felt she needed to leave us all, then, damn it, I want to hear it!"

Mr. Landry nods in my direction before taking his seat again. "Go on, Auden."

I nod back at him, his words giving me the courage to keep going.

"I've made some decisions since that day that I'm neither proud nor ashamed of and some of you may even hate me for them. But I won't keep running from my past, and I won't allow the Montgomerys to threaten me or my family any longer. The day I left Monroe was on my own eighteenth birthday. I drove myself to a clinic nearby, and I had an abortion before heading straight to the airport and starting my life over in Minneapolis, completely alone." The whispers around me grow louder, and I can feel the tension building with their judgmental eyes.

I look over in Brad's direction, and his eyebrows have narrowed, his expression looking no longer stiff and angry but maybe even showing a small bit of sadness.

"Taylor had written to me once a year, every year since I had left, but she never found an address to send them to. That's a regret I will have to live with for the rest of my life because if she had been able to reach me, if I had known before it was too late what she was going through married to Brad, I would've been back faster than you can say molasses. I would've helped her leave him before it was too late."

"This is all a bunch of fucking lies, Auden, and you know it," Brad shouts as he paces back and forth behind his father. Mrs. Montgomery and Trevor, the youngest Montgomery son, all stand by Mr. Montgomery's side, their chins held high as they continue to glare at me in anticipation of what might come next.

"The only lie here, Brad, is your statement that you actually loved Taylor. I've stood by and listened to you fake that your heart is broken, and you don't know how you can ever go on without Taylor. But we both know she was nothing but a shiny plaything to you and would never be anything more. You held her back from going to college, you held her back from every dream she ever had, and even after she caught you cheating red-handed, you held her back from having her own emotions when you convinced her she needed the same anxiety medication she used to kill herself."

The voices surrounding me grow louder, whispers of "No, Lord" and "Oh, sweet Taylor" blowing around me like a small gust of wind, but I keep going. I can't stop until it's all out and Taylor can be remembered for who she truly was.

"And in the end, you put her in the same position that you put me in. She was pregnant. She was pregnant, and she made the decision to protect them both by taking them straight to Jesus, the one person who never failed her."

My lip starts to quiver, and it takes all of the strength I have left to hold myself back from releasing my tears full of anger and guilt.

"We all failed her. None of us were there for her when she needed us most. All of us just assumed that Taylor was a happy, young girl and would stay a happy, young woman without any of us actually stopping and asking the question. She was pushed into the idea of the perfect romance with a boy who was himself raised by a monster. She was left in a house all alone for months at a time, and you all thought the expensive wallpaper and wrap-around porch was enough to fill her with happiness, not taking a moment to recognize her pure emptiness and loneliness. How did we even get to this point? How can we sit around sharing endless stories of a girl who is defined as the representation of blissfulness when she ended her own life to escape the torture of living another day by herself. None of us saw her for what she really was and the least we can do is give her the respect of being honest about that."

  Everyone is silent. There are no longer any sounds of dishes and silverware being collected and washed, no cigars are being puffed on in the back of the lawn, the water in the pool hasn't made a wave in minutes, and even the Montgomerys are standing in complete silence.

  I swallow, knowing that my time is about to come to an end, and my tone starts to soften.

  "Taylor's dream since we were little kids was to grow up and change the lives of the future generations of Monroe. She wanted to be a part of building a better future, and I'm standing here today because I want to ensure that she still makes that happen. That *we* make that happen for her. Because maybe if when I was still only seventeen and saw a girl who was brave enough to keep telling people that she was taken advantage of until someone finally believed her, then maybe I would've had the courage to keep telling until I was believed as well." I reach my hand out and squeeze Asher's. "I may have been believed a lot sooner than I realized. But here I am, six years later, and I'm telling you all now. I'm taking my truth and Taylor's and I'm telling every little girl, teenager, and woman that what happened was not okay and you will be believed. I believe you. Just don't stop telling."

As soon as I finish speaking, my body feels weightless, like I'm floating. I can't remember what I said. Asher holds onto my arm as I lower myself onto the grass, stepping off the chair.

Suddenly, a slow, loud clap breaks the silence.

Mr. Montgomery begins to descend the patio steps, heading towards me with a forcibly calm demeanor. My heart races in my chest, and I instinctively move closer to Asher, who stands beside me.

"Well, wasn't that just a wonderful performance," he says, continuing to clap and walk forward until he stops where Mr. Calhoun is currently seated. "Is there anything you'd like to say, Mr. Calhoun?"

Mr. Calhoun bows his head away from Mr. Montgomery and stays silent.

Mr. Montgomery plants his hand hard onto Mr. Calhoun's shoulder, leaning down and repeating, "Mr. Calhoun, isn't there something you'd like to say about these wild accusations?"

Mr. Calhoun closes his eyes for a moment before bringing himself to a stance and taking another second to clear his throat as he searches for his response.

"Uh, yes, there is," he starts, smoothing down the front of his plaid sport coat. "Miss Sterling, unless you have some evidence here to back up your very serious accusations, I'm going to have to ask everyone here to ignore everything said against the Montgomerys."

Mr. Calhoun turns in the direction of Sheriff LeBlanc, "Isn't it true that everyone is to be considered innocent until proven guilty, Sheriff?" he asks.

Sheriff LeBlanc nods his head, "Yes, that is true," he replies, his tone unconvincing.

"Brad forced me to do things I didn't want to do as well," a female voice suddenly projects from the opposite side of the lawn. We all turn to see who just yelled, and our gaze lands on a tall blonde with a round, naturally beautiful face, dressed in a cream maxi dress.

"Kelly Anne," I hear whispered from behind me.

This time I join in on the crowd's gasps, looking over at Sarah whose jaw is hanging open as she continues to record. I scan my table, seeing my mama's eyes as they fill with tears as she looks back and forth between Kelly Anne and me, everyone at a standstill, unsure of what to do with this new information.

"You rat whore!" Brad screams, causing my head to snap back towards the steps where he's already descending, weaving through the tables towards me. Asher steps in front of me, and my father quickly rises from his seat.

"You're both lying because you regret spreading your legs!" Brad's gaze is icy, fixated solely on me.

"Brad took a photo of me drinking when I was still underage. He told me it would ruin my father's career if it ever got out. He made me do things with him to keep him from sharing it", Amelie LeBlanc says, standing up from her seat and looking directly at her father, the Sheriff.

"Is that true?" the Sheriff asks her, his fists balling up and his voice full of concern.

Before the Sheriff can react, Mr. Calhoun interjects, "Now, Sheriff, unless any of these ladies have proof of these accusations, then the only thing I see happening here is a whole lot of he said, she said."

Mr. Montgomery walks closer to the Sheriff, his chest puffed and his shoulders back as if he needed to remind him of his self-proclaimed authority. "I want each one of them arrested, Sheriff, now!" he barks.

The Sheriff closes his eyes while he slowly shakes his head side to side as he contemplates what to do next, his knuckles drained white. "I don't see any evidence to arrest any of these women." He stands and takes a step in Mr. Montgomery's direction, the veins in his neck proving the strength it's taking him to remain calm. "And since my own daughter has now accused your son of sextortion, I can no longer be legally involved."

"Is a recording enough evidence?" Millie Dupont asks, standing up from her seat at the table directly behind Brad.

Brad turns, getting closer to Millie and she takes a step back. "What the hell are you doing?" Brad asks her, his tone grasping for control.

"It does in the great state of Louisiana!" Sarah chimes in.

Millie steps out of Brad's shadow, turning her attention back to the Sheriff. "Two nights ago, Brad took me to the same spot where he took Auden and forced me to pretend to be her," she confesses, her fingers twiddling in front of her stomach as she speaks, and her face flushing with shame. "I didn't realize what a disgusting role I was playing, and now I feel sick to my stomach realizing it. He recorded the whole thing so he could rewatch it later."

Brad keeps his gaze fixed on Millie, ignoring the rest of us. It's clear he's contemplating how to escape the public exposure of his past crimes.

"You disgraceful excuse for a man!" Mr. Montgomery bellows, spitting in Brad's direction. "You have embarrassed this family for the last time."

He heads directly for Brad, using both hands to grip the back of Brad's shirt and starts to drag him in the direction of the Sheriff, pushing Brad down until he's on his knees at the Sheriff's feet. "Get him the hell out of here, Tom," he says.

The Sheriff looks over at Millie, his eyebrows creasing his forehead. "Millie, would you like to press charges against Brad Montgomery?"

Millie looks around the lawn, first at Kelly Anne, then over to Amelie LeBlanc, and then she turns her head, very slowly, until her eyes meet mine. Her eyes look as if they're swirling with a mixture of terror and shame. My lips curl up as I give her a silent signal that she isn't alone in this, that each of us standing, although we're practically strangers, is now connected forever. We will support her every step of the way. She nods her head once, before turning back to Sheriff LeBlanc, her posture straightening before she replies, "I want to press charges for Taylor," as she turns back in my direction. "I want to press charges for Auden because I had the smallest taste of the secret she has lived with for too long now." She pauses for a moment, pulling her seat out a little further and walking until she can face Brad, who's still kneeling down in front of the Sheriff. "And I want to press charges for every girl you've ever found something to hold over their head. But most of all, I want to press charges for me. Because I deserve so much better than a future of feeling like I deserved every moment that you forced me to degrade myself and compromise my worth. No more. I want to press charges for the Millie I was before you saw me as a weak opportunity. I'm taking my strength back."

My eyes start to fill with tears as I witness the empowerment building in Millie's heart.

The Sheriff leans down and grabs Brad's arm, raising him up before aggressively pulling both of his arms behind his back and cuffing them.

"You will always be weak," Brad whispers. "You were nothing without me."

No one even attempts to whisper at this point as each guest starts to share their own opinions on the current situation. Mrs. Landry rises from her seat, slowly pushing her chair out, and walking in the direction of Brad, Mr. Montgomery, and the Sheriff.

Asher gently wraps one arm over my shoulder, pulling me tightly into his side as we prepare for what his mother is about to do.

Growing up and being around Mrs. Landry frequently, I had a good understanding of what kind of mother she was. She always loved her children, but her way of showing it was not always the most affectionate. Her focus was more on ensuring they had a bright future and were respected members of society, in the hope of making their lives easier. She seemed hesitant to let them explore new things or take risks. My mom and Mrs. Landry were classmates, and one evening, as I vented about Mrs. Landry, I remember my mom telling me that Mrs. Landry was one of the strongest women she had ever known. However, something had happened in her life that had dimmed her light, and now only a few fortunate ones get the chance to witness it. Today, I realize I am one of the lucky ones, and I'd do anything to have Taylor here to see it too.

"Sheriff, if you're going to arrest Brad, then you better look into the beast who made him as well."

The sheriff looks confused, and Mr. Montgomery lets out a vindictive laugh. "What the hell are you talking about, Helen?" he asks.

Mrs. Landry doesn't even acknowledge the question and keeps her eyes focused on the Sheriff. "Dale and I had dated for a few months in high school. When I got to college and became engaged to Charles, Dale drove up to my campus to express his disappointment. When I rejected his advances, he forced himself on me and raped me in my own dorm room. I stayed silent about it because I didn't want to lose Charles, but after hearing what a mess not holding him accountable has made, I want it to be known. I want to take responsibility for my part in the pain that inevitably spiraled into my daughter's life."

Brad lunges toward her but the Sheriff holds him back by his cuffs. "You're a whore bitch just like your murderous, pathetic daughter!" he screams, his voice so loud that it starts to crack.

His words, as he attempts to break Mrs. Landry, who bears a striking resemblance to Taylor, push me over the edge. This could have been Taylor's moment if only I had seen her and recognized her need for help like I had always done throughout our childhood. She could have been standing here years later, alive, ready to confront Brad for all he had taken from her.

My feet are moving, and my arms are shaking as the rage builds in me.

She should've never had to feel like she was trapped and alone, stuck so deeply in the Montgomerys' grasp that death was the only option she felt she had left.

Tears start to flow from my eyes, burning the hot skin on my cheeks as I feel my arm pulling itself back and shooting forward as I watch Brad's jaw slamming against my fist, his body hurtling backwards into the table behind him.

All I can hear is the sound of the entire town starting to clap in a thunderous roar.

Epilogue

Taylor,

It's been six years since you passed away. There isn't a day that goes by that I don't think of you.

Life has been so good to us.

You would be proud of Asher. He became the Deputy Chief at the Monroe Fire Department last fall. He misses you and still visits you every Saturday with a mimosa and picnic. We finally got a new headstone two years ago, and I think you would approve. We switched to granite so that it shimmers in the sun, just like you used to bring such light into our lives. I also added a small replica of the Ectomobile in front of your headstone that Asher and I found when we returned to Minneapolis. We thought it was better than leaving fake flowers. You made people want to stop and smile whenever they noticed you during your life and we felt it was only fitting that your headstone did the same thing. Sometimes I sneak in at night like we used to do together when we'd go to visit my grams and I eat an apple, leaving half behind for you. Asher doesn't know it's me who does it, and I hope I never get caught because I doubt he'd be too happy bailing me out of jail again. Your funeral reception was one night too many in my opinion.

Okay, let's be honest, a night in jail for a perfect uppercut was more than worth it!

Jane from the Minnesota Coalition Against Sexual Assault saw the video of Brad's arrest and called me a week after your funeral with a job offer. She said she was already planning on calling for a second interview after my intriguing, but abrupt, departure from my first interview. However, after seeing me stand up and share both of our stories, she said she needed to have me. I went back to Minneapolis to talk more with her and after a lot of discussion with both her and Asher, I made the decision to move home to Monroe. Jane helped me set up a nonprofit here instead. The Taylor Landry Foundation for Truth, The Taylor Truth for short. We help survivors get justice for their sexual assaults, and we also provide support, shelter, and any other assistance they may need. Sarah Underwood helped raise the money to start it up through her own connections and a gofundme highlighting the video Mike Taylor posted to The Monroe Daily.

But the majority of the funds came from Trevor Montgomery. When his father, Brad, and DJ had enough cases built up against them, Mr. Montgomery transferred the family estate into Trevor's name. It turns out that Trevor isn't anything like the rest of his family. He was so torn up about what had happened that he set up an account that sends funds every month straight to The Taylor Truth account. He sold everything, bought an old traveling van and hit the road. He checks in every once in a while, and I like to hear where he's been exploring.

My good friend Dec and his boyfriend come down and spend the winters here with us. Dec teaches a free dance class to the kids through church during winter break. Mama made a deal with him that if he does the free class, she'll let him cut bouquets from her flower beds once a week. You would've loved Dec, and you'd think he knows you by how often he talks about you and asks about our past adventures.

We see your parents every Sunday when mama cooks dinner at their house. It's become one of our favorite things to look forward to. It would bring you joy seeing both of our families together like we are now, and I believe we have you to thank for that. There isn't a Sunday that goes by that we don't laugh until our bellys ache telling stories about you.

Thank you for trusting me with your truth, and thank you for bringing us all together.

We pray as a family every single night for you

Until we meet again,

Auden, Asher, and your niece, Taylor

Acknowledgements

As I'm sitting in my living room, trying to come up with the perfect acknowledgments, I realize how incredible it is that I even have the opportunity to acknowledge anyone. So here we go.

First, to Rachel, my editor. Rachel, I know I ended most emails with "you're a badass," but I want to say it again: YOU ARE A BADASS! Thank you for believing in me, guiding me through this journey, and introducing me to a new Mexican restaurant in the process. You have made my dreams come true.

To my Papa, who passed away in April of 2024, thank you for always believing in me and reminding me that I can do anything; I just have to choose to do it.

I want to thank my husband for continuously giving me the time and space to follow my dreams. You are the reason I was able to do this, and I will forever be grateful for your support.

Thank you to my children for allowing me to take over the living room so I can write in my sunny spot on the couch. You put up with a lot during this last year, and I appreciate you both for giving Mom her space.

To my girls, thank you for taking the time to read and give me your input. The hours of texts about characters, the inspiration behind them, and helping me tweak every aspect have meant the world to me. You are all my favorites.

To my sister, thank you for reading my stories back when we were in third grade and pushing me to do it again in our thirties. This book wouldn't have happened without your support. I will cherish the texts and photos of you crying over the chapters for the rest of my life.

Thank you to my bonus dad, Bill, for staying up way too late so you could read another chapter. Thank you to my grandma for taking the time to read.

Thank you to my dad for reading and always getting excited about whatever new adventure I have decided to embark on, and for forcing me to read as a kid.

Lastly, thank you to my mom for the hours of proofreading, suggestions, and endless amounts of love. I wouldn't be here without you, and I definitely wouldn't be able to say I wrote a novel without you.

And to all of my future readers, THANK YOU!

Authors Note

This story resonates deeply with many aspects of my life, as I'm sure it does for many of my readers. Unfortunately, there are many of us out there who are Audens and many who may have been a Taylor at some point. I myself have been both.

When I was sixteen years old, I didn't believe two of my close friends when they told me about being assaulted. Not only did I not believe them, but I proceeded to go out on a "date" with the boy they said had taken advantage of them. By the end of that evening, I too had experienced my first assault.

I was embarrassed.
I was ashamed.
I believed them.

I fell for the nice guy act that many had fallen for before me. His nice smile and popularity were enough to make me trust him over two friends I had known since elementary school.

Eventually, I spoke up.
Eventually, I found my own strength to speak up.

Was I believed? Not by most. But it was no longer a secret I had to keep to myself. There were more Brads after that. There will always be more Brads out there in this world. It's up to us to decide if we want to be an Auden or not.

If I can leave you with anything, let it be this: Trust the person who confides in you. Speak up as loudly as you can for yourself and for others. Never allow a Brad to silence you. You are not alone, I promise.

Just don't stop telling.

Made in United States
Cleveland, OH
07 July 2025